C90
D0548216

A COLD CASE IN AMSTERDAM CENTRAL

Also by Anja de Jager

A Cold Death in Amsterdam

A COLD CASE IN AMSTERDAM CENTRAL

ANJA DE JAGER

Constable • London

CONSTABLE

First published in Great Britain in 2016 by Constable

1 3 5 7 9 10 8 6 4 2

All characters and events in this publication, other than those clearly in the public domain, are fictitious, and any resemblance to real persons, living or dead, is purely coincidental.

A CIP catalogue record for this book is available from the British Library.

ISBN: 978-1-47212-063-2 (hardback)
ISBN: 978-1-47212-064-9 (trade paperback)

Typeset in Bembo by Photoprint, Torquay
Printed and bound in Great Britain by
CPI Group (UK) Ltd, Croydon CR0 4YY

Papers used by Constable are from well-managed forests and other responsible sources.

Constable
is an imprint of
Little, Brown Book Group
Carmelite House
50 Victoria Embankment
London EC4Y 0DZ

An Hachette UK Company
www.hachette.co.uk

www.littlebrown.co.uk

In memory of my grandfather, who printed an underground newspaper during the Second World War, got arrested and miraculously survived the concentration camps.

Chapter One

The street lights made the deadly spikes of glass shine and sparkle. It was almost nine p.m. and darkness had invaded what had been a bright spring day. I tried to walk along the edge of the lake of shards but misjudged it, crushing splinters underfoot. I was lucky they didn't pierce the soles of my shoes. High up, seven floors above to be precise, two man-sized glass panels were missing from the balcony. It was probably referred to as a roof terrace in the marketing material for the almost-completed office block. Those two missing panels were here, in a million pieces at my feet. The fragments covered everything in a ten-metre radius: the pavement, the square wooden flower planters and the body.

The dead man lay on his back amidst the sea of glass. I grabbed a large piece of cardboard that was propped against the building and created a bridge so I could get near him. His hair was rusty red. He was young. Early twenties was my guess. He was like a young, snub-nosed version of Boris Becker. Apart from the blood on his face, he looked like someone asleep after having fallen into bed drunk. Too young to be dead. I looked up towards the seventh floor.

How long did it take to plunge from that height? For how many seconds had he known he was going to die? The thought of how frightened he must have been as he was falling made me wrap my arms around my waist.

Paint splatters on his shirt and arms shouted out his profession, along with his thick Timberland boots. His face was bruised and cut in several places. There was glass all over him. If it weren't for those shards, I would have pulled up his trouser leg to check for impact wounds. In the majority of falls from this height, the legs carry the brunt. The impact can break the tibia and fibula and often cause compound fractures that pierce the skin. I had seen them before, especially with suicides. If you jump, you're likely to land on your feet and the energy from the fall will shatter your legs.

This didn't look like a suicide but a workplace accident. Especially with those missing glass panels. Maybe the man had been installing them.

We couldn't get on to the building site as the door was locked. The building manager was on his way with a pass. There were many offices here, as this part of Amsterdam was close to both a tram line and a mainline station, Zuid WTC, and only two stops from Schiphol airport. When I'd gone to university, on the other side of the tracks, the station had only just been built and none of these towering blocks had been here. The one we stood next to had an unusual shape: two seven-storey sections placed on top of each other, with a four-metre sideways offset that created a corridor on the ground floor and a terrace on the seventh.

My colleague Thomas Jansen was talking to a witness on

the opposite shore of the glass lake. We had driven here in an uncomfortable silence that had become harder to break with every second that passed and every street we crossed. A pale centimetre of skin showed where the dark hair on the back of his neck had been shaved away. He had a tan he hadn't had yesterday. This morning he'd been filmed for our recruitment video. Everybody else had been from a minority. The next Matt Damon, he'd called himself. Should have had the haircut before the tan.

What did he see when he looked at me? A woman who wasn't getting any younger, back at work after four months off. When I said hello yesterday morning, it was clear that he wasn't happy I'd returned. I even wondered if he had testified against me in the internal investigation. It must have been a tough decision to balance his desire to disclose what he suspected with the need to not make a murder case collapse. A case that had largely depended on my witness statement to imprison the man I'd been so desperately in love with. Discredit me and you discredited my testimony that he'd confessed.

Now Thomas came over.

I stayed on my cardboard life raft by the body. I hadn't seen a dead person in the last four months. Nor had I seen any criminals or victims. Or maybe I had seen them but hadn't recognized them as such. I'd been a normal civilian, or as normal as you can be whilst recovering from a gunshot wound.

'Who called it in?' My words were rusty but at least I'd said something.

'A guy in the office opposite.' Thomas's voice sounded final.

Out of a childish desire to needle him, I kept going. 'What's the witness's name?'

'Maarten Schuur.'

'Victim's name?'

'Frank Stapel.'

'Next of kin?'

'Wife.'

Even before it all happened, Thomas and I hadn't been the best of friends, but standing here with him now felt like being at a dinner party with a partner you'd cheated on. Both of us wished there was somebody else, anybody else, who could have gone instead. Like an old married couple, maybe we'd get to a point where we could put the deceit behind us.

Five of our uniformed colleagues, the fluorescent-yellow stripes on their dark jackets clear from a distance, made sure that anybody sick enough to want to look at the dead man wouldn't get a chance.

'It was an accident,' Thomas said.

Most of the buildings around us were only half lit, with dark windows showing that nine-to-fivers had left hours ago to have dinner with their families. Not many people lived here.

I looked up towards the roof terrace. 'What did the witness see?'

'I saw him fall.' The man who spoke stood to my left, where the glass stopped. He wore pale trousers and a blue blazer. From my crouching position there was no missing his orange boat shoes. 'I looked up from my screen and he was . . . you know . . . already in the air.'

'What time was this?'

'Not sure. After eight o'clock.'

We would get the exact time he'd called from Dispatch.

He folded his arms and kept his eyes to my right, deliberately looking away from the body. 'Those glass panels came down right after him.'

'You don't know what made him fall?'

'No, I couldn't see that. I'm working over there.' He pointed to the building opposite. 'We've seen this one go up. I've been watching it for months. But the glass panels are reflective. On purpose, I guess, to give people some privacy.'

'Which floor are you on?'

'I'm on six.'

Someone from a higher floor might have been able to see on to the roof terrace, but all those floors were dark.

A young police officer came up to us, confident in his dark-blue bomber jacket with yellow stripes even though acne still clung to his skin. The gun on his hip added a swagger to his walk. His boots dealt with the glass much better than my shoes had.

I stood up.

He started to ask my name but stopped himself. 'Detective Meerman,' he said. 'Sorry, I didn't recognize you.' He held his pen and notepad as if he was going to ask me for my autograph. 'I've followed all your cases,' he said, 'especially—'

'Thank you,' I said.

'So you're back?'

'Second day.'

He nodded, kept his face serious. 'We've got the man in charge of the building site just here.'

'Great,' I said. 'I'll—'

'I've got this,' Thomas interrupted. He walked towards a bulldozer of a man who had his hands in his pockets but needed to keep his arms away from his body to give his biceps room. His neck was like a chimney going straight down from his ears.

'His name is Kars van Wiel,' the young officer in uniform said as he followed Thomas.

I stayed behind with the body.

Sometimes the dead were easier to deal with than the living, I thought an hour later as I pressed the doorbell that had the label *Frank and Tessa Stapel* next to it.

'Have you forgotten your keys again?' I heard the smile in the young female voice.

'Police,' I said. 'Can we come in?'

'What's it about?' Any hint of levity had gone.

'Can we just come in?'

The flat was in one of a line of pale-yellow three-storey blocks that had been placed at angles to pretend that they had been playfully dropped there rather than carefully planned. Outside the centre of Amsterdam, half an hour's drive from where Frank had died, these rent-controlled apartments were all owned by the same pension fund and provided it with a steady and predictable income stream. They were around the corner from where my mother lived in a similar block.

The buzzer sounded and I pulled open the communal door to a long hallway. Thomas stepped past me as if I was the doorman. I hoisted my handbag higher up my shoulder and followed him along the stretch of matching red doors.

Halfway down, I stopped. The wall of the corridor was newly painted in a magnolia colour that nobody could object to. The weight of my gun, hidden under the jacket of my suit, reminded me that I'd had far worse encounters than the one coming up. Still, the thought of the pain that we were going to inflict caused a sensation like goldfish were swimming inside my gut.

Thomas looked round. 'Don't worry, I'll take the lead,' he said over his shoulder.

I swallowed my annoyance at being treated like a rookie. After all, we were equal in rank and he was younger than me.

Provided with the choice between putting away a child killer and ending the career of a colleague, Thomas had chosen the former. The more time off I had to take, the more he must have thought he was going to have it both ways. I took a grim satisfaction in having spoilt that.

He knocked on the door of number 7.

Tessa Stapel opened it. Her grey eyes were so wide with worry that they seemed to take over her whole face. She couldn't be older than twenty-five. 'Yes?' she said.

Thomas showed his badge.

She pulled up her eyebrows until they were safely hidden under the fringe of her long dark hair. Even though it was late in the evening, she was still wearing office clothes – a white shirt tucked into a grey skirt – but had swapped her shoes for pink moccasins. She pushed her hair behind one ear and showed a small pearl earring. A jacket that matched the grey skirt hung over a chair.

'I'm sorry,' Thomas said, 'there's been an accident.' His tone was matter-of-fact, like a doctor delivering grave news. Was it only because I'd been away that it sounded callous and uncaring?

Her hand flew to her mouth. 'Oh God, are you taking me to the hospital? Let me get my coat.'

'I'm sorry.' Thomas stopped her with a hand on her arm. 'He's dead.'

Tessa's mouth opened in a silent scream that turned into a snarl, and her hands flew open-palmed against Thomas's chest. He put an arm out to keep hers at bay and took a step back.

'It's not true. It's not.' As her arms swung, they pulled the shirt out of the front of her skirt. 'You're lying!'

I caught one of Tessa's wrists in front of her but was annoyed with myself when the momentum allowed the other to slip through my grip. At the second attempt I pinned it against her stomach. I restrained her easily. She howled; a high-pitched sound that was almost loud enough to shatter the glass of the coffee table. I tried not to make my fingers too tight on her wrists, but we couldn't have her hurt a police officer or try to go for my gun. Her hair flew around with the fierce shaking of her head, as if denial would make her husband's death less true.

The *NOS Journaal* on the TV in the corner broadcast the demise of hundreds of Syrians into her front room, all far away and anonymous.

'Shh, shh,' I said. 'I'm sorry. I'm so sorry.'

She pulled with the intensity of an angry toddler in the grip of a tantrum: fierce, muscles tensed. Thomas stepped further back. His blue eyes were half closed, judging me as if he had to write a report afterwards to dissect how I'd handled the situation. I nodded at him that I had her and gave her enough space to fight out her grief. This was how much it hurt when you were suddenly alone. When my baby died, I'd screamed as well. When my husband left me, I'd only cried. Compared to that, being shot had been easy.

Tessa dropped her head forward and shook with her sobs. My eyes burnt in sympathy but I bit the inside of my cheek to keep the tears inside. Thomas would interpret it as a sign of this incompetent rustiness he kept mentioning.

'Are you calmer now?' I said. 'Ready to listen to us?'

She nodded.

I released her arms. Her face was the same colour as the paper of the cigarette smouldering in the ashtray. 'He fell from the roof terrace. At the building site,' I said. I gave her a tissue.

She collapsed on to the leather sofa and wrapped her arms around her stomach as if she'd been punched. 'He wouldn't have. He wouldn't have left me like this.'

I sat down next to her and put my arm around her

shoulders. She rested her head against me. Thomas was still standing like a scarecrow in a field. I offered her the glass of water that stood next to the cigarette. She refused.

'Can I get you anything else?' Thomas said. 'Something stronger?'

'I don't drink,' she said.

'Cup of tea?'

'No.'

'Here's my card,' I said. 'If you need anything, call me.'

She accepted it without making eye contact.

Three days later, she took me up on my offer.

Chapter Two

On TV, they were showing a man running on to a football pitch during a game. His jeans were low around his hips, showing the top of his underpants. Francine Dutte had lowered the sound when her husband called but could still tell that the commentator was shocked. Even without any volume, she knew exactly what he was saying. She was curled up on the sofa with the phone hugged to her ear. She rubbed her left foot, which always hurt after a long day.

'They called me back. They want me in Qatar on Sunday,' her husband said. He sounded upbeat. It was mid-afternoon in New York, evening in Amsterdam.

The pitch invader had come close to the central defender. His face was turned away from the camera and only the short stubble on the back of his head was clearly visible. He lifted his arm to hit the player.

'Great,' Francine said. Her husband didn't sound as if he was a continent away. He seemed deceptively close, as if he was calling from the house next door instead, or maybe just from the Amsterdam ArenA, the Ajax stadium, which was being shown on TV. From their house she could see the floodlights in the evening and faintly hear the roars when the home team scored. No sound today. The footage was months old. Francine took the remote control from the arm of the sofa and turned the volume up.

'The Qataris are concerned about what's happening in Bahrain,' her husband said.

The defender, in the yellow away strip, turned round, saw the man coming and floored him with a swipe of his leg.

'They want to make sure everybody knows about their attempts at political reform,' he said.

The man was trying to get up but the football player landed a few kicks in his midriff.

'Francine, are you even listening to me?'

Francine's eyes stayed fixed on the TV. 'Of course I am. Qatar on Sunday.'

'You're not listening, you're watching TV. I can hear it in the background.' His voice was raised.

'Darling, if I wasn't listening, how could I repeat what you said?'

'You're watching TV.' He was silent for a few seconds. 'I can hear what it is. You're watching *that* again. Have you recorded it? Do you have it on a permanent loop?'

'It's the news. It's on the news.'

The hooligan was hauled from the ground by the stewards, dragged off with his hands behind his back. They were supposed to have stopped him coming on to the pitch but had been too cowardly to do anything to get in his way. Now that he was down, they were there in force, supporting each other; a gang of them against one man. Francine turned the TV off.

'Stop watching it,' her husband said.

Francine put the remote control back on the table. 'It's gone.' She knew that if she hadn't switched it off, she would have kept staring at it, unable to draw her eyes away from the screen. It was easy for Christiaan. He was far away, not in the front room. He would have watched it too if he'd been sitting on the sofa next to her.

'It was finished, wasn't it? The footage. It had finished anyway.'

'Darling, I'm listening to you. Tell me more about Qatar.'

'I'm sorry if I'm not as interesting as the TV.'

'It's not the TV. It's—'

'That particular clip. I know. Anyway, I'll be home in time for the trial.'

'We're not going.' As she said the words, her eyes hurt. They'd been to all the previous ones. But no longer. She didn't want to go, and Sam definitely didn't want them there.

'We're not?' Christiaan said.

Her dark-blue work shoes lay on their sides in front of the sofa. The leather of the left was stretched out of shape by her bunion. Her misshapen foot had worked on the shoe until that was equally warped. She picked it up. Turned it over. The edge of the heel had been walked off. She placed it back under the table. She'd get it fixed tomorrow.

'Are you sure?' he said. 'We can talk about it when I get home.'

'I don't want to go any more,' Francine said. How many

men had she seen come through the court? All so similar to her brother, all with that feeling of intense boredom, that nothing was ever exciting enough, that normality was dull, that fitting in was for losers. A job was for those who conformed. Not for them. They wanted the excitement of drinking, fighting, setting up times to meet with the other groups before the games.

'Does Sam know?'

Sam. Sam D. they called him in the press, not being allowed to use his full name. Her husband kept telling her she should go under his name and drop the surname that had gained notoriety. If Francine hadn't seen so many of the others, she might have thought it was her parents' fault. Or maybe her fault: that she'd mothered her little brother too much, that having two mothers had made her brother rebel. But she had seen the other parents, and apart from the few who were always used as stereotypes, most were decent, law-abiding people like herself. Sometimes you couldn't help what your children were like.

'Sam doesn't care if we're going or not,' she said.

'And your father?'

'I don't want him to go either.'

'It'll be nice to spend some time together,' her husband said. 'Or do you have to be in court all day?'

'I've taken the time off. I'll pick you up from the airport.'

'Don't, I'll take the train.'

'No, I want to. You're landing at eleven, right?'

'Eleven oh five. But really, Francine, don't bother. It's easier by train.'

'Don't be silly. I'll meet you there.'

'Last time—'

'I'll be there.'

'Okay. And Francine . . .'

'Yes?'

'It's good we're not going.'

She knew that her husband thought they weren't going to the trial because she'd finally come to her senses and given up on Sam. In reality, it was because Francine couldn't stand to be in court and meet all her colleagues. They would smile sympathetically, say that they were all supporting her, that having Sam D. as a brother shouldn't make a difference to a prosecutor. But Francine knew they didn't believe it. She also knew they were right. Every time she asked for a sentence for someone like Sam, she looked at the defendant and pictured her own brother in their situation.

And asked for a longer sentence.

Chapter Three

Amsterdam Centraal station's newly restored main hall formed the high-ceilinged nave of this nineteenth-century cathedral for public transport. I crossed the blue-and-white-patterned tiled floor and skirted past mobile chicanes of students and tourists. Before the station improvements, a departure board would rattle its turning metal strips whenever a train left. I missed the sound.

After the light and spacious main hall, the stored luggage area was a 1970s throwback, with strip lighting and bad air. All oxygen seemed pushed out of the room by the low ceiling, which I could touch if I raised my arms even halfway. The only pattern on the floor here was that made by discarded chewing gum stuck on the dirty linoleum. Tessa sat on a chair in the guard's office, separated from the luggage lockers by thick yellowed Plexiglas.

She looked over her shoulder at something I couldn't see. Her feet dangled ten centimetres off the floor. The last three days had cut themselves into her face. She probably hadn't eaten or slept since her husband died. Her face was gaunt and drawn; all colour had been sucked from her skin by grief until only the red around her eyes was left.

'She refused to pay,' the security guard said. He stood close enough to her that he could act if she tried to leave. He towered over her. He could have lowered his chair.

At least she wasn't crying any more. She had been when she called me. When I'd seen her previously, she had been a well-dressed young woman, but now, in a large jumper marked with paint stains and ragged gashes, she looked like a runaway teenager. The too-long sleeve, unravelled at the edges, partially disguised the mobile phone she clutched in her left hand. The security guard had probably thought the sleeve was hiding needle tracks.

I showed my badge to defuse the situation. 'Her husband died in an accident three days ago,' I said.

'That's what she told me. But I thought . . . It's no excuse for . . .' His uniform was immaculate. It looked new. He'd probably only been in this job for a few days. I remembered what those early days in new employment were like: you wanted to do your best and apply all the rules to the utmost of your ability. You hadn't learned to judge yet when bending them made everybody's life so much easier.

Tessa looked across at me. 'He wouldn't let me get Frank's stuff. He wouldn't let me . . .' Her voice started defiantly but disappeared in a sob.

'Too young to have a husband,' the guard said. He himself didn't seem much older than Tessa. He rubbed his wrist. 'She looked . . .' He shrugged and didn't finish his sentence. He didn't have to. I understood why he'd refuse to let a woman who looked like Tessa get luggage from a locker without paying the fee. It was a scam that many junkies tried: steal bags from stored luggage with old tickets or those that people had dropped on the floor.

'I'm sorry, Detective Meerman,' Tessa said. She clutched the luggage ticket in her right hand, as if that small piece of paper was the last part of her husband that she could ever touch. Her wedding ring shone brightly. It should have told the guard that she wasn't lying; had she been a drug addict, it would have been the first thing she'd sold. 'He says I have to pay. That Frank had only paid for one day.'

'Yes, the machine—'

'It's okay,' I interrupted him. I was keen to get Tessa her husband's possessions. I wanted her to have the answers she was looking for, and I really hoped that the contents of the locker would ease her pain. I wasn't sure what would make it better; maybe something he'd bought for her that he'd stored at the station so that he could pick it up on his way home, because he hadn't wanted to get it dirty on the building site.

Over the guard's shoulder I could see a group of young girls, students or tourists, with open luggage. Oblivious to her surroundings, one of them was getting changed, stripping off to her underwear and putting on clean clothes from her suitcase. Her two friends turned to look at me. They must have sensed the tension, seen the shiny new guard, the grey-faced, dishevelled young girl, and me, the woman who was old enough to be the girl's mother.

'Let's get that locker open,' I said. Whatever Frank had stored there, we should find out what it was.

'It's thirty euros a day,' the guard said. 'It's been three days.'

'Her husband died. Can't you waive the fee?'

'No, I'm sorry. As I explained to your friend here' – at the emphasis on the word 'friend', Tessa kicked her legs and rotated the chair, to turn her back to the guard and his official stance – 'I can't open the locker until the money's paid. Only my boss can. She's out for lunch.'

'Give me the ticket,' I said to Tessa.

She stared at it for a while without really seeing it, and her fingers crushed the slip of paper as she balled her hand into a fist.

'Tessa, I'll open the locker for you.' I could raise the paperwork, or I could pay up myself.

She straightened the piece of paper out, caressing each of its creases. At one time it had been folded in four. Where had she found it? 'I'm really sorry,' she said. 'I didn't mean to cause any trouble, but I got so angry when . . . well, when I had to pay.' She rubbed the ticket with her thumb, reluctant to let go.

I held my hand out. When she passed me that slip of paper, the size and shape of a cashpoint receipt, it felt warm to my skin.

Tessa turned to the guard. 'It's so unfair.' She sounded like a petulant teenager, acting up against her father or a teacher. She was reacting to the station guard because he was there and her husband wasn't any longer.

The ticket said 'C7'. I walked to the left-most bank of lockers, scanned the paper slip in the machine, paid the extra money on my cash card and listened out for the soft whirr of an electronic mechanism unlocking. A medium-sized door to my right swung open. Inside I could see a large bin bag.

I knew that whatever was inside it, it might not give Tessa the answers she was looking for. Sometimes accidents were just accidents. I had seen it many times before in upset relatives: the stubborn desire to prove that the death of their loved ones had meaning; the refusal to acknowledge that some things just happened for no reason whatsoever. The autopsy report had said there'd been no alcohol or drugs in Frank Stapel's bloodstream. He'd had multiple fractures of his skull, nose and jawbones. The point of impact hadn't been his legs but his head. All his injuries were perfectly in line with a fall from a great height, especially after those panels landed on top of him. We'd released his body to the family.

I stopped thinking about Frank, stepped aside and let Tessa get the bag out. I looked the other way to give her privacy. The three young girls, now all fully dressed, were hoisting their suitcases into one of the larger lockers. From behind me I heard the rustling of plastic. It was a sound of such normality, the once-a-week sound of bin night.

Then Tessa started to scream.

Chapter Four

When Tessa dropped the bag on the floor, whatever was inside rattled. It sounded just like the old departure board in the main hall. The bin bag sat on the floor like a fat bulbous time bomb. The yellow tie-string was a garish addition, like a cheap bow on a particularly nasty present. She stepped away from it. Her hands were shaking.

I asked her if there was anything dangerous in the bag. She shook her head, then sank to the floor, huddled against the lockers as far away from the sack as she could, and cried, hysterical keening cries, interrupted by a sound like a hiccough every time her breath caught on an inhalation. She covered her head with her arms.

I took a pen from my handbag and used it to open the bag. I'd been holding my breath, but the smell wasn't bad, only the faint petrol odour of the bin bag itself.

Inside the sack, bones were piled up with a skull on top. It had tipped on its side and the empty eye sockets were staring the other way. I could see the back, which was smooth, apart from a circular hole, just above the base. I imagined there would be a matching hole on the other side. Even though I had no idea whose remains these were, or why they were in a bin bag in a locker at Amsterdam Centraal, that hole at the back of the skull clearly showed how this person had died.

'I thought . . .' Tessa whispered, 'for a second I thought . . . that it was Frank.'

'It isn't. It's old,' I said.

'I know,' she said and buried her head in her arms again.

I got my mobile out and called Thomas. 'There may be more to the death of Frank Stapel than we originally thought,' I said.

'That builder? There isn't,' Thomas said. 'He just fell off the roof terrace. An accident. Nothing suspicious.'

'There's a human skeleton in a locker he hired at Centraal. That suspicious enough for you?'

'Is it real?'

'Looks real to me. Better come over. Bring Forensics.' I didn't wait for his reply but cut the call off. I turned round to talk to Tessa, as I thought she might need comforting, but I saw that the security guard had done what I'd done three days ago: he'd put his arm around her shoulder and held her. He was talking to her softly, and I could just make out that he was murmuring that soothing lie that everything was going to be okay.

Tessa raised her head. 'I told you, didn't I? I told you Frank wouldn't just have fallen. Now do you believe me?'

I wanted Tessa out of the way before Forensics got here. It would be best for her to be gone when they started sorting through the bones. We could take her fingerprints later.

She'd only touched the outside of the bag and maybe the door of the locker. 'Is there anybody you want to call? Someone who can pick you up?'

'Eelke,' she said. 'Frank's brother.' She pulled up the sleeve of her jumper and used it to wipe her eyes. The tears made a dark mark next to a bleached patch where someone had scrubbed the material to get something else off. Maybe spilled paint or plaster. 'I'll call him.'

It was another time of waiting: waiting for Eelke, waiting for my colleagues in uniform to close off this area of Centraal station, waiting for Forensics and waiting for Thomas. I'd become an expert at waiting during the time I'd been off work. I had to wait one hundred and twenty-four days before they'd finally cleared me to go back to my job. The same young policeman I'd talked to at the site of Frank's accident was the first to arrive. 'Detective Meerman,' he acknowledged before cordoning off the stored luggage area.

There was shouting in the distance. A man in a suit flapped his luggage ticket around as if it was a flag to get the guard's attention. He barked that someone should get his bags for him, as his train was leaving in ten minutes. The guard looked at Tessa. He made sure the brother-in-law was answering the call before doing the pragmatic thing: he took the ticket and got the man's bag out of the locker for him. He was clearly a fast learner, as that was not according to the rules.

Eelke turned out to be a skinny young man with hair the colour of a polished two-cent coin. He carried four balls in a net and the studs of his football boots clicked as loudly as stiletto heels on the station floor. The cut of his seventies-retro Adidas tracksuit only emphasized his lack of bulk. He led Tessa away.

Then the Forensics team arrived and filled the stored-luggage area. The three girls who'd got changed in there earlier were still hanging around on the other side of the cordon, taking photos on their iPhones.

Thomas turned up five minutes later. 'You know he just fell,' he said. He wore a slightly different blue shirt every day, because his wife had once told him it brought out the colour of his eyes. Today's shirt was cornflower blue.

'He placed these bones in the locker the day he died.'

'What time?'

I checked the ticket. 'Thirteen fifteen.'

Thomas nodded. 'His boss said Frank was working late because he'd taken the morning off.'

'Where did he get the skeleton from?'

Thomas stared at the bones again, then tapped the nearest forensic scientist on the shoulder. One of them had started by dusting locker C7. That set of prints should be fairly clear, and then we'd be able to tell if Frank Stapel put the bones in there himself or if he was just the holder of the luggage ticket.

Edgar Ling, part of the Forensics team, stood up from his crouching position by the bag. He was short and bulky and the Tyvek coveralls weren't particularly flattering. His eyebrows and eyelashes were so fair they were barely visible, and his eyes were glossy, as if marbles the colour of wet soil had been inserted into his skull.

'What do you think?' Thomas said.

'About what?'

'Age of the bones?'

'They're old,' Edgar said.

'How old?' I asked.

'I can't be sure until we get them to the lab.'

'But at a guess? Are we talking decades or centuries?'

'Oh, I think decades. They're old, not ancient.'

'And they're human, right? They're real, I mean.'

'It's a very good fake otherwise. If I had to guess, but it's just a guess, I'd say Second World War. I've got some experience with those.'

Behind the cordon, from a distance, curious commuters stared at the bones. Many of them, like the young girls, were taking photos. Tomorrow – no, within seconds, these would be posted and seen by people all over the world: photos of the skeleton in the bin bag on the floor of Centraal. I tried to see it with their eyes: the dirty station floor, the white plastic sheeting, the bones of the skeleton, the forensic scientists walking around like Martians in their white Tyvek suits, and that one dark-grey bin bag. At least I'd saved Tessa from being in the photos by sending her home.

Forensics bagged the bones up, ready for transport to the lab.

What kind of person would stuff a skeleton in a bin bag and then put it in a luggage locker? Even if it was from the Second World War. It wasn't that unusual for an old war skeleton to turn up. Most were found during building work, when gardens were turned over or fields ploughed. The law told any finder to call us, and they normally did. They'd found a few when they'd dug the new metro line. But Frank Stapel hadn't called us and he hadn't bothered to show these human remains any respect. He'd stuffed the bones in a bin bag. As if they were rubbish to be thrown away. Why had he kept them? And what had he planned to do with them?

We went back to the police station and I just had time to grab a cheese sandwich before I was ambushed by the call that the boss wanted to see me.

Chief Inspector Moerdijk seemed to have lost even more weight after running the Rotterdam marathon on Saturday. His zealous pursuit of health made him look permanently ill. I paused in the doorway to his office.

'Good afternoon, boss,' I said.

'Sit down, Lotte. I just need to finish this.'

I took a seat at the other side of his large dark-wood desk and rested my notepad on my lap. The boss's head was low behind a stack of paperwork. He'd had a pre-race haircut, and the shape of his skull, every dent, every bump, was covered by only a millimetre of hair, short like a recently mowed lawn. I drew circles. I filled in the outer ring and adorned the edge of the paper with a garland. Behind the boss, rain drops started to blot the window, falling from a grey sky more suited to autumn than April. The nice weather we'd had over the last few days had finished and a week of rain was forecast. I added a square to my notepad and filled it with dots to represent where water was hitting the glass. 'How was the run?'

'Not bad. Just under three hours fifteen.'

'You wanted to get out of Rotterdam as quickly as you could. I understand.'

He didn't smile at my joke but at least put his pen down and pushed the paperwork to the side. 'How was your first week back?' He looked at me over the rim of his reading glasses the way a doctor might look at a terminally ill patient.

The first morning had been awkward; I'd paused on the threshold of the office I used to share with Thomas Jansen and Hans Kraai. Hans was the only one who'd come to see me in hospital, but he had left the police force and moved away from Amsterdam to run his father's farm. There were things on his desk – a handbag, some files – so someone else had moved in and taken Hans's old desk by the window.

'It's as if I've never been away,' I said now.

'Good. That's good. You're feeling well?' the CI said.

'Perfect.'

'Good. And now there's this skeleton.'

'Yes, we found it in—'

'I know. I've heard. I'm glad Internal Investigations cleared you.'

'Yes, me too.'

'But not everybody sees it the way I do.' He pulled his glasses from his nose and rubbed his eyes. 'Some people said that maybe you weren't coming back.'

I added dots to my doodle for the new drops of rain that had fallen as the CI was talking.

'I'm glad they were wrong,' he said. 'Work with Thomas on this case. Tidy it up. Make everything right.'

The thought of Thomas's pretty-boy face made my shoulder muscles tense. I nodded as I weighed up the CI's words.

'Do your best,' he said, 'even with the skeleton. Not much of a chance of identifying it, but with the current drive to name unknown bodies, well, we should definitely try our hardest now that we've found a new one.'

Forensics departments all over the country were busy digging up cadavers previously buried in anonymous graves. From one of Amsterdam's cemeteries they'd raised seven coffins in one week alone.

'I want to look at Frank Stapel's accident again.' It was hard to make identifying an old skeleton my top priority.

'Focus on the bones in the bag. The burgemeester will be on the phone as soon as he hears about it.'

'Don't you agree it puts a different light on things?'

'We need to know where the skeleton came from, certainly.'

'I didn't mean that. I meant that we should investigate Frank Stapel's death.'

'Lotte,' here was that doctor's look again, 'identify the skeleton. Don't waste your time looking into something that was obviously an accident. It's not worth it.'

'Got it,' I said.

I strolled along the long corridor back to our office.

Ingrid Ries stood outside. She was the new addition to our team and now had the desk next to mine. She reminded me of an Eastern European high-jumper. Her face had the pronounced cheekbones and wide jaw of a Slavic woman and her body looked stretched to the point where there was no flesh left for any curves. I remembered when half the girls in my class had suddenly shot up and acquired that same shape, all legs and arms, no hips yet and no breasts. Real-life stick figures. How old had we been? Fourteen? Fifteen?

But it wasn't Ingrid who made me slow down. It was the fact that she was talking to Justin de Lange right there outside the office.

'Hey, Lotte, congratulations,' Justin said. 'We cleared you.' He smiled, and his small mouth almost disappeared in the shadow of his nose. What must it be like to work for the one department that everybody hated?

'Thanks,' I said.

'I hope it wasn't too difficult.'

'What was? Coming back to work? No, that's easy.' Through the open door was the safe sanctuary of my desk.

'I didn't mean that,' Justin said.

'I know what you meant.' I turned back to face him. 'You meant was it difficult to talk to you. About what happened.'

He seemed pleased that I understood him. 'Yes, that's what—'

'It was, so let's not mention it again. Is that okay with you, Justin?' I escaped into our office and sat down at my desk. Maybe I should ask him if the files and tapes could be destroyed now that I was no longer being investigated.

I had just started up my PC when Thomas came in.

'We should talk to Tessa Stapel,' he said.

'That poor girl,' I said.

'I'll go with Ingrid. Then you don't have to worry about her.'

'No, I'll come.' A few days ago I would have gone out of my way not to be alone in a car with Thomas again, but I felt sorry for Tessa. I wanted to look out for her, even though it would cost me.

Chapter Five

'Sorry about the mess.' Tessa Stapel's long hair was pulled back in an untidy ponytail and as many mousy-brown wisps drooped by the side of her face as had been gathered into the elastic band. When we had first told her about her husband's death, the flat had been tidy. Now it had changed as much as Tessa herself had. Clothes were scattered all over the floor and the drawers of a sideboard yawned half open, its contents obscuring every centimetre of spare surface area around it. If a hurricane had occurred indoors, it could not have caused more complete chaos. She couldn't have done this in the few hours since she'd come back from the station. This was the work of days. 'I was trying to find something,' she said.

'Something you should have told us about last time?' Thomas asked.

Tessa didn't respond. We followed her further into her home and had to step over hammers and paintbrushes. On the table a large toolbox had all its compartments open. Screws and washers, screwdrivers, pencils and pliers were strewn across the white tablecloth. Three screw bits had rolled off the table and dropped on to the floor.

'Can I get you anything?' she said. 'Tea? Coffee?' Her fingers caressed a man's coat – a brown leather jacket – that was hanging over the back of a tall chair.

'No thanks,' Thomas said. There was nowhere to sit that wasn't covered with clothes or pieces of paper. To make space, he grabbed a thick blue jumper that had been thrown on to the seat of the sofa.

Tessa shuffled a chair away from the table and picked up a Stanley knife. She pushed the blade out and ran it over the flesh of her thumb. She didn't flinch when the metal cut through the skin but only looked mesmerized at the drop of blood that welled up from the thin red line.

'Tell us about the ticket,' Thomas said. 'Did you know he had something in a locker?' As he asked the question, he folded the jumper. He turned it into a square, the sleeves secured inside, with three quick movements of his hands.

She brought her thumb to her mouth and sucked away the blood. 'I looked for anything.' She reached behind her for the leather jacket, pulled it from the back of the chair and put it around her shoulders. 'Anything at all that would make sense.' Her voice was soft but calm. Her eyes never left Thomas's hands as he tidied her late husband's clothes. She pulled the jacket closer around her. The leather was cracked around the elbows. 'We'd only been married for six months.'

'The locker ticket,' Thomas said.

She tugged at the jacket again. 'It was in the left pocket.'

'Inside pocket?' I asked.

Tessa nodded and turned the left-hand side of the jacket over to show a pocket that could be closed with a zip. 'This one. I only found it this morning. I was in bed, wearing it.' She looked at me. 'It was his favourite. It still smelled of him. I couldn't sleep. I'd checked all the pockets of his clothes already but I hadn't noticed the inside one.' She was quiet for a bit. 'I hadn't noticed it until I felt the zip against my skin.'

'You opened it and found the ticket?'

'I thought maybe the answer would be in the locker. And it was, wasn't it?' She looked at me. Asked me to confirm that the skeleton in the locker had somehow helped us to understand why her husband had died.

'We don't know,' Thomas said.

She nodded. 'You don't know. Of course.'

'Did your husband mention anything—'

'About the skeleton? He didn't talk about it over dinner if that's what you mean.'

'Did he talk about it at all?'

'Hold on, I nearly forgot.' Tessa got up and came back with her handbag. She rummaged around in it until she found her wallet. 'Here, Detective Meerman.' She held money out to me.

'What's that for?' Thomas said.

'She paid for the locker,' Tessa said. 'I like to pay my debts.'

I hesitated before taking the notes. I looked for the receipt for the luggage storage. I offered it to Tessa.

'What's that?' Thomas said.

'Luggage receipt.'

'We have to keep that. It's evidence.' He pushed back the floppy fringe that had fallen into his eyes.

The only information the receipt showed was the exact time I'd opened the locker. 'It doesn't really tell us anything—'

'Yes it does. Time, amount paid, we need to keep it.'

There was nothing important on the bit of paper, but I went through my wallet again and found the second part to the receipt, which showed the transaction on my card. 'What about this one?' I said. 'Evidence as well?'

His eyes narrowed. 'No, but you might not want to give that away. You should shred it.'

I ignored him and wrote on the card receipt: *Paid back by Tessa Stapel.*

Thomas turned back to Tessa. 'So, where were we before this little financial transaction took place?' He was making an effort to keep his voice light. 'Did he talk about the skeleton at all, I think I asked.'

Tessa sat back down and smiled at me. She had a gap between her front teeth. I hadn't noticed that before. I hadn't seen her smile before.

'Did he mention the skeleton, Tessa?' The lightness in Thomas's voice was becoming more strained.

'No, no he didn't. Never.'

'Do you know where he got it from?'

'No.' She put the receipt in her wallet. As it opened, I could see a small photo.

'That's Frank, isn't it?' I said. I had only seen him after he had died. I wanted to see what he had looked like when he'd still been alive.

She held the wallet out to me. It was a passport photo. Frank looked like a child; an annoying child, the one who would always be in trouble.

'Let me show you a better photo of him. You can't smile in those.'

We followed her out of the room, across the hall and into the bedroom. A large photo of Frank was garlanded by flowers, and a semicircle of tea lights threw moving shadows over the image. He looked happy in the photo. Young and healthy. He was on the beach; the wind had ruffled his hair, his bare feet were dug into the sand. The sunlight had thrown freckles over his cheeks. His hair was paler than his brother Eelke's, more reddish blond than polished copper. He had his arms extended, cigarette in one hand, ready to hug whoever was holding the camera. I tried to push to the back of my mind the image of how his body had looked after the fall, but my brain kept slipping it over the photo. Blood had splattered from his mouth, his neck had snapped, and those fingers that held the cigarette in the photo had been broken. The impact had killed him instantly.

'Anything he was involved in that was—' I started to say.

'No, nothing. Never.' Tessa picked the photo up, moved into its offered embrace and kissed the glass in front of Frank's face.

The duvet on the bed had been kicked to the bottom. A pile of clothes pushed into the shape of a person covered the left-hand side of the bed. Only the right pillow was dented.

'Nothing apart from this skeleton,' Thomas said.

She put the picture back. Ran a finger along the frame. 'Maybe it wasn't even his. Maybe the ticket, the locker, they weren't his.'

'We'll test the ticket, we'll test the locker. Test for fingerprints.'

'Then you'll see they probably weren't his.'

'Did you find anything else? When you searched the flat? Anything that showed he was depressed?'

'He wouldn't have left me. He was happy.'

We followed Tessa out of the bedroom. In the hallway, she paused. 'But you'll have to investigate it properly now, won't you? My husband's fall?'

'We'll investigate where the skeleton came from, why it was in his locker. It's a crime to move human remains,' Thomas said.

Tessa went straight to the sofa, took the folded jumper from its arm and put it on top of the toolbox.

'Did your husband only work on that site, the one in Zuid?' I asked.

She moved her eyes from the jumper to me. 'He worked on two different sites. He did specialist work, carpentry and decorating, and they didn't need him all the time.'

'Could you give me the other address, please?'

'I don't know. Hold on.' She pulled a pile of papers towards her. 'Here. Two sites. The one in Zuid . . .' She fell silent.

We all knew that 'the one in Zuid' was the one where he'd died.

She took a deep breath and expelled the air again slowly, pulling her ribs closer together as if that would keep her emotions inside. 'These two here.' She gave me a piece of paper covered with a man's handwriting. 'Maybe some others.'

'Can I keep this?' I asked.

'No.'

I didn't argue. We'd already met Kars van Wiel, who ran the site where Frank had fallen to his death. The name of the second property developer made me pause before I wrote down his telephone number, but Mark Visser was a common name. There had been two Mark Vissers in my school alone.

'You said that the ticket, the locker, could have been someone else's,' Thomas said. 'Any idea whose? Any friends your husband was close to?'

'What do you mean, close?'

'For someone to give you the ticket to a locker with a skeleton inside, I guess they have to trust you particularly well,' he said.

'Not his colleagues.'

'His brother?'

'Yes, they were close. But why would Eelke have a skeleton?'

'Anybody else?'

'Maybe Robbert. Robbert Kloos. It could be a kind of joke. Robbert, of course.' She nodded to herself and smiled. 'Robbert likes to play jokes. Maybe it wasn't a real skeleton. Just to scare Frank?' She looked at Thomas, somehow hopeful.

'It seemed human, but Forensics are testing it now.'

She took the jacket from her shoulders and hung it over the back of the chair again. She walked to the large window that overlooked the grass at the back of the blocks of flats. She hummed softly to herself for a few seconds. 'Can you talk to Eelke?' she said. 'He lives next door.'

Chapter Six

We talked to him around his kitchen table, Thomas and I at one end, Eelke at the other. I'd positioned my chair so I could watch Thomas and Eelke simultaneously.

'Tell us about your brother,' Thomas said. 'What was he like?'

'Hard-working, normal guy.' Eelke looked so much like his younger brother that I could picture him lying on that pavement instead of Frank, beads of blood staining his mouth and chin.

Eelke sprawled on his wooden kitchen chair, one arm draped over the back, fingers stained yellow. He was fidgeting. Maybe he'd like to light up but didn't think it was polite to do so even though he was in his own home. His eyes darted between me and Thomas like a mouse trapped between two cats.

'Just a normal guy? What about this skeleton?' Thomas shifted his body forward, suddenly looking alert, to indicate that this was what he really wanted to know. 'Is that normal?'

'Why are you here? Why are you accusing my brother?'

The colour shot to Eelke's face, an instant flash of red. He sat up straighter. It hadn't taken much.

'We're not accusing anybody.' Thomas sat back. He pulled a hand through his floppy hair and smoothed it back.

'What about the site manager, Kars van Wiel? Why aren't you talking to him?' Eelke slouched back in his chair.

'We went to the building site,' Thomas said, 'immediately after your brother's death. There were warning signs all over. Their safety records were exemplary.' He looked back through his notebook as if he were searching for inspiration for what to ask next.

'Until my brother died.'

'He fell,' Thomas said. He didn't look up from his papers. 'It was an accident. Unless you think it was suicide?'

'The insurance company would like that, wouldn't they? But Frank didn't kill himself. Isn't someone liable? Responsible for his death?'

'Accidents do happen. Your brother,' Thomas said, 'he worked in two different places?'

'Yes, that site in Zuid, and one in the centre, I think.' The wall behind Eelke was covered in photos of Ajax players. Some were from the golden era: Marco van Basten, Frank Rijkaard; and there were some newer players I recognized but couldn't name. Twenty photos in frames, four across, five rows down. A sea of red and white. From what I could see, all the photos had been signed.

'Did he work anywhere else?' Thomas said.

'No.'

'Are you sure?'

'Just those two places.'

'Okay, but painters, decorators, they often do little jobs here and there.'

'Frank didn't.'

'Cash-in-hand jobs? Off the books?'

'Frank didn't.'

'Did you know about the skeleton?' Thomas said.

'No.'

'When did you last talk to Frank?'

'Night before he died. He came to the flat.'

'What about?'

'Nothing in particular.' Eelke looked down at the kitchen table. 'Just catching up.' He was still in his studied relaxed pose. He'd stopped looking at me several questions ago and that made his pretence more convincing, without the twitching eyes to give him away.

'He didn't mention this skeleton?' Thomas repeated.

'No.'

'Or any plans he had to make some extra money?'

Eelke sighed. 'The only plans he had were to do his job. He was an honest guy, worked hard, on two building sites.'

'An honest, hard-working guy with a skeleton in a locker.'

'Maybe he was holding the ticket for someone.'

'His fingerprints are all over the bag.'

I'd been watching Eelke, so I couldn't tell if Thomas's face changed during the lie. We hadn't spoken to Forensics yet.

'Nobody else's?' Eelke said.

'There are always other prints.'

Eelke's head shot up. 'Look,' he said, 'I don't know why he had that skeleton. It was probably just a prank, or most likely it wasn't even his. But he's dead now, the funeral is tomorrow and you need to go to the building site. Find out if there's something not right there. Because you must wonder, now that you've found this skeleton, you must start to question—'

'There are two things we want to know.' Thomas looked Eelke straight in the eye. 'One,' he held a finger out, 'where the skeleton came from, and two,' second finger, 'why your brother had it in his possession.'

'You don't care about his death.' Eelke sounded as if he'd only just realized that.

'He fell.' Thomas wrote something in his notebook.

'Tessa said you were like that.' Eelke's eyes locked with Thomas's. An unhappy smile crept on to his mouth. 'When you talked to her three days ago you were like that too. You don't care. You're all like that. Siding with the establishment. Looking after the rich. Forgetting about the common man.'

'And what do you do?' I asked.

Both Thomas and Eelke looked at me as if they'd completely forgotten I was in the room.

'Sorry?' Eelke took one hand out of his trouser pocket, put the elbow on the table and tipped his head sideways. He scratched the back of his neck.

'Your job. What do you do?'

'What does that have to do with anything?' Eelke said.

'Just answer the question,' Thomas said.

'I'm a teacher. PE teacher.'

'And a big Ajax fan.' I nodded at the wall behind him.

'Yes, love the photos,' Thomas said. He got up to examine them more closely. 'Cruyff. Wow.' He turned back to look at Eelke. 'How did you get Cruyff to autograph a photo for you?'

'Well,' Eelke smiled, 'I actually bought that one.' He looked comfortable for the first time since we got in. 'But the others, they were signed just for me. At the stadium. Started as a kid.'

'Great collection.' Thomas went back to his chair and sat down. 'Did you see the game on Sunday?'

'What a mess, wasn't it? That AZ goal was clearly offside.' Eelke's shoulders dropped, happy with the football conversation. Was he one of those guys who was only interested in sport? There was no evidence of a woman in this flat. No pictures, no ring on his finger.

'How well do you get on with Tessa?' I asked.

'Why?' His dark eyes darted back to me.

'When you picked her up from the station, did she say anything? Had Frank told her anything about the skeleton?'

'No.'

'Would she have told you?'

'Maybe.'

'If your brother had a money-making plan . . .' I said.

'He didn't have a plan.'

'But if he did, would he have told you?'

Eelke chewed his bottom lip. 'He didn't have a plan.'

* * *

'What the fuck questions were those?' Thomas said as soon as we got outside the block of flats and had closed the door behind us. '*What do you do for a living?*' He said it in a nasal, sing-song voice. 'I'm happy for you to tag along, but don't interrupt me. I was questioning him about his brother's accident and you want to know what he does for a living?' He set off towards the car at a pace that I had trouble keeping up with.

Tagging along? Was that how he saw it? 'You didn't want to know what kind of work he does?' I said.

'I really couldn't care less.' He smiled at me with the grin of a fighter eyeing up a much smaller opponent. His squat build would make him a good boxer, but he'd never go anywhere near the ring; he'd be too worried it might mess up his perfect hair. 'And that stuff about Tessa, was that really necessary?'

'She called him.'

'So?'

'It was worth a question. You don't think that's useful?'

'No, clearly not.' He unlocked the car doors with a beep.

'Why not?'

'There's nothing there. Builder finds skeleton on building site. Doesn't want to delay the boss, sticks the bones in a bin bag, stores them in a locker for a day, aiming to chuck them out later. Has an accident and dies. End of. There's no plan, nothing that he'd tell either his wife or his brother. There's nothing. There's an accident. That's it.'

'But—'

'I know you want to think this is important, but it's not.

I want to get it off the books and move on to something more meaningful.' He opened the door.

'A skeleton, a dead man. What more do you need to make this meaningful, Thomas?'

'A Second World War skeleton and an accident. I guess I'd need a crime.'

'Moving the skeleton not crime enough for you? You don't get out of bed for anything that carries less than a twelve-month sentence?'

'I'm less interested when the guy who did it is dead.'

'Frank Stapel's death is odd, though, don't you think?'

He stopped, one leg in the car, the other still outside, hands on top of the door frame. 'You're dragging this out beyond any reason. We went to the site. We interviewed the widow and the brother. We're done.' He sat down behind the wheel.

I was done too. Done for the day. 'You go back to the office,' I said. I tapped the roof with both hands. 'I've got something to do around here.'

Thomas opened the passenger door from the inside. 'Get in.'

I didn't even know if he'd heard me. 'No, you go. I'll see you tomorrow.'

He pulled the door shut. Just as I was about to walk away, the window whirred down. 'Why did you come back, Lotte?'

The comment buffeted me like a storm-force wind. I'd had to fight hard to be allowed back in. I needed to make up for the mistake that had nearly ruined my life. 'I've been cleared.' Getting things out in the open could be the first step towards an improvement in my relationship with Thomas. I took a deep breath to work up the courage. 'Thanks, Thomas.' He'd been the person closest to finding out the truth about me. He'd listened to the tapes of the conversations I'd had with the murderer. Of course not all the conversations had been recorded, and Thomas knew that.

He raised his eyebrows. 'Thanks for what?'

'For not saying anything.'

He shook his head. His eyes narrowed and his eyebrows pulled together. 'I wasn't going to jeopardize a conviction. Go to another team. We didn't want you back.' He closed the window again and drove off.

My cheeks burnt as if I'd been hit in the face. I watched the car disappear. I hoisted my handbag higher up my shoulder. There was something I should do. I was only two apartment blocks away from my mother's flat.

Chapter Seven

In nature, the first rays of warm sunshine had brought bumblebee queens and solitary bees out of their nests. In my mother's flat, spring had brought forth a multitude of boxes. Large, old-fashioned pieces of furniture crowded the place at the best of times, and now I couldn't even get in the door. 'This a bad time?' I said.

'Of course not.' Her tone belied her words and I waited for her to make an excuse, but she pulled a large box out of the way to clear a path. The ease with which she did it said more about her than her white hair. 'You can help. I could do with a hand.' Too thin for seventy-four, she looked fragile, but I knew she was really a steel rod with wrinkled skin around it.

I carefully stepped over another box to get to the oak table.

'How's your shoulder?' My mother put a basket of rags – old T-shirts shredded into cloths and a few ancient socks – in front of me.

'Fine.' Our relationship had been strained these last few months since I'd been reunited with my father. I hoped we could get back to how we used to be.

She sat down with her own basket of cloths and her own cardboard box. 'What did the doctor say?'

'He said it had healed well.' I chose a cloth from the basket in front of me. In a previous life it had been a thick white tennis sock. I balled my hand and shoved it inside the sock. The circle that my index finger made with my thumb showed through the hole that my mother's rough-skinned heel had worn in the fabric. I held it out. 'That's what my scar looks like: a circle inside smooth tissue.'

She pushed my hand away. 'That's not funny.'

'I'm not being funny.' I looked at my hand again within the sock. I examined it from a different angle. 'It's pretty accurate actually. But more like the exit wound. The entry wound is much smaller.' I reached over to the cardboard box on the floor and raised the lid. My toys. I'd put them in this box when I'd made room for my university books. It had been an indication that I'd grown up, even if I hadn't been able to afford to move out.

I pulled the lion cage out of the box. I caressed its plastic bars with the white sock.

'You look tired,' my mother said.

'Thanks.' I concentrated on the yellow vertical rods.

'How's your father?' My mother was cleaning the fake Barbie doll I'd never liked. It had a similar figure and facial features to the real one but had been less than half the price.

'He's fine.'

'And his wife?'

'Mum, please.' I moved on to the lions themselves. The two plastic animals were stuck in a soundless roar.

'Is she fine too?'

'She is.'

'And work?'

'First day back last week.' I told her about the skeleton.

'I hope you can identify it. Give the family something to bury,' my mother said.

'If there is a family.' I fished the large pool out of the box. It was a grey plastic kidney shape with a blue slide in the middle.

'At least you're doing something worthwhile this time, not just running after your father.' She had moved on from the dolls to the small collection of Playmobil. She rubbed the head and legs of each little man and woman with a piece of an old T-shirt.

'That was important.' I wiped the dust from the penguin enclosure.

My mother didn't respond.

I passed the penguins themselves through my tennis sock and arranged them in a line on the table. 'I'm really concerned about the widow. The skeleton, it's old anyway.' I kept them as far away from the lions as possible.

'You always care about the strangest things.'

'My boss told me not to look into her husband's death. And my colleagues would probably agree with you.' I grimaced at the memory of Thomas's words. 'But she's so young, and I have to admit, the skeleton makes it all the more intriguing.'

'You need to be careful. After all that drama with your father, just do what your boss wants.'

'I want to do something good for a change. Make it better for someone. Give this girl the answers she needs.'

'And the family of that Second World War skeleton?'

I shrugged. 'That's old news.'

'Don't talk like that. It doesn't feel old to me.' She finished cleaning the twenty little men and women.

I didn't bite and didn't give her another chance to talk about the war. She'd only been a child when it ended, but she'd told me about the hunger so often. How there'd been no food at all that last winter, no electricity, no gas. How I should be grateful not to have lived through that. I packed the zoo back into its cardboard box. I gestured to another one close to me. 'This one next?'

She nodded.

I opened the cardboard flap; inside were my earliest books, large and bright. *Pim, Frits en Ida.* They had been my favourite. The series of adventures of two brothers and their little sister. I used to dream of having brothers.

'Sorry, Lotte, I lost track of time. I'm having some visitors soon.'

My mother always had people from her church over. 'Anybody I know?'

'I'm babysitting.'

I stared at the books but left them in the box. 'Who for?'

'Nadia.' She stared at me with her duck-egg-blue eyes as if challenging me to object. 'She's dropping her daughter off.' Her eyes were almost the same colour as the walls in my flat.

'Nadia?'

'They're going to the cinema. I've been babysitting—'

'They? My ex-husband and his new wife?'

'Well, you're meeting *my* ex-husband,' she said.

'Your ex-husband just happens to be my father. A bit different, don't you think?'

'Nadia needed the help.'

'How long have you been talking to her?'

'Arjen called after you'd been shot. He'd read about it in the papers. He called to check you were all right.'

'He didn't call me.'

'You were in hospital. He and Nadia came to see me a month after. I told them you were on the coast and I hadn't seen you for a while.'

I tore the white tennis sock from my hand and threw it on the table. 'You told them you were lonely.'

'I told them I hadn't seen you; they drew their own conclusions and came over. With the girl. She's so sweet. She's almost two now.'

'Mum, please.' I closed my eyes. My own daughter had never made it to two. After her death, my marriage had fallen apart.

'You asked me why I was meeting them.'

My mother knew exactly where my weak spots were. It would have hurt less if she had taken a knife and jammed it into my shoulder.

'I babysit once a week. Arjen drops her off, Nadia picks her up.'

I looked at the boxes full of my old toys.

'And a few extra evenings. Now that she's back at work.'

'Sorry, Mum, got to go. See you next week.' I picked up my coat and moved to give my mother a kiss on the cheek. She backed away. I pulled the box with the toys towards me. It was the most precious one. The books would have to stay. I wrapped my arms around the box, hoisted it up on to my hip and carried it down the stairs.

My mother shouted after me that I shouldn't be so childish.

I ignored her.

I was halfway between my mother's flat and the tram stop when I heard someone else call out behind me.

'Detective Meerman!'

It was Tessa. She darted across the grass that edged the block. When she got close, she pointed at the box. 'Can I help you with that?'

I shook my head, kept the box in front of me, both arms wrapped around it. 'I'm only catching the tram.'

'I saw you,' she said, 'and knew this was our chance to talk. Were you interviewing other people in the area?'

'I was visiting my mother.'

We crossed the road side by side.

'You will take my husband's death seriously now, won't you? You won't just say it was an accident, like your colleague? I talked to Eelke just now. We both think . . .' She had her set of keys in her hand and the metal ring that held them together was slipped over her middle finger.

'Tessa, maybe it was purely an accident.' We arrived at the tram stop and I put the box down.

'But what if it wasn't? If you won't even investigate . . .'

I looked down the road in the direction the tram would arrive from. 'We'll investigate.'

'You'll do it thoroughly? You? You personally?'

I stopped looking along the tram rail. The wind blew Tessa's hair around her face. She drowned in a man's parka.

'Please,' she said. 'You have . . . experience. You've been in all the papers. If you decide it was an accident, I'll believe you.'

Unlike doctors, the police could never make things better. Unless we could prevent a crime, the best we could do was to punish perpetrators and give those left behind some justice. In Frank's case, his death could well have been an accident, but I could give Tessa answers about what he had been doing on his last day and that might help heal the wounds that his loss left behind. If I wrote off the very first death I'd seen once I'd come back to work, then why had I bothered to return? Helping this young widow come to terms with her husband's death might not be in my job description, but it would even the universe's score against me.

In the distance I heard the bell that announced the tram was coming around the corner. I lifted the box back on to my hip.

'Promise me.' Tessa's eyelashes were darkened by unshed tears.

'I promise.' It was partially a promise to Tessa, but more than that it was a promise to myself that I would do some good.

She gave me an awkward one-sided hug over the box of toys. She smiled her gap-toothed smile. I got on the tram and through the window I watched her drift back to her flat. She had her parka wrapped tightly around her and took each step slowly, her head bowed as if she had to examine every blade of grass to decide which one to trample. A group of children ran with a football right next to her, a different species altogether. Then the tram turned a corner and I couldn't see her any more.

The tram rattled through central Amsterdam for fifteen minutes then turned the corner that would take me to my stop. As I got off the tram and walked along my canal, I saw the pile of furniture outside our communal door. I lived in a seventeenth-century house that had been split into three apartments, and the downstairs neighbours, an American family, had moved out while I was at work. They'd gone back to the States and abandoned whatever they couldn't fit in their removal truck. The shipping costs must be high and it was probably cheaper to buy these things new. A nice sofa, four kitchen chairs in good condition, a couple of cardboard boxes and a pet carrier. There were always students who could use free furniture. Most of that stuff would be gone by the morning.

As I stuck my key in the lock, I heard a sound. A soft meow. Behind the carrier's fenced front was the black-and-white face of downstairs' cat, Pippi. She looked just like the one from the Felix ad, but with a black nose. I pushed a finger through the wire and rubbed her forehead. 'Hello, girl,' I said. She bumped her head against me.

Unlike the furniture, the pet carrier was labelled. A big sticker on top said *Urgent, animal, treat with care* and the address where she was going to go. A cardboard box roughly the same size as the box of toys I was carrying had similar tags and said *Pippi's things* on the side. 'When are they coming to get you, puss-puss?'

The cat meowed again, as if to indicate that she was tired of waiting.

'I know Pippi-girl, it's horrid.' I read the labels, which said that couriers would pick her up to reunite her with her owners in about ten minutes. I gave her another small tickle. 'Bye, Pippi, good girl, they'll be here soon.' I was surprised the neighbours hadn't taken her themselves rather than leaving her outside.

I hauled my toys up the stairs, let myself into my flat, sat down on the sofa and hugged the box. I rested my forehead on the cardboard lid and thought about the interview: Thomas questioning Eelke, asking about the skeleton. I'd interrupted and asked about his job. PE teacher. I had broken Thomas's rhythm to get that really useful information that Eelke was a PE teacher. He'd been carrying a net of footballs when I'd first seen him at Centraal station: I could have figured out he was a PE teacher without asking.

A guy finds some bones on a building site. He puts them in a bag to throw away later. Then he falls. It wasn't a suspicious death but an accident. Sure, sticking human bones in a bag is a crime, digging them up without calling the police is even a crime. But a small crime and, as Thomas said, the guy who'd done it was dead.

I put the box of toys on the floor and picked up the book I was halfway through. I found it hard to keep my mind on *Surviving Your Elderly Parents*, even though I needed all the help I could find on how to get on with my mother. Frank Stapel's death kept demanding my attention, more interesting than the page talking about frail health and how that could affect people's feeling of self-worth.

I gave up on the book, went to my study and clipped a fresh white sheet of paper to my architect's table. It was one of the items that the interior designer who'd owned my flat before me had left behind. She needed the money and I needed furniture and a place to live. I took over everything she had. It was the best interior design decision I had ever made: not to change anything in the flat, just to move in with my clothes and my pots and pans and leave it at that. I left all my other belongings behind in the house I'd shared with my ex-husband.

I tilted the table. I hadn't thought it would be useful, but what a great tool it had turned out to be. I moved my hand over the pure white sheet of paper and started to write in large letters with a blue felt pen. I wrote *Frank Stapel* in the middle of the page. I drew a box around his name. Something didn't make sense: if you wanted to get rid of an unwanted skeleton, where better than at a building site? Why dig it up and put it in a locker if you could, for example, just pour cement over it and be done with it? People did whatever was easiest, and in Frank's case, surely the easiest thing would have been either to call the police and take a week's delay on the project, or maybe even less; or otherwise leave it in the ground and ignore it. Instead he dug it up. He put it in a locker. There must have been some other reason.

I linked Tessa and Eelke to the box with arrows. I made

a note, in pencil, of the two places where Frank had worked. From there, I drew a squiggly line to the word *skeleton*. I knew I didn't have anything to go on, but standing here, looking at the drawing, I could see so many questions that there might even be something to investigate.

I woke up at 3.57 a.m. Pale light was peeking around the corner of the curtains. There was noise outside. Men's voices. Loud, boisterous. On their way home after pub closing time. I got up and yawned as I opened the curtains just a fraction. Apart from a narrow pavement, the curved one-way streets on either side of the canal were just wide enough for a car. The canal was like an extreme central reservation at twice the width of each lane. In the seventeenth century, when the canal had been dug, it had been a moat around the city and had doubled up as the main route of transport. The water had been important, the road an afterthought.

Two men stood by the leftover pile of furniture, lit by the street light above them. One of them sat down on a kitchen chair. Their laughter was raucous. I opened the window and their voices streamed in.

'Here, puss-puss-puss,' one of them said.

'Let's chuck it in the canal.'

I switched on the light and looked for my slippers.

'Think it'll swim?'

'Dude, it's in a cage. It's not going to swim.'

I grabbed my keys and ran down the stairs. I pulled the outside door open.

The guy on the kitchen chair jumped up.

The other one, who held Pippi in her basket, stood and stared at me. 'What do you want?'

'Put the cat down.' Even to my own ears it sounded silly. Two men. Both taller than me. The one who'd jumped up from the chair at least didn't have a shaven head. He made eye contact. Not aggressive. The other one was the problem. A tattoo snaked around his neck.

'What's it to you? It's not your cat, is it?' Mid-twenties. Drunk. Pippi meowing loudly in her carrier in one hand, can of beer in the other. Two of his friends, who had been further up the canal, came back and joined in now that there was some excitement.

Four against one. The odds were getting bad. 'Put the cat down.' The front door was right behind me but I had no intention of backing off.

'I was thinking of taking it home.'

'Mate, you weren't. I heard you. You were going to throw her in the canal.'

The guy with the hair said, 'Let's go.'

'Yes, boys, go. Give me the cat.'

'Who are you to tell us what to do?' Tattoo took a step in my direction.

All remnants of sleep left my body. 'I'm a police officer. I've got a gun upstairs. Don't make me get it.'

Tattoo stood his ground. 'I'm not doing anything illegal. This stuff's abandoned. The cat would die if it was just left here. I'm rescuing it.'

Tattoo's two mates stood in the road. There were no cars

at this time of night. Nobody else was walking along the canal. Tattoo's eyes moved down from my face. I didn't fold my arms over my front but stood up straight and tall in my light-blue fluffy slippers. I was acutely aware that I was wearing a large T-shirt with Nighty Night printed on the front, matched with a pair of stripy pyjama bottoms. Tattoo moved into my personal space. His breath smelled of booze and his chin was covered with a mixture of blackheads and dark stubble.

I put out my hand. 'Give me the cat.' My voice was as strong as it had been four months ago when I'd asked for someone's gun. I pushed the thought to the back of my mind that that had got me shot.

The guy with the hair put a hand on Tattoo's arm. 'Come on, Jack.'

Tattoo waited, staring at my hand, as if to show that he wasn't afraid of me. My shoulder muscles tensed. He was a good head taller and a lot wider than me, so I was convinced that I didn't worry him in the slightest. He swung the pet carrier towards me. I reached out to grab it.

At the last moment he skipped away, towards the canal, as if he was in a bowling alley, rocked the carrier back with the momentum and let it go at the highest point.

The splash when it hit the water was followed by Pippi's loud howl.

'Woo-hoo!' Tattoo shouted. 'Bull's eye!' He ran away. His friends followed him, whooping as if throwing a cat in the canal was a major achievement.

'You fucking cowards,' I shouted after them. Then I rushed

to the water's edge. The carrier plunged but bobbed back up, partially afloat. 'Shit shit shit.' The image of submerged shopping trolleys and junkies' needles shot through my head. The pavement was sharp under my feet after I'd kicked my slippers off. I dropped my keys. During freshers' week, one of my university classmates had dived into a canal and broken his neck. He'd never returned to class. I jumped after Pippi.

The cold water took my breath away and my skin contracted closely around my bones. My feet never reached the bottom and the dark water closed above my head. I kept eyes and mouth closed until I kicked my way back to the surface. I scanned around me to locate Pippi in the dark. To my left I heard her low-throated yowl. The carrier was sinking quickly. My T-shirt had engorged itself and tried to drag me under. The brown water came up to my chin. I closed the distance and scrambled to grab the handle on top before I couldn't see it again. I was barely staying afloat with only one arm free to swim. My muscles were shaking. I lifted the pet carrier as high as I could. Hopefully it would let Pippi keep her head above the water. The canal pulled on my feet.

'Help, somebody.' No reply. The cowards had run away and left me here. The light from the street lamps bounced off the water and showed me where to go. 'It's okay, girl. Don't be scared.' Water slopped into my mouth. I spat out as much as I could. Four more strokes and I would be at the canal's edge, an arm's-length above my head. 'I've got you.' This was nothing like dragging dummies to safety in a swimming pool. For one thing, the dummies never moved. Something brushed against my arm. I hoped it was a fish or a semi-decayed plastic Coca-Cola bottle, but it could just as easily be a used condom. My fingers burnt with the strain. There was silence inside the carrier.

'Pippi?' I said softly. 'Pippi?'

Nothing. Had she drowned? My eyes stung from the canal water.

I was nearly at the edge, pushed myself as high out of the water as possible and swung the carrier on to dry land, less carefully than I wanted to.

I held on to the canal wall and rested my forehead on the cold stone. Then Pippi growled. Relief surged through me and came out in the form of a laugh. I waited a few seconds to get the strength back in my arms. I was worried about what my fingers would touch on the bank, but I felt only brick. I pulled myself out of the canal as from a swimming pool. On dry land, I stayed kneeling down, head bent, with water streaming from my hair. Pippi whimpered. I got to my feet and picked up the carrier. She was as soaked to the bone as I was.

'The worst is over now, sweetie.'

She meowed bravely.

I wanted to take her out and hug her, but I was worried that she'd make a dash for it. I left a trail of water behind as if I was a swamp monster that had been cut at each step by the sharp pavement. Worse than the cold and the discomfort of the cobbles under my bare feet was the smell of rotten fish that clung to my hair, skin and clothes.

It was a miracle that my slippers were still there with my keys inside.

As I carried her up to my flat, Pippi whimpered hoarsely, as if she'd given up. My legs were shaking but I went down the two flights of stairs once more to get her box of things, then I put her carrier in the bathroom and unhooked the metal grille. Pippi looked like a cross between ET and a rat, but then I didn't look much better. I sat down on the floor. Her green eyes were enormous now that all her fur was plastered against her skull. I dried her a little with my towel until she told me with a pathetic little hiss that she'd had enough and took over herself. I opened the cardboard box, found bowls, cat food, litter and a tray. I put it all out and gave her water. Then finally I had a shower. It took a lot of shampoo before I could no longer smell the combination of algae and fish in my hair.

I rolled into bed but found it hard to sleep. Even after the long hot shower, my teeth chattered so loudly that the sound could have kept the neighbours awake. At some point in the night, Pippi curled up against me and started to purr. Her fur had dried but she reeked like week-old sushi. I stroked her little face. I'd have to get a book on looking after cats. Cleaning her would be a job for tomorrow.

A call on my mobile woke me at 8.57 a.m. I must have turned off my alarm.

'When you have a second,' Edgar Ling said, 'could you pop down to the lab?'

'I'm in the middle of something but I can be there in half an hour.' I tried to sound as if I was at my desk instead of still lying in bed. 'Why?'

'There's a problem with the skeleton.'

Chapter Eight

In the basement lab, I shivered and hugged my arms around my waist. I was sleep-deprived and in desperate need of coffee. After Edgar's call had woken me up, I'd thrown on a suit, fed Pippi and dashed over here. It had taken me a little less than the half an hour I'd told Edgar, as I hadn't stopped by the office.

'It was when I'd laid them all out.' Edgar Ling's eyes shone even more than when I'd talked to him at Centraal station, and his face was flushed pink. His blond hair showed the tracks of a comb. 'When I put them together like that, it was immediately obvious.'

I looked at the skeleton to see what 'immediately obvious' looked like. They were just bones to me. The forensic lab's artificial bright light didn't show me much difference between them.

'Do you see it?' he said.

I shook my head. Some of my colleagues were squeamish about bones, but for me there was nothing revolting about them. Dead bodies were no different. Only the very first forensic examination I'd watched had been tough. Our class had been warned beforehand not to dress in our favourite clothes, as we'd always associate them with the smell.

'Oh, well.' His excitement didn't falter just because I was too blind to grasp what he was trying to explain to me. 'Look at this.' He pointed at a bone. 'Can you see now?'

I tried, just for the guy's sake. 'It looks different.' It seemed the most logical thing to say.

'Exactly. It looks different because it *is* different. It isn't from the same body.'

That didn't make any sense. 'Are you kidding me?'

'It's actually not even the right bone. Humerus. Upper arm.'

'So this is another old bone? Does that mean the skeleton came from some Second World War mass grave? Have you managed to get that confirmed? That this is from the war.'

'The main skeleton is from around that time. There could be five years either side, but it seems most likely. But this extra bone isn't. This is much more recent. It's between five and ten years old. I've run a couple of quick tests this morning, as it took some time to find someone from your team. This bone is from a man. And can you see this line here? That's where it was broken before. It's the bone of a man who'd once had a broken arm. Isn't that amazingly interesting?'

'Five years? That's all?'

'That is the earliest, but yes. These bones were buried directly in the ground. That's why it decomposed to a skeleton in a relatively short time. When a body's properly buried in a coffin, it takes a lot longer.

'And there's only one bone?'

'No, these as well.' He pointed at two more. 'The ulna and radius. All from the right arm.'

'Age?' Last night's lack of sleep was still hindering my ability to think, but I was slowly realizing this could be a significant find.

'Not sure yet. We're doing some more checks. Not young I think, though.'

A middle-aged man with a broken arm. 'Was the arm cut off?'

'Oh no, there are no signs of trauma on any of the bones. No cuts. No sign of knife markings.'

I rubbed my face as if that would help me understand what Edgar was showing me. 'So the man whose arm we have here is dead?'

'That's a distinct possibility.'

There were a number of men who had gone missing over the last ten years, if we used Edgar's upper limit. Maybe we had found one of them. Someone who had been killed and buried together with a war victim? Or just an arm that had gone astray. That didn't make sense. 'And the rest of that skeleton?' I asked.

Edgar shrugged. 'Who knows. Still buried, maybe, or in another bin bag.'

'I don't understand: how do three bones from a recent skeleton get mixed up with a wartime one? Were they at the same place?' If the man with the broken arm had died of natural causes, I couldn't think of a reason why those bones had got combined.

'I'll run some more tests.' Edgar pointed at the humerus with the back of his pen. 'See here? There is soil residue on all the bones. Attached to it, not contaminated from being in the same bin bag.' He nodded as if to himself. 'We'll be able to tell if it came from the same place.'

My mobile rang. It was Thomas.

'Where are you?' he said. Maybe he had hoped that I wouldn't have come back to work after yesterday's little heart-to-heart.

'I'm with Edgar Ling.' He'd probably looked at my shift schedule to see when I was supposed to be at my desk. 'There's been a development. Where are you?'

Thomas told me he'd just got back to the office. I said we'd be right up.

'Come with me,' I said to Edgar.

He grabbed a folder and followed me up the stairs.

'A man's bones,' I said. Our office had four L-shaped desks in it, pushed together to form a plus sign. Ingrid was to my left, by the window.

'More old bones. It doesn't matter.' Thomas hung up his coat on the coat rack behind me. I had my old seat back, closest to the door. He sat down at his desk diagonally across from me. Behind him was the newest piece of art to adorn our office. State subsidies to artists translated into their works covering walls in many governmental buildings. I could imagine the desperate sighs when this latest monstrosity had turned up. They cycled round every few months, so hopefully it would go away soon.

Edgar slumped at the spare desk opposite mine. I was embarrassed about Thomas's lack of interest for Edgar's sake. 'They're not old,' I said. 'Ten years at most. A man was buried more recently alongside an old war skeleton.' I'd stared at the painting the whole week that I'd been back and still hadn't managed to discover any meaning or pattern in the red and blue swirls and dots of paint, surrounded by a square of black. Half-eaten guppies in a fish tank maybe.

Thomas stopped typing. 'Was it just an arm?'

'Humerus, ulna and radius,' Edgar said. 'Only the right arm. No sign of trauma.'

'So the rest of the skeleton is still somewhere.' I knew I'd jumped ahead, but I needed Thomas and Ingrid engaged. 'We need to go to the sites where Frank Stapel worked.' I held out the piece of paper with the names of both property developers that Tessa had given us yesterday. The whiteboard on the wall to my right was still empty, as evidence that Thomas didn't think this was a case. 'That's the best place to start. Double-check if the skeleton we found in the bin bag came from either site.'

I expected Thomas to object, but he nodded. 'Okay,' he said, 'we'll do that. Edgar, what else have you got on the old skeleton?'

'The main skeleton is most likely Second World War,' Edgar said. 'It's a man, around thirty years old. We could tell from the wear on the teeth.' He handed round photos from a cardboard folder. It showed the skull from various angles. If I hadn't known how old it was, it could have been a recent professional hit, as the bullet mark showed a shot to the back of the head from close distance.

'Was he a soldier?' Ingrid asked.

'Can't tell. There are no fabric fibres of any kind on that skeleton. I did find some on the humerus of the recent one. I got good soil samples too, still stuck to the skull. I've mainly worked on the skull,' he said. 'It's ironic. Second World War skeletons used to be my job. Before I came here.'

'That's a job?' Ingrid asked.

'Army Identification Unit. To deal with the bodies of soldiers. Identify them and bury them.'

'A full-time job?' Ingrid said.

'Less and less so. I heard there were six or seven people employed in the late fifties, when they found a handful of bodies a week. Especially around Arnhem and closer to the German border. Now they deal with a couple a month. Did you know there are still thousands of soldiers missing, last deployed on Dutch soil?'

'I had no idea,' Ingrid said.

'What's the chance of identification?' Thomas finally turned away from his computer screen. After all, that was the main thing the boss cared about.

'If it's a soldier, about twenty per cent. When they're buried with some of their belongings, there's a better chance. It's hard when they're in the state our skeleton is in.' He got two photos out of his folder and put them in front of me. 'No uniform, no insignia.'

'They're normally found with their things?' Thomas said.

'If only. Diggers go out around Arnhem, search the battlefields with metal detectors to find memorabilia. Some of the ruthless ones will dig up the bodies, strip them of their lighters, watches and anything else that they can sell on eBay and leave the remains behind.'

'People buy that stuff?'

'Have a look on eBay when you get home tonight,' Edgar Ling said. 'There are people willing to pay a lot of money for something that's been stolen from a dead soldier.'

I shivered. 'That's what could have happened with this body then? Someone dug up the war skeleton and left the newer one behind but picked up recent bones by mistake?'

'I don't think so,' Edgar said. 'If that was the case, I would have expected some of the clothes to be there. Socks, shoes.' He smiled, but it was only a movement of the lips out of politeness, as if to show what he thought of those diggers. 'In my experience, war skeletons are normally found for one of three reasons: first of all, when a new road or house is built. Then the diggers, of course. But sometimes we find them because people feel remorse and tell us where bodies are buried.'

'And what about fingerprints?' Thomas asked.

'There were no prints on any of the bones. On the bin bag we found Frank's and Tessa's.'

'So he wore gloves when he dug up the bones but not when he carried the bag to the station?'

'You could draw that conclusion,' Edgar said.

'Can we go back to these extra bones? Can you tell if they came from a building site?' Thomas asked. 'And the same for the old bones?'

Edgar folded both hands together and pressed them against his mouth. 'I'll do some tests. Get the National Forensic Institute involved too. We can even detect pollen, you know, see what plants were growing close by.' He fished a piece of paper from the pocket of his jacket and scribbled a reminder to himself. 'So yes, we've taken a DNA sample from the skull. The one from the arm bones should be here tomorrow.' He shrugged. 'It's a day behind, as I'd thought I was only dealing with one skeleton at first.'

'What are the chances of identifying him through DNA?'

'All we need is one descendant who's a criminal. That's all.'

'When will you know?' Thomas said.

'The computer is churning through it as we speak.' He looked at each one of us in turn, like a schoolteacher checking to see if his pupils had any questions. When we didn't, he closed the cardboard folder, put it on my desk, and left.

Chapter Nine

We should probably have gone to Kars van Wiel the minute we found the skeleton. It would have been our last chance to take the manager of the building site where Frank Stapel had died unawares. Now he knew what we'd found in that luggage locker.

At least nobody knew about the extra bones. Nobody knew about the rest of the skeleton that was probably still buried somewhere.

Our skeleton had been on the news last night. This morning it was all over the papers. Was it a Second World War body? Was it the result of a gangland killing? Was it a body that had been dug up at one of Amsterdam's cemeteries last month? Was it a prank by some students? There'd been no comment from the police, of course.

A photo taken on a kid's iPhone had accompanied the piece in *De Telegraaf.* It showed me from the back, my head close to that of one of my colleagues in uniform, seemingly whispering in his ear.

'Have you seen this?' Thomas showed me the photo before we left to visit the building site again.

'Of course.'

'Didn't know you liked them that young.'

'If you look closely, you can see that I'm actually in front of him and talking to Edgar Ling.'

Thomas grinned. I shook my head. We drove back to Zuid. We parked and walked over to the distinctive office block where Frank Stapel had fallen to his death. A man waved at us as soon as we approached. Even from a distance I recognized the man who seemed as wide as one of his bulldozers.

'You want me to show you everything again? You miss something last time?' Kars van Wiel grinned, then rubbed his eyes. Now that I was standing close to him, his bulk was even more noticeable. His eyes were red and swollen, as if someone had socked him. 'I always tell my guys that it saves time to do everything right first time. I guess it's the same for the police.' His voice was nasal.

'We didn't miss anything,' Thomas said. 'There's new information.'

'Of course. That skeleton.' Kars inhaled sharply through his nose and cleared excess snot into the back of his throat with a gurgling sound.

'Yes,' Thomas said, 'there's that skeleton. So show me around the site again. I want to see if Frank could have found it here.'

'Here?' Kars scanned the area as if trying to spot a bone sticking out of the ground. 'Unlikely. Not at this stage. Tone . . . hey, Tony!' he shouted out at a man carrying a clipboard. 'We didn't find a skeleton here, did we?'

The clipboard looked out of place in Tony's hands, which were made to break breeze blocks in half. His skin had the pitted red surface of a brick.

'My brother.' Kars pointed at him with a thumb.

I wasn't sure if I'd hire the brothers to run a large-scale building project, but if I ever needed anybody to destroy a wall by hand, I'd know who to call.

'We found some bones on our last project.' Tony's voice was surprisingly light, coming out of such a big body. 'But that was on fallow land. We found them early on, when we were putting the foundations in.'

'Soldiers?' I said.

'There were no insignia, so your guys said they wouldn't be able to identify them.'

'How long did work stop for?' Thomas asked.

'A week or so. Because they weren't army. No risk of ammunition or bombs lying around. But it was a bloody nuisance.'

The foundations of this building would have been dug and hammered into the ground months ago. Amsterdam's soil was soft, and concrete underpinnings were always necessary. A children's song spoke of Amsterdam as the city built on poles. This particular new office block was already taking shape: the walls were up, the floors placed, the roof done.

'They put the bones in one of those unnamed graves,' Kars said. 'And now they're digging them up again, I read in the paper. Waste of money. They couldn't identify them a year ago, so why they think they can now is beyond me.'

'New technology,' Thomas said, 'so we can bury them with some dignity rather than just dumping them in a nameless grave.'

'No, that isn't it,' Kars said. 'It's to keep people in a job. That's all. Thanks, Tony.'

Kars guided us to the front of the building. To the right, two doors down, smartly dressed men and women were dripping through revolving doors into a tower of office space. Most of them had their eyes cast down to their mobiles, as if it was important to have a final check of their emails before they reached their destination. It was the building where the witness Maarten Schuur, the man with the orange boat shoes, worked. By the time our colleagues in uniform had got here, people could be split into two groups: those who stopped and stared and those who walked quickly by and avoided looking at the broken body on the ground. When Thomas and I arrived, most people had left.

'This is the only place where we're digging.' Kars gestured to the cordoned-off area. They were adding the final touches: lifting a few street tiles to put in the bike racks and a raised flower bed. 'But we had to stop. After Frank . . . after Frank's death.'

The drawn outline was still here, right next to the plants. They were in bloom, clumps of bright pink tulips, edged by purple violets. This was where Frank had landed. I couldn't think of it any other way. His body had missed the corner of the flower planter by a metre or so. I looked up to trace the trajectory of his fall. 'What was Frank working on?'

Thomas looked at me with a deep frown, lips pursed. I'd told Pippi this morning as I fed her that I definitely would not ask any questions about anybody's job.

'As I told your colleague here the other day,' Kars said, 'he was plastering on the seventh floor. Just on the second tier. We want to have that area done so we can show people round. The view's great. I still don't know why he was out on the terrace. To have a smoke, maybe.' He shrugged.

I looked back up, glanced at the roof terrace. I'd never had a head for heights and couldn't understand why someone would walk around there just to smoke. 'Did anybody see him?'

Kars shook his head. 'He'd bunked off in the morning, so was making up the hours. Everybody else had already left.'

'Can we go up?' I said.

'Sure.'

Kars took us to the back. We walked around the outside area. There were gaps where they'd stopped laying new tiles, an area where the soil was visible, but there were no signs that it had been dug up in the last week or so. Stamped down, evened out, yes, I could see that, but dug up? There was no way the skeleton could have come from the flower bed. It wasn't big enough. No, if it had come from this particular site, it must have been dug up months ago, when they'd put the foundations in. But then what had Frank done with it in the meantime?

Kars opened a door with a swipe card. We took the goods lift up and got out on seven. The cement floor was fish-scale grey and the bare walls amplified our footsteps as if we were in a cave. It smelled of paint but there was nobody working. A pile of deserted building materials had taken over one corner. Otherwise the floor was empty. It would be impressive once there were some walls and furniture, but now it was only a cavernous space. A fireproof door led to the terrace. Large safety signs were plastered all over the door: *Hard-hat area, do not enter without safety equipment.* I hesitated before I pushed the door open. I didn't go out. Heights always seemed to pull on my stomach, as if gravity were tempting me to jump.

'Were these signs already here?' I said.

'Yes,' Thomas answered. 'When I came up here on the evening of Frank's accident, I saw all of these.'

'I was probably a bit hard on Frank making him work that late,' Kars said to Thomas. 'But I was annoyed that he'd taken the morning off. We were waiting for him. He was holding everybody up.'

'I know what that's like,' Thomas said.

'Right. And I thought: it's not fair on everybody else.'

'That they have to work harder because someone is doing stuff for themselves, you mean? Pursuing their own aims, their own goals.'

'That's it. That's exactly it,' Kars said. 'And sometimes a guy will come to me saying he can manage his own time, but they never can.'

'They always have difficulty judging when they're wrong,' Thomas said.

'Or when to—'

'Any CCTV up here?' I interrupted them. I glanced round but didn't see any obvious cameras.

'No point,' Kars van Wiel said. 'There's nothing here to steal.'

Thomas walked around on the terrace. From the safety of the door, I looked at the missing panels, the gap now covered with plastic sheeting. I was glad when Thomas finished his tour and came back in. We said goodbye to Kars van Wiel, told him we'd be in touch, and headed back down.

On either side of the path to the car park, office buildings full of workers towered over us. After we'd passed two of the buildings, I could see that the next one had a ground-floor canteen. I bet it was overpriced: here was a captive audience and not many places to eat, unless you wanted to sit outside on the concrete steps and munch on sandwiches you'd brought from home.

'Coffee?' I said. It would give me the caffeine boost to make the upcoming car journey with Thomas bearable.

He looked at his watch.

'Just a takeaway,' I said. 'I wouldn't want to keep you out of the office for too long.'

His look turned into a grin. 'I didn't think you were quite awake,' he said. 'You didn't ask that many pointless questions.'

We went in.

'I would have said "stupid questions",' Thomas said as we were waiting in the queue. 'But you'd be offended. You think you only ask clever questions. That's why you're checking my work, isn't it?'

'I'm not checking anything.'

'So why—'

'I'm not checking your work,' I said. I gave my order and looked at Thomas. 'What do you want?'

'I'll get my own.'

'We need to find that man's skeleton,' I said.

Thomas ordered his coffee and seemed completely engrossed in watching the girl make it.

'Was Kars different the last time you talked to him? He seemed pretty relaxed to me, for the developer of a site where someone's fallen to his death.'

'It was an accident.' Thomas put a plastic lid on his paper coffee cup.

'Right, but he didn't seem upset at all. If one of your workers died, wouldn't you at least stop joking about giving him a hard time?'

'Depends on whether you liked them or not.' He raised his cup to his lips and the coffee gurgled through the lid, sounding remarkably like Kars van Wiel clearing his nose.

I took a sip of mine. The caffeine felt good. 'So you don't think Kars liked Frank Stapel much?'

'I don't know. He seemed more concerned on Friday. More . . . Not sure how to describe it.' He shrugged. 'Made more of an effort, I'd say.'

My mobile rang. It was Edgar Ling. He sounded out of breath. 'You won't believe it,' he said. 'The skeleton. We've got a match.'

Chapter Ten

Francine Dutte looked ready to go out, probably to work. Unless she wore a leather jacket and matching boots inside the house. She had masses of dark hair and looked more Mediterranean than Dutch, as if Gina Lollobrigida had suddenly taken a job as a prosecutor in Amsterdam.

'Thomas,' she said. She only glanced at me for a second.

'Hi, Francine.' On the way over, he'd filled me in about her. He'd worked with her on two cases, both drugs-related. She was going places in the prosecution department. Very ambitious but had a brother who was trouble: a football hooligan, convicted many times over. The brother in the DNA database.

'This really isn't convenient. It's my day off, and the Kamphuis case isn't due to go to court for a month or so yet,' she said.

'It's not about that.' Thomas reached out and touched her on one leather-clad arm. 'Francine, can we come in?'

'Is it Sam? I know his trial's today, but—'

'Let's go inside, Francine, and we'll tell you.'

She combed both hands through her intensely waved hair

and cradled the back of her head as if that would help her think. 'Okay, but you'll have to be quick.' Decision made, she took her hands from her head and the released hair bounced back into a cloud around her face.

It was difficult to guess Francine's age. Her make-up was thick but flawless. There was some creasing around her eyes, but her forehead was wrinkle-free. We followed her down the corridor. A golden chandelier dangled from the ceiling. Maybe it would have looked fine in one of the canal apartments – we just about got away with it in the communal hallway of my flat – but hanging from the low ceiling of a sixties terraced house in Amsterdam East, it was completely out of place.

She didn't ask us to sit down, so we stood in her front room and formed an awkward triangle. Thomas stood close to Francine. She looked at her watch.

'It's about a member of your family,' Thomas said. 'Maybe your grandfather.'

'My grandfather?' She frowned. 'He died ten years ago.'

'No, not him. We found the remains of a male member of your family, a close relative, who died in his thirties or forties, possibly during the Second World War.'

'You . . . what? You've found what?' She grabbed a pen and a lipstick from the table and put them in her handbag. The bag matched her leather jacket. 'Sorry, I don't understand.'

'Did you hear about the skeleton we found at Centraal station?' he said.

'Yes, the one in the locker. So?'

'We did a DNA test and ran it through the database. It came up with a match. Your brother.'

'How could it possibly be? If this is your idea of a joke, Thomas . . .'

'No joke. Do you know of any member of your family who died during the war? Or a few years either side?'

There were a few photos in her front room. One was a wedding portrait, a young Francine and a man who looked older. Francine was looking at him; he was looking at the camera. Then a photo of a young woman smiling outside a building I recognized: the same university I'd gone to, the one just outside Amsterdam Zuid train station. No photos of the brother.

'From the age, we think it must be your grandfather or great-grandfather, or a great-uncle.'

'Oh for goodness' sake.' She looked around, eyes darting about the room, over the table. Looking for something else to stuff in the bag. 'This is so inconvenient. I really have to go.'

'You and your brother have the same parents, don't you?'

'It would have been rather better if we didn't.' She grimaced. 'But I don't have that excuse.' She snatched her smartphone from the table. 'Is that all? Can we talk about this later?'

'Is it possible—'

'Yes, yes, it's possible. My grandfather disappeared in the final months of the war. He was in the resistance.' She rummaged around in the bag and came up with a set of keys.

'My grandmother was picked up and died in a concentration camp. Westerbork. Quite late in the war as well.'

'Your father escaped?'

'Yes, he was only seven at the time, but he walked all the way from their house to his aunt and uncle's in the north. It was seventy kilometres and it took him a week to do it.' She zipped up the handbag and hoisted it on her shoulder. There were hardly any creases in the leather of the bag. Likewise there were none in the jacket. I was reminded of Tessa pulling her husband's jacket around her shoulders. The front had been cracked from use, the elbows rubbed and faded. Francine's was different. When Thomas reached out and held her arm, it would have felt soft to the touch. 'But he got there,' she said. 'It's a story he tells a lot these days.' She frowned. 'At least it's a good story.'

'We'd like to talk to your father,' Thomas said.

'I can't allow that.'

'We need to take a DNA sample—'

'My father isn't well. He's in a nursing home.'

'Come on, Francine,' Thomas said with a smile. 'You know what the procedures are.'

She seemed to melt, her smile wide, the tip of her tongue running over her teeth. I thought she was going to give us her father's address. But the magical effect only lasted a few seconds, then the smile fell from her face and she stuffed her hands in the pockets of the leather jacket. 'There's clearly no need,' she said. 'My grandfather's remains have never been found. You've got a DNA match with my brother, so that's the end of the story.' She did the zip of her jacket up and took a scarlet scarf, already folded, from the table. She held the middle against the front of her neck, wrapped it around twice and made a knot in the front. She didn't look down at her hands once; all the movements were done with a fluid and practised precision. 'You're right, Thomas, I know the procedures as well as you do, and I know that what you've got is a positive ID. Now please.' She pointed to the door. She couldn't have dismissed us any more effectively.

'Your DNA then, Francine.'

'Thomas, there really is no need. If this was a case, I'd press for a conviction based on the evidence you've got.' She held her keys out. 'How about I come to the police station later?'

'Do you have anything of your grandfather's? Any photos?' I asked as we walked to the front door.

A curt shake of the head was all the reply I got.

'Thanks, Francine,' Thomas said.

'Thank you,' she said. 'We'll talk later.'

'She won't leave it that much later,' Thomas said after we'd left. 'She'll be ringing in half an hour. An hour max. She'll tell you it's a disgrace that his skeleton was in a bin bag, will ask if there's any movement on the case. She won't leave you alone for a second.'

'She doesn't even know my name. She won't leave *you* alone, you mean.' Not only had she not asked my name, she'd used Thomas's four times in ten minutes. She hadn't even bothered to answer my question. There was no way she was going to call me.

Thomas grinned. 'She's a good prosecutor because she always finds the weak spot. She'll call you.'

'I don't mind. I'm the one taking this seriously, remember?'

'Excessively so.'

'I want to get her some answers. Tessa. Find out what happened to her husband.'

Thomas shook his head. 'Wanting to find the more recent skeleton I understand, but you should know better than to think we can get everybody the answers they want.'

'Maybe the answers they deserve?'

We got back to the police station just before lunchtime. At our office, Thomas popped his head around the corner and said, 'Coming?' to Ingrid. The two of them left. Ingrid looked over her shoulder at me but didn't invite me along.

A little later I went down to the canteen. Cheese sandwich and glass of milk on a tray, I sat down at my favourite table, from where I could see the traffic outside. It was raining, and a woman with a green golfing umbrella was walking her dog along the canal: a large German shepherd with an unambiguous plan of where he wanted to go. The dog reminded me of Thomas.

'Mind if I join you?' Edgar Ling said. He put his tray down without waiting for my answer. 'How did he take it?'

'Who?'

'Sam Dutte.' He took a large bite of his sandwich. He'd brought his own lunch: four sandwiches, in a blue-and-white striped box. An apple and a banana to the side.

'We talked to his sister, Francine. Thomas knows her.' I

could hear him eating. The grinding sound of teeth on food. His jaw clicked on every move.

'What's she done?' he said.

I laughed. 'Francine Dutte's a prosecutor. Hasn't done anything as far as I'm aware.'

'She must have been excited.'

'No, just in a rush to get rid of us.'

'Really?' He put his sandwich down. 'I thought the family would be pleased.'

'I guess the grandfather's been dead a long time. Francine never knew him.'

'Are her parents still alive?'

'Her father is. The son of our skeleton.'

'What did Francine know about her grandfather?'

'She didn't tell us much. Grandfather was in the resistance, grandmother died in a concentration camp.'

Edgar picked his sandwich back up and the clicking noise returned. It was the clacking of bones, but different from the sound the ones in the bin bag had made. This was a muffled sound, with the flesh and skin around the joints working as a dampener. 'It's possible that he was executed,' he said.

Executed. It made it worse somehow that the skeleton of one of the good guys, of someone who had been executed by the Nazis, had ended up in a locker at the station. What would I do if the country was overrun tomorrow by an invading army? Would I do the right thing and stand up, or would I just go on with my daily life, try to ignore the violence around me, try to ignore the fact that all the men were taken away to work in the factories of the enemy and that some ethnic groups were decimated? I liked to think that I would act, but you never really knew until you were faced with the situation. I used to talk to my mother about the war. The south of the country had been liberated, the north had been starving. Francine Dutte's family, stuck in Amsterdam, would have been right in the starving part. It must have been even worse when the grandfather disappeared.

'There's no obvious exit wound,' Edgar said.

'I saw that from the photos,' I said. 'Probably out through the throat?'

Edgar nodded. 'Yes, out through the throat, gun at the back of the head, from up high. I imagine the man on his knees, on the floor, classic for an execution. The only thing that's wrong is that he couldn't have had his head bent down, because then there'd be an exit mark. Alternatively . . .' He shrugged. 'Alternatively, the other way round.'

I picked up his line of thought. 'In through the throat. From under the jaw.'

He nodded again. 'Yes, throat or mouth. Classic suicide.'

I thought of my shoulder, where the star shape on my back showed quite clearly where the bullet had left. The surgeon had said I'd been lucky that it had been a small-calibre gun and therefore had made less mess. 'The size of the hole, can you tell anything from that?'

'I'd say handgun, but I'm not sure.'

'Anything about the rest of the body?'

'I've mainly been concentrating on taking the DNA and looking at the skull. It's been interesting. Do you remember we talked about the ground that the body had been in? Well, I found tulip pollen.'

'Tulips? So it was buried in a garden?'

'Not necessarily. It could have been a tulip field. Or a park.'

There had been tulips in the flower beds around the building site in Amsterdam Zuid.

'The arm as well?'

Edgar nodded. 'The man and the Second World War skeleton: they were buried in the same place.'

I looked at my watch. Frank's funeral was in an hour. Maybe his colleagues could tell me something.

Chapter Eleven

Her husband stood, suitcase by his feet, on this side of the barrier. Among the throng of people, he was the only one looking towards the exit. Everybody else was staring through the glass partitions at the people waiting for their luggage the other side of customs, anxiously anticipating their loved ones' arrival. Those were the people who'd turned up on time. Francine hated airports, because there was always stress involved. On the way over, she'd been worried what her husband was going to say. Whatever it was, he would sound more tired than angry. He never got angry. Even when things in their relationship had been bad, he hadn't got angry. He wouldn't argue. He would just walk away. That frightened her most, that one day he would not come back from a business trip.

When he saw her, he just nodded at Francine's apology for being late, looked at his watch and sighed. She wanted to tell him that she'd tried to be on time, had even seen a flash so had probably picked up a ticket for speeding, and still she'd arrived at Schiphol half an hour after he'd collected his luggage. She didn't say anything, however, because she knew he'd argue that she wouldn't have had to speed if she'd only left the house on time. They'd had that conversation so often before. He probably wanted to tell her that he'd almost be home by now if he'd taken the train, but that she'd insisted on picking him up. If she'd listened to him, he would have been in a better mood. This was all taking place in her head and she didn't want to start their time together with an argument. 'Darling, I'm so sorry,' she said, 'but you won't believe what happened. It was the police.'

'I knew it was work.' The words broke forth from his silence. He didn't look at her but walked quickly through the obstacle course created by the other people at the airport. 'You always say that I work too hard, but really it's you who . . . Never mind.'

They walked past a woman with a string of heart-shaped balloons. Was that what Christiaan would have preferred, Francine thought, for her to be waiting for him here with balloons? She'd taken two days off, she wasn't going to her brother's trial, what more could he want? In the back of her mind she knew she was being unfair, that he hadn't asked her to collect him, that it had been her idea and that she had screwed it up.

'I'm parked at the Cheese,' she said, inwardly cringing at mentioning the parking area named with tourists in mind. Cheese, Windmill, Clog, Tulip, these were the zones you could choose from. What was wrong with a, b, c and d? 'Would you like me to carry your bag?' She'd planned it so differently. She was going to be here early, he was going to give her a tight hug as soon as he saw her; it would be the perfect start.

'Don't be stupid.' He set off at high speed towards the travelator.

'Have you read any of the papers? The Dutch papers, I mean.' Her feet were hurting in her new boots. The high heels, so sexy when she'd tried them on, had seemed perfect for the meeting she'd envisioned. They would make her that little bit taller so she would fit exactly into his embrace. Now she was almost running to keep up with him and they weren't quite as ideal for that.

'Not really, haven't had much time.' He swerved around an elderly couple.

'Did you read about the skeleton?' She was getting out of breath. 'The one they found at Centraal.'

'No, I didn't. Is that your new case?' He sounded utterly uninterested in the answer.

'Thomas came.'

He started kneading the back of his shoulder with the hand that wasn't dragging the suitcase along. Somehow it hardly slowed him down. 'Thomas. I should have known.'

She could have kicked herself. She should have said that Lotte Meerman had come to the house. Francine had recognised the detective instantly and Christiaan would have been interested in her. 'He came—'

'I thought you'd taken the day off?'

'Yes, and he was with a colleague.'

'More work?'

'No.' She stopped and let the travelator carry her towards

the car park. It suddenly hit her, what Thomas had told her. All the time he and Lotte had been in her house, all she could think of was getting rid of them and getting to Schiphol before Christiaan came through customs. Then, on the way over, her mind had been on how annoyed he would be with her. Only now, on the way to the car park, with announcements of flights taking off and flights landing and a delayed flight circling overhead, did Francine finally realize that what they had come to tell her was something monumental.

She didn't know whether to laugh or cry. This was the man her father had told her stories about when she'd been a child: about how her grandfather had been a hero who'd stood up to the Nazis. Whenever there was something that Francine or her brother were having problems with – fights with kids at school, or teachers they didn't get on with, or homework they wanted to skip – their long-dead grandfather was held up as a shining example of how to overcome adversity, of how you had to work through your difficulties and find something you could do. Not that it was said in those words, but the stories about How Grandad Fought the Germans were told like parables but with an extra level of resonance: this figure who was related to them had done those brave things. The message in the parables had always been the same: stop slacking and do some work. Francine couldn't say that it had been the only thing that shaped her, but her grandfather had been a big influence on her. For her brother it had turned into something to kick against, but then he kicked against everything.

'This skeleton, the one they found at the station, it's my grandfather.'

'Your grandfather?' Christiaan had walked on, pulling his bag behind him, but now he stopped too and turned round. They made eye contact for the first time since she'd arrived.

'Daddy's father. You know the story he tells, how his father was in the resistance, how he disappeared?' The sign above the travelator showed a picture of a piece of cheese and an arrow to the left. 'I'm parked there.' She walked to the elevator and pressed the button.

'And now they've found his skeleton?' Her husband put an arm around her shoulder. 'Let's get home, you can tell me all about it.'

As they waited for the lift to arrive, Francine leant in to him, put her arm around his waist and her head on his shoulder. The sound of his breath, so near, gave her tingles in her stomach. Her pelvic floor muscles tightened with the memory of his face next to hers, tucked in the corner of neck and shoulder; the feeling of the rasp of his stubble, like an exfoliator on her cheek. It had been too long. She loved the way he smelled when he'd just come off a plane: the smell of a T-shirt that had been worn two days in a row no longer hidden by the hint of his rosemary and lemon shampoo. She also knew he would hate it if she told him that. It was the smell of having two people in bed instead of one, of a morning when she could reach out and touch him, feel his bare skin.

They took the lift one floor down and got in their car.

As she negotiated the exit from Schiphol, Christiaan said, 'I guess it's had a lot of publicity, this skeleton?'

'What do you think?' She let two cars go past before she joined the ring road. Her husband was so close. She'd only have to stretch out her hand and move her arm a little bit. She wished she didn't have to pay attention to the traffic. 'It's been all over the papers.'

'You should do something with that. Get your name out there. Maybe do some interviews.'

'Why?'

'Don't you want to move up? Don't you want to have a career? So far, if people know anything about you, it's that you've got a brother who's a football hooligan.'

'Sam's . . .' She swallowed the rest of her brother's defence. He was a football hooligan. It was a fact. The whole world was allowed to say it. She shouldn't get angry at her husband for voicing it. She stopped her indicator, no longer in a rush to overtake the green car in front of her. The anger was gone, and with the anger the need for speed.

'You know it's true. Especially after that article asking if a prosecutor with a criminal brother could possibly be objective. You can't even blame the journalist. So why not use this to get some positive publicity for a change? The papers would love to write about it.'

'What am I going to say?'

'Tell your father's story, about how he walked for a week to escape. Your grandmother died in a concentration camp. How's that not a story the papers would give an arm and a leg to write about? It's April. Next month we have

Remembrance Day and Liberation Day. It couldn't be better. Maybe they'll ask you to say something during the ceremony.'

She treasured how words now flowed from him. 'You think it will make a difference?'

'People will know you. Maybe you can go on some of those talk shows. You deserve some good publicity. You work so hard, but all your colleagues talk about is your brother. How about they talk about your hero grandfather for a change? Tell them how he inspired you to become a prosecutor, to do something for society, just like he'd done. Stand for good, stand against evil, just like your grandfather. How's that not a story?' She heard the excitement in his voice. 'I'd love to run with that,' he said.

'I don't know,' Francine said. 'Are you sure it's appropriate?'

Chapter Twelve

The crowd in the church was small, probably some of Frank's colleagues, his family and a few friends. I'd slipped in the back without making anybody look round. The few people who knew the hymns made a frail sound that echoed through the half-empty church. I didn't sing along. The afternoon light picked out the colours of an abstract stained-glass window. At the top of this religious grotto, a bald vicar talked about a man he'd probably never met.

When he'd finished, Eelke stood up and straightened out a piece of paper with notes. He wore a black shirt with dark trousers. No tie, no jacket. Still a huge improvement on the tracksuit bottoms he'd been wearing yesterday. He walked to the front of the church. He looked down at what he'd written, then turned the page over and seemed to put it aside.

'My brother and I were close.' His voice broke. He kept his eyes down and coughed. 'We were close. We had to be. Especially as kids.' He rubbed his hair. 'We were red-haired, had no father and a drunken mother.'

The hall was wider than it was tall, eleven rows of seating, furnished in an unrelenting modern style with bare pine-wood benches. Actually, bench was too grand a word for one slat to sit on and one to rest your back against. Near the front was an elderly woman with tears streaming down her face. Was that the drunken mother?

'Sorry, I shouldn't have said that, but those were the words the other children in school used. I'm older . . . sorry, *was* older than Frank. It was bad enough when I was at school alone, but when Frank joined, I had to defend him as well as myself.' He grimaced at the memory. He looked at Tessa. 'Even then I was skinny. Just like Frank.' His grimace turned into a smile. 'I worked hard to get a bit bigger but it hasn't done much good. I'm sure at work his friends still had to carry Frank's heavy gear for him.' A guffawed laugh burst from a man on the third row who could well have been one of those colleagues. He had a gnarled face like an ancient leprechaun. A woman with smooth blonde hair sitting next to Tessa turned round to stare at him.

'Anyway, at school there was just us. Eelke and Frank against the world. He helped me so much. We lived next door.' He looked at Tessa. 'He was my anchor,' he seemed to say just to her. 'Helped me keep my life together. Now he isn't here any more and I'm alone. We all miss him.' He looked over to the vicar and gave him a nod. He stepped down from the podium and took his seat. Through the slats that formed the backrest, I could see that Tessa slipped her hand into his and squeezed it tight.

Large tapestries made by the funeral director's children or an artist severely lacking in talent hid part of the grey-painted bare-brick walls. One of the hangings seemed to depict Noah's Ark. At least, unidentifiable blobs were lined up two by two. Blobs like two little boys.

The mourners filed out of the hall and I watched them pass. Tessa and Eelke walked side by side. The blonde woman who might be Tessa's mother was right behind them.

'That was kind,' the mother said to Eelke, placing one hand on his shoulder. She seemed to know him well. 'Really touching.' She paused and looked back at the coffin. 'I hate cremations. What's wrong with a burial? At least you accompany the coffin to its last resting place. Just the thought of the body burning.' She shuddered.

Tessa swayed and Eelke gripped her tightly. He held her upright and supported most of her weight. 'Mrs K. Please.'

'Sorry.' The woman took two fast steps to catch up with her husband and linked arms.

Eelke stopped, turned Tessa round and wrapped both his arms around her. She rested her head on his shoulder. I could see that her body was shaking with sobs. My eyes stung too. Eelke put his cheekbone against the crown of her head. They stood like that as everybody else left the hall. I stayed in my seat at the end of the row and felt like a voyeur watching their shared pain. I was glad they didn't look my way when they finally walked out.

I waited until they'd left before I followed them into the room at the side of the church where everybody had gone for coffee and cake. The squabble broke out only a little later.

Tessa was talking to the gnarled man who was probably Frank's colleague. She was asking him a stream of questions about the skeleton. Why had he given it to Frank to look after? It wasn't real, was it? The man responded that he didn't know anything about it, but Tessa wouldn't accept it. Eelke stared at them from a distance. He held a piece of cream cake on a saucer but didn't eat it.

Tessa's mother walked over to join them. Eelke moved, but too late to intercept her.

'Was Frank good at his job?' Tessa's mother asked the colleague.

The man nodded. 'One of the best. Couple of property developers we work with were always asking him to do more jobs. For them, their family, their friends.'

A waitress handed me a cup of too-strong tea. I refused the cake.

'What were you working on recently?' Tessa said. Her smile disappeared. 'Other than the one . . .'

'Sure. Well, we're working on an office refurbishment. Turning it back into a residential property. It's lovely to make something that was standing empty into a place where families can live again. We're also working on a pretty unusual house.'

'He can't have been that good,' Tessa's mother interrupted just when I got interested in what the colleague had to say. 'He must have been clumsy. To fall like that.'

'Mother!'

I put my teacup down and was just about to join them when an ancient woman with purple hair, balancing an enormous piece of cake, came up to me. 'Isn't this a lovely party?' she said.

'He wasn't clumsy,' Tessa said loudly. 'Someone pushed him.'

'Darling, I know you want to think that, but if he wasn't clumsy, maybe he jumped.'

'Aren't you listening to me?' Tessa shouted. 'Someone shoved him. Shoved him hard. Pushed him off that building.'

Could that have happened?

'Such a nice party,' the purple-haired woman muttered. 'But who are these people?'

'Mark Visser,' the voice on the other end of the line said. The other property developer. The other address where Frank had worked. As always, my breath caught when I heard the name. My initial reflex was to put down the phone again and hide, followed by an intense feeling of guilt and an internal stern lecture that I shouldn't be so pathetic.

'Detective Meerman, Amsterdam police,' I said. 'We'd like to talk to you about Frank Stapel.'

There was silence.

'Frank Stapel,' I repeated. 'He worked for you, didn't he?'

'Detective Meerman. Of course. Today is difficult, but if you could come to this address . . .' Mark Visser explained why he couldn't meet us where Frank had worked and asked us to come to another building site where he would be tied up all day.

I agreed we'd meet him there. Frank Stapel's place of work could come later.

'I wish I could come along,' Ingrid said. 'I would love to see you interview someone.'

'You can go in my place,' Thomas said. 'I don't need to go.'

I googled Mark Visser and his company. I found a website with a picture. I stared at the image, looked at it with my eyes slightly closed, but even so I couldn't say if this was the same Mark Visser I'd known.

I tried to call up a clear image of the boy who had been two years older than me. All I got was a series of images of dark hair and blue eyes. He'd had a straight fringe, a blunt line across his forehead. Uneven teeth, still trying to adjust to the size of his mouth, but then we'd all had those. The hair of the Mark Visser on the screen was trapped under a bright-yellow hard hat. He looked like a tall man of wiry strength. Unless they'd made him look like that on purpose: the type of man who'd be able to build you a house.

'Lotte, what do you think?' Ingrid said.

'I'll go with Thomas,' I said. Unable to tell whether I knew him or not, I had to make sure that Thomas was coming with me. Internal Investigations might have cleared me, but that didn't mean I was off their watch list.

* * *

When Mark Visser opened the door, I still wasn't sure. He was the right age, a few years older than me, but it was hard to see the boy in such a tall man. At his firm handshake I had to tip my head back to look at him. His blue eyes were shielded by small circular glasses that rested on pronounced cheekbones, and he wore a charcoal-grey suit over a black polo-neck jumper.

Then he smiled at our introduction, a broad smile, and it transformed his face. His teeth were still uneven and he suddenly looked so much younger that all my doubts disappeared. The shape of his mouth hadn't changed, even if everything else about him had. Would he remember me? My stomach muscles tensed with the anticipation. He didn't give any indication that he had.

It had been a short drive to get to this polder from Amsterdam, but the city felt a hundred kilometres away. The main characteristic of this landscape was that it was relentlessly flat. You could see the curvature of the earth if your eyesight was good enough. It was impossible to tell where one bit of reclaimed land ended and the next began.

The road to the house Mark was building was a straight line cut through the countryside. Thick clouds, bin-bag grey, formed a flat surface, parallel to the ground. I relaxed: there was no corner from which people could shoot at me, no buildings in which someone could hide. Even driving was easier, as you could see cars coming from kilometres away. It was all here, open to the eye. The straight line of the road was beautiful. Only one bend spoiled the perfection, where a small house jutted out.

Now, as we followed Mark Visser into the farmhouse, Thomas asked him about the kink in the road.

'Old Karel's house,' Mark said. 'He kept holding out for more and more money when the government was buying up the land. In the end they decided it was cheaper to build the road around his house. He killed himself.' His tone was matter-of-fact. At one point he had been my friend. 'Traffic noise drove him crazy. And this was more than sixty years ago, before there was that much traffic. Come through. This way.'

He walked stiffly as if his suit was as comfortable as a straitjacket. I didn't think he was wearing it for our benefit. He half turned and addressed us over his shoulder. 'There's a lesson there for all property developers.' He pointed a finger to the ceiling, which he could touch if he stretched his arm out fully. 'Know when to sell.' He laughed.

Thomas met my eye, raised his eyebrows and shook his head.

Mark showed us into his office at the back of the house. I couldn't hear the traffic any more because it was drowned out by the boom of machines driving metal poles into the ground. Even that noise was challenged by the pounding of my heart against my chest.

'You wanted to ask about Frank Stapel?' Mark sat down. He hooked his feet behind the legs of the chair and I noticed that he was wearing brown hiking shoes that didn't go with the suit. 'Yes, we're looking into this skeleton,' I said. My mouth was dry.

'And of course those who find skeletons are all evil

project developers.' He smiled at Thomas. He avoided looking at me. His skin had a pallor under the tan. Was he hung-over? Or was he worried because we were here?

'We're checking the places where Frank Stapel worked,' Thomas said.

'Yes, sorry about that.' Mark put a folder on his desk. 'It is an interesting one. We're turning offices and a flat back into a single dwelling.'

'Did you dig up a skeleton?' Thomas said.

'No we didn't.'

'If you had—'

'We didn't.' Mark said the words with extra emphasis. A frown emerged between his eyebrows. It was oddly diagonal, starting just below his left eyebrow and ending above the right. He ran a finger round the collar of his jumper, pulling it out as if to give him room to breathe. 'We haven't altered any of the foundations of that building. I've heard of people finding those Second World War skeletons, but it's always in farmland.' He got up, took the suit jacket off and put it on a hanger. The jumper was tight-fitting. His shape reminded me of the boss, those same thin muscles of a fanatical runner or cyclist, but hopefully without the desire to win at all cost.

'You're changing the foundations here,' I said. Through the window behind him I could see mechanical diggers riding to and fro. One of them could easily have hit on a skeleton.

Mark sat back down. 'We could have found one here, but—'

'But Frank Stapel didn't work here,' Thomas said.

Mark's eyes flicked to me and he saw that I was watching him. He switched his glance back to Thomas. 'No, he only worked on that refurb,' he said 'Plastering, painting, the finishing touches really.' He brought his thumb to his mouth and bit on a hangnail.

The tea I'd had at the funeral was pressing against my breastbone. His hand was completely different now – rough-skinned, large and strong – but it still reminded me that the last time I'd seen Mark we had touched. I'd held that hand. We'd both been upset.

He caught himself and folded his arms. 'It's not just builders who find skeletons,' he said.

'You're the ones,' I said, 'who put a house on every patch of green you can.' The diggers at the back were driving metal rods into the soil as if they were drilling for oil. Laying new foundations.

'What about farmers?' Mark said. 'They plough it over.'

'It's not the same. I wouldn't want to live so close to another house that I could see what they had for dinner.'

'Where do you live?'

'Golden Bend,' Thomas replied for me, using the name for my canal area favoured by guidebooks and estate agents.

'Didn't know the police paid that well. Anyway, you should visit the refurbishment that Frank worked on. That's probably more to your taste.'

'The site where Frank actually worked. Yes, we wanted to go there,' Thomas said. 'You insisted we came here.'

'Yes, sorry, I've got some people—'

'Did Frank Stapel ever come here?' Thomas said.

Mark sat back in his chair. 'Not that I know of. He'd have no reason to. We're not ready for decorating yet.'

'He worked for two employers. No conflict there?'

'Happens all the time. We don't have work for everybody continuously; it's not a daily job like yours. Feel free to take this folder,' Mark pushed the file closer to Thomas, 'but the skeleton didn't come from here.'

'If I need it, I'll come back.' Thomas took the folder and got up. Interview ended.

Mark hung back. I was starting to thank him for his cooperation when he said, 'I mentioned to my mother you were coming to ask me some questions. She said to give you her regards.' He scratched the short stubble on the back of his head. The criss-cross wrinkles under his eyes deepened with his smile. 'She still remembers you.'

So he'd known after all. He looked awkward. The professional front from earlier had gone, replaced by something more like the face a teenager would pull when introduced to a stranger. 'Maybe I shouldn't have brought it up,' he said.

The sound of digging stopped, and in the distance I could hear the cars driving along the straight road, the noise that had driven Old Karel crazy. From behind the house, a bird, a blackbird maybe, called out loudly that all intruders and possible rivals should stay out of the way. Thomas waited a few steps down the corridor. He was grinning at me with raised eyebrows.

'How is your mother?' I was glad my voice was under control.

'Old. What can I say? She asked if you would come visit her some time. She'd like to see you again.'

'I don't know.'

'You have to make it soon. Really soon.' His voice dropped. 'Cancer.'

I nodded. I couldn't think of anything else to say. The past wasn't a good topic of conversation.

'Can we go now?' Thomas said.

Mark looked round and seemed surprised to see him still there. 'Of course. Sorry.' He stood aside and let me leave the office.

'Well, that was just charming,' Thomas said once we were in the car. 'That wasn't your ex-husband, was it?'

'No it bloody well wasn't.' I clicked the seat belt in place and looked at my watch. The interview had lasted exactly half an hour. I stared at the landscape going by. The thick clouds that had threatened rain all day were still running across the sky. Mark Visser after all these years.

The last time I'd seen him, his mother had been screaming, I'd seen his dead sister's body.

I'd failed to save her.

Chapter Thirteen

'Are you going to tell me?' Thomas had his hands clenched around the steering wheel and kept his eyes focused on the straight road ahead, which at some point, hundreds of years ago, had been under water.

It ought to be oppressive, the realization that as soon as the dykes burst, this part of the country would drown again, but to me it gave a feeling of power. A sign that everything could be beaten, even something as mighty as the sea, as long as you used the right methods to conquer it.

'Nothing to tell. Hadn't seen him in over thirty-five years.' We would never let the land return to water, regardless of how much the sea level rose over the next decades. We would just build our defences higher and keep the water back.

'University boyfriend?' Thomas grinned.

'Very funny.' Not that there was any sign of the sea here. The only water in sight was the drainage ditch and the canals that ran along and across each of the fields. Herons kept watch at waterway crossroads, tall, stately birds with long feathers on the back of their heads, floating behind them like my old teacher's ponytail.

Thomas was still talking about our interview ten minutes later when we got back to the office. 'It was so charming,' he said to Ingrid as he hung his coat up. 'Like love at first sight, but a lifetime later.'

Ingrid looked at me with a watchful stare. Maybe she felt sorry for me, or maybe she was checking that I was okay with being teased.

'And I was there to witness it. The meaningful glances across the desk, the lingering handshake. My wife reads all these books, you know, where women sink into the dark eyes of someone they meet—'

'She's reading those because she's bored with you,' I said.

Ingrid laughed.

'At least she's got someone to be bored with.' His voice lost its playful edge.

'But apart from Lotte meeting this man, did you get anything?' Ingrid said. 'Anything more on this skeleton? Where it could have come from?'

'No, but thanks to Lotte,' he tipped his head in my direction, 'we've met the widow, the brother and have gone to two building sites where they couldn't possibly have found it. Real progress, I think.'

'And what would you have done?' I asked.

'I would not have driven out to the polder to meet my ex-lover at a site where the dead man had never even been.'

'He's not—' I clenched my teeth together and stared out of the window. It had started to rain again.

The whiteboard taunted me with its blankness. I needed to write something to make sure Thomas and Ingrid saw this as much like a case as I did. I stood up and got a blue marker pen out. 'On Friday, Frank Stapel falls to his death. On Monday, I open a locker at Centraal station and find a skeleton in a bin bag.' I wrote *Frank Stapel* and *skeleton* on the whiteboard. I added an arrow and the words *extra bones*.

'The girl must have known something. Tessa.' Thomas got up and wrote her name down.

'I don't think so. But either way, we need to look further into Frank's death. If we know why he died—'

'He died because he fell.'

'Sure, he fell, but maybe someone gave him a hand.' I'd been fairly certain it had been an accident, but Tessa's words at the funeral did make me wonder if we had drawn that conclusion too quickly. 'Either way, we still need to know where the rest of that second skeleton is buried.'

I pushed the file on the Second World War skeleton to the side and opened the one on Frank Stapel's accident. I turned over the first photo. The body wore a T-shirt and jeans. The next one was a close-up of Frank's leg at an unnatural angle. Then that face with the mouth and chin covered in blood. I picked up the picture and examined it closely. His face was as I'd remembered it and yet subtly different. He was now a case, no longer real life. The skin grazed. All his injuries consistent with a fall from seven floors up. Immediate cause of death: broken neck. The statements and documents from the building site showed that, as Thomas had said, they'd had a perfect safety record until Frank's death. I stuck the photo on the whiteboard.

'I'm heading out,' Ingrid said. 'Want to come for a drink?'

I shook my head. 'I'm going to have another look through these.' I gestured at the second set of photos, the ones of the Second World War skeleton that Edgar had left on my desk. 'Maybe some other time.'

I went back to the photos that showed the skull from the front. When I'd first seen it in that bin bag, I'd thought there would be a corresponding puncture wound at the front of the skull, but as Edgar Ling had said, and the photos showed, there wasn't one. I could picture the man, Francine Dutte's grandfather, on his knees with the gun pressed to the back of his head.

'I'm glad you're so interested in that old skeleton,' Thomas said. 'That means Ingrid and I can concentrate on the missing man.'

'That's a change of heart, isn't it? Finally acknowledging that I was right? That this is important?'

He left without replying.

It was eight o'clock in the evening when my doorbell rang. I put Pippi on the floor, got up and pressed the button on the intercom.

'Hi, Lotte, it's Ingrid. Can I come in?'

'Hold on a second. I'll come down.'

'But—'

I cut her off and ambled down both flights of stairs. I opened the external door a fraction. 'I brought you these,' Ingrid said and held out a bunch of fire-red tulips.

'You shouldn't have.' I kept my hand on the doorknob.

'We got off on the wrong foot.'

Over her shoulder I could see the canal. A tourist boat came past. Now, in high season, one came by every fifteen minutes or so, on its circular route through Amsterdam. 'No, not at all,' I said. 'What makes you say that?'

'I told Thomas you should have the desk.'

'It doesn't matter.' Hans's old desk by the window. No longer with my back towards the door. I didn't want to tell Ingrid that I wished nobody had taken that desk, so that it would still be free when Hans got bored with farming.

'Whose sofa is this?'

The four abandoned kitchen chairs had disappeared during the day. Someone must have taken them home. The sofa was still there, getting sodden in the drizzle. If nobody had taken it by tomorrow, I would call the council to have it removed.

'My downstairs neighbours moved back to the States and left a bunch of furniture behind.'

'Thomas said . . .' Ingrid's voice faltered. 'I only relocated to Amsterdam two months ago.'

'You're not in need of a sofa, are you?' It was a poor joke. I was dry in the doorway, but mist from the drizzle was forming in Ingrid's hair. Then a raindrop fell on a short dark strand and beaded up like dew on a blade of grass. 'This is stupid,' I said. I should have accepted her invitation for a drink. 'Come on in.'

'The rain doesn't matter.' She wiped a big drop from her eyes. 'I don't mind.'

'To the right. Up the stairs. I'll get you a towel.'

She stepped into the communal hallway and looked at the

chandelier and the black and white tiled floor. 'This is nice,' she said.

I climbed the stairs. Amsterdam's houses were tall, the steps narrow and the stairways long. Ingrid's footsteps echoed close behind me. As I pushed the door open, I could hear her puffing.

'This is a great place you've got,' she said.

'Thanks.' I was proud of my flat, pleased with how it looked even now that the warm honey colour of the floorboards was dimmed by a thin layer of dust.

'Give me the tour,' she said.

'This is the front room, as you can see; my bedroom is through here, spare bedroom,' I indicated it with my hand, 'and here's my study.' I gave her a brief glimpse of the large architect's table and the rows of books. 'Come through to the kitchen.'

'Have you lived here long?'

'A couple of years.' I filled the kettle and switched it on. 'I was lucky.' I rested my hip against the dishwasher. 'Sorry the place is such a tip. Haven't had time to clean. I've only been back a week.'

'Don't worry about it.' Ingrid put the bunch of tulips on the work surface. The pollen stained the green paper they were wrapped in. All the colours of the crayons we used in primary school: red, yellow, green.

'Cup of tea?' At least the kitchen wasn't too much of a mess. The dishwasher whirred behind me.

'Yes, that would be great.'

I reached past her, and took two mugs from the cupboard.

'Shall I put the tulips in some water?'

'No, leave them there. I'll do it later.'

'No, let me,' Ingrid said. 'Got a vase?'

I took the tea towel, entirely white, from its hook. Lifting it to my face, I was relieved that it didn't smell mouldy. I rubbed the dust from the two white mugs. The dishwasher clicked to warn that it was going into its drying cycle.

'The boss says it's important to identify the skeleton,' she said.

'I know. He said the same to me. But that was before we knew there was another body buried somewhere.' I went into the front room to grab a vase and some scissors. 'Plus I'd like to get Tessa some answers. About what happened to her husband.'

'You've got a lot of books,' Ingrid said, looking at my bookshelf and pulling out *How to Be a Woman*.

I didn't answer that they helped me make sense of the world.

'Thailand, Indonesia . . .' She trailed her finger over the row of travel guides. 'I would love to go.'

'My father's in Thailand at the moment.'

'You've been?'

I shook my head. 'No, never.' I just liked reading the books.

'So what can I do to help?'

'Nothing at the moment.'

She took her coat off. Held it in the crook of her arm. The sleeves of her shirt weren't long enough and exposed the knots of her wrists. 'What about Frank Stapel?'

'His wife asked me to investigate. His widow, I should say.' Frank Stapel seemed more real after I'd seen the photo of him on the beach with his feet dug into the sand; no longer just a body or a victim.

I remembered that feeling of the beach between my toes, the way my feet would suddenly hit cold sand as soon as they'd gone through the layer that the sun had warmed up and found the water level. I had enjoyed my four-month stay on the coast. Every day I'd walked a few kilometres on the beach, trying to time my stroll to low tide so that I could walk on the firm footing between the sea and the high-tide mark of shells, stranded jellyfish and seaweed.

'We did a project at school about Second World War corpses.' Ingrid filled the vase at the tap. Unwrapped the tulips, spread them out on the countertop and cut a few centimetres off each stem. 'They used to find them all the time, soldiers from both sides. But it's been a while now. The war, I mean.'

I turned to watch the kettle. I missed my old one with the whistle that could cut through conversations and memories. This one only clicked off. I poured steaming water into the mugs. I moved the tea bag up and down in one mug then the other, holding it by its label until the tea was the same colour as Frank Stapel's leather jacket. I opened the bin with my foot, shook the tea bag above the mug until it stopped dripping, and threw it away. I put Ingrid's mug next to the tulips.

Ingrid pointed with her shoe to the bowl on the floor. 'You've got a cat?'

'Just temporarily. Rescued her from some thugs last night.'

'What's her name?'

'Pippi.'

'Ginger?'

'Black and white. '

'Pippi, Pippi,' Ingrid called in the hallway, but Mrs Cat was too wary of strangers to appear. She was probably hiding under the bed in the spare room.

Ingrid put the first tulip in the vase. She'd cut it too short. The flower, its petals still closed and shaped more like an arrow than a cup, only just peeked over the glass edge. Yellow snaked through the red, from the stem to the arrow's tip. 'So Thomas,' she said. 'What's his problem?'

Thomas's problem with me was that he'd seen my mistakes in a previous case and had listened to tapes that had recorded my poor judgement. Tapes that could have got me fired. My problem with Thomas was that he knew what I had done. My other issue was that I cared. 'Is there a problem?' I said.

'Why did he insist I take the desk by the window?' She put all the flowers in. Spread them. Lifted them up so that they held their heads high above the water. Let go. They slipped back down.

'What difference does it make?'

She moved the flowers up again, entangled the stems so that the friction of leaf on leaf kept them up. She smiled, pleased with her handiwork. 'Is he afraid of you? Scared because you're too good?'

I smiled. 'I doubt it.'

'Because you are, you know. Much better than he is. You solved that financier's murder. What has Thomas done?'

'He worked on a spate of armed robberies. Plus it wasn't just me. It's never just me. It was a team of people.' I hoped Thomas didn't see things the way Ingrid did. I remembered what he'd said, that I was checking his work.

'But you're the one in the papers,' she said. 'You did the interviews. You did such a great job, we all followed it. You're the one whose name everybody knows.'

'Let's go through,' I said. 'Sit down.' I carried the vase and placed it on the table, my typical single-person dining table, with a place mat on one end and a pile of papers on the other.

'They look nice,' Ingrid said. 'Cheer the room up a bit.'

The red was too bright. It made the pale blue of the walls, the colour of the sky in March, look insipid and cold.

'How do you know Mark Visser?' Ingrid said. 'I felt bad when Thomas was teasing you, but I didn't know if I should interfere or not.'

This conversation had started to feel like an interrogation. 'No need.'

'You've only just come back. If there's anything I can help with . . .'

'We have a man's body to find. We need to find out where the skeleton came from. There's enough to do.'

'I meant with Thomas. Or with the boss. I chatted to Justin de Lange yesterday. He said there'd been some resistance.' She caught my sudden look and shut up. 'I shouldn't have said that.'

I shivered. The room was chilly, but I wasn't going to turn

the heating back on in April. Wasn't everything I'd told the Bureau for Internal Investigations confidential? 'It's not your fault. It's his. He shouldn't have mentioned anything.' Justin de Lange knew too much about me. I had known there would be a meeting with his department even before my first day back: we'd agreed on that as soon as I'd given the CI the date on which I'd return to work. In that interview, three weeks ago, there had been two of them in the second-floor meeting room: Justin de Lange and a woman, neither one of whom I had met before, neither one of whom looked sincere when they smiled.

I had a mug of coffee with me and sat down on the other side of the table. The BII agents sat opposite me, their notepads in front of them to make sure it was clear who was conducting this interview. The woman was dressed in a light-grey suit over a bright-green shirt, probably inspired by the leaves of the tulips at the stalls on the square. The man didn't wear a suit or a tie; his pink shirt was open at the neck and tucked into brown trousers. Maybe he was trying to brighten the department up a bit. Years of only meeting with criminals and colleagues would drum it into him that grey was a more appropriate colour to wear than pink.

'We won't take much of your time,' the woman said.

I didn't reply. Silence was always the best option when you doubted your best response in a meeting with Internal Investigations.

'How's your shoulder?' the woman asked.

'Much better.' I moved my hand to rub it, but stopped myself and picked up my coffee mug.

'Can you give us the details?'

So that was part of the interview. 'The doctor said I'm fit for work. In his view, the wound has healed well and there will be no lasting damage.'

'You've been out for . . . ?'

'Four months.'

More nodding. Their heads moved in tandem. 'It's great that you're physically able to work again. Do you feel mentally well enough?' The man looked at me.

'Absolutely. Can't wait to get back.' Those four months had felt like a century. Now at last I'd be back with the team. Then I could show them I was still good at this job.

Justin wrote more notes. 'There was a suspicion that you were still unbalanced after the strain of the previous case, and a concern that this might have caused you to make, shall we say, the wrong choices.'

I stared at a painting covering the place on the wall where a window should be. It was modern art and resembled a dismembered doll inside a shopping bag. 'I'm fine now. Four months of rest did me the world of good.'

'Let's talk about your last investigation. After that we can come back to your state of mind. That's more something for Justin to focus on anyway,' the woman said.

I took my eyes off the painting to stare at the woman. I'd clearly missed something at the introduction, because I hadn't realized they didn't have the same roles. 'Sorry, why is Justin focusing on my state of mind?'

The woman's eyes left mine and moved down to her notepad. 'For now we want to talk about—'

'I'd like to know what Justin has to do with my state of mind first.' The pink shirt should have been a giveaway. Justin must be the internal do-gooder, the police's own social worker.

'Maybe I can schedule a follow-up with you, Lotte? Is that okay?' he said.

I didn't like that he was using my first name. I didn't like the idea of having a follow-up with him. I also didn't like not working. 'Sure,' I said.

So I met with him. I met with him four times to be precise, four times in two weeks, and we discussed previous cases, getting shot, a failed marriage, a lost child.

And now he'd been talking to Ingrid. What had he told her?

'It wasn't anything confidential,' Ingrid said, as if she'd been reading my mind. 'Just office gossip. Actually . . .' She picked up her mug of tea, blew on it, took a small sip. 'No, never mind.'

'Actually what?' I held my mug between both hands, warming up skin that had suddenly felt cold. From the kitchen the dishwasher whirred and clicked.

'I was going to say: if you know Mark Visser, shouldn't you report it to the BII?'

'There's no conflict of interest. We were at school together. Not even in the same year.'

'Sure, but,' she folded her long body forward, dug her pointy elbows into the flesh just above her knees, 'shouldn't you be careful?'

'I am careful. I'm taking Thomas with me to every meeting.'

She nodded. 'Okay. But if you ever, you know, don't want Thomas to come along, for whatever reason, I'd be happy to help.' She closed her eyes for a second. 'I would love to help. I really want to help. That's all I wanted to say.' She finished her tea and got up.

'Thanks for coming round,' I said.

I listened to her footsteps go down the stairs. I went to the bathroom and took my jumper off to grab a quick shower. In the mirror I caught sight of the scar marking my right shoulder. There was another one, larger, on my back. The surgeon had asked me if the scarring would be an issue. I'd said it wouldn't be. I touched the scar with the index and middle finger of my left hand, ran skin over skin, felt the ridged circular scar and the puckered surroundings. Red lines flared from the circle, creating an image of a sick sun. Not just the bullet hole, but the signs of the operations to repair the nerves. They were slowly starting to look less angry.

I pulled back the shower curtain. Pippi shot out from under the taps and I leapt back so far that I stepped on my jumper and nearly slipped. 'Oh, cat!' I said. She hadn't been in the spare room then. 'You're such a silly girl.' The towel by the side of the shower was now used by Pippi-puss as her bed. 'Your dinner's in the kitchen.' I shouldn't get too used to her being here; her owners would surely want to have her back soon.

I turned on the tap and stood under the hot water. My heart rate was slowly getting back to normal. After my shower, I put on a bathrobe and brought my face up close to the mirror. I had dark circles under my eyes; I'd hardly had any sleep last night. My hair had grown so long that I could almost tie it back again. I needed to decide whether to cut it or let it grow.

I went into the study and looked at my drawing. I wrote down *Kars van Wiel*. I wrote down *Mark Visser*. Mark had mentioned my name to his mother. They'd talked about me. Talking about what was painful was the worst thing to do. The more you talked and thought about something, the more it created a path in your brain, like water running over soft soil, until it had cut a ravine of remembering. Stuffing it away, deep inside you, until you forgot, that was the way to deal with bad memories. I wondered how well Tessa Stapel was dealing with her pain. I squiggled lines from both the property developers' names to the box with the word *skeleton*, even though I couldn't see how the skeleton could have come from either site. Had Frank worked somewhere else? On another job?

Pippi stuck her little black-and-white face around the corner of the door.

'Hello, Pusskin.'

She took a careful step into my study and stared at me. Then, spooked by something I couldn't see, she ran away.

Chapter Fourteen

'It wasn't like that,' Francine's father said.

It was the interval and they were standing in the foyer of the cinema, eating their ice cream as they did every time they went to the movies. Francine would have to tell him that they'd found his father's skeleton, she just had to find the right moment. He was an old man. She was worried how he would take it. He looked smart in his suit and tie, overdressed compared to everybody else, but he was attired the way he thought you should look when you were out and about. On the rare occasions he was freed – as he put it – from the nursing home, he wanted to dress properly. Because he'd been out in the sun and his face had a rosy hue, he looked the picture of health, even though he wasn't. His white hair was still thick.

'I'm sure it wasn't like that at all.' Francine wondered what the people she worked with would say if they saw her now. She'd considered cancelling now that her husband was home, but it was difficult to deny her father his once-a-week outing. She'd also thought that it would be easier to tell him here about his father's body. That had been a stupid idea.

She should have talked to him in the nursing home, where there was help around if the shock was too much.

She took a scoop of her vanilla ice cream. It wasn't made with anything that had ever been close to a real vanilla pod. Her father had bought ice cream, as he did every week, in an attempt to fatten Francine up. Or so he said, anyway. It was probably because he fancied a chocolate ice cream for himself. It had been easy to fall into these weekly patterns, work permitting, having a chat on Sunday after her run and going to the cinema on Tuesday, where she paid for the tickets while her father covered the snacks.

'They always put the break in at a stupid point,' he said. 'I want to know what's going to happen on the other side of the door.'

'You wanted to go to this cinema. We could have gone to one that doesn't have breaks.'

'I want my ice cream. Plus, well, I need to go. You know. That's what old age does to you. You need to go more often.'

'They probably put the intervals in to keep ice cream producers happy.'

'For the cinemas to make more money. They won't start the second half until the queue for the popcorn has gone.'

The decor of the cinema dated from at least a decade before the smoking ban: plenty of cigarettes had been stubbed out on the red carpet. The faded glory of the place was in sharp contrast to the ultra-modern special effects of the movie.

Francine's father had wanted to see the latest war film. His favourites were war and sci-fi. Nothing to do with the courtroom, he always said, as it reminded him too much of his daughter's work.

'What do *you* think is on the other side of the door?' he said. The interval lights had come on just when the young hero had been about to go into the bedroom of a bombed house in Berlin.

'No idea. Nothing good, I imagine. Did you do anything like that: go into bombed-out houses?'

'Amsterdam wasn't bombed, but I'm sure we got up to lots of stupid stuff. I was a young boy when the war started.'

'You were still a young boy when it finished.'

'I can remember that last winter, when there was no food.'

'The Hunger Winter.' The ice cream felt sinful as they talked about other people starving, even if it was now long in the past. She took another scoopful, pushing the little plastic spoon into the solid mass, and tried to enjoy the sensation of the ice cream melting on her tongue. She had to tell him now or wait until the movie had finished.

Her father continued eating until the scraping sound of the plastic spoon on the bottom of the cardboard pot indicated there was nothing left. 'Aren't you going to finish yours?'

'Sorry if I'm not eating it without taking a breath.'

Her father smiled. 'You still look good. You don't have to worry about what you eat.'

'I'm looking after myself. Actually, Daddy, there's something I need to tell you.'

'Is something wrong? With Christiaan or Ruth?'

'No, everybody's fine. It's about the skeleton they found. The one at the station.'

'The one in the locker?' He read the paper every day, front to back.

'Right, that one. They did a DNA test on the bones.' Francine took a deep breath. 'Don't be upset, Daddy, but it's Grandad.'

Her father went pale. His eyes widened and his Adam's apple moved up and down.

'Daddy?' She shouldn't have come out with it like that.

Her father shook his head and rubbed his hand over his face. 'Are you sure?' His voice sounded thin, like a muted trumpet.

'Yes. They linked the DNA to Sam's.'

'How . . .' Her father shook his head again. 'Of course. I get it. Sam's in the database.'

Francine nodded.

'Dad went missing in '45. I never thought . . . I read in the paper that he'd been shot.'

She put her hand on his, the one still holding his plastic spoon. 'Yes, he'd been shot. I'm so sorry.'

'Don't be.' Her father took a deep breath and visibly struggled to pull himself together. 'He's been gone for so long. I never thought we'd find his body. And someone dug up his skeleton.' He remembered the part that Francine had hoped he'd forget. 'They dug him up and put his bones in a bin bag and stored them at Centraal station?' He sounded as if he couldn't believe it. 'Why would anybody do that?

Who would do a thing like that?' Tears glistened in his eyes. 'My father. Why?'

'We'll find out who did this, Daddy, don't worry. They won't get away with it.'

'But there's only the skeleton, just the bones? No clothes?'

'Just the bones.'

Her father closed his eyes. He whispered something, too soft for Francine to catch. The gong chimed to announce that it was time for them to go back in. She let her father go first, then chucked the leftover ice cream in the bin and immediately felt guilty for throwing away perfectly good food.

When they were back in their seats, her father said, 'Remember that movie we saw a few years ago? The one about Iraq and the bomb disposal squad?'

'*Hurt Locker*?'

'Yes, that's the one. That one was real. In the first five minutes, the famous person died.'

'Oh yes, I remember. I thought he was going to be the main character and then he got blown to bits.'

'Right. And that's how it was. That's what I remember of the war: the people you think are going to live for ever, they're the people who don't survive.'

The lights in the cinema dimmed, saving Francine from having to respond. She reached out for her father's hand. Then the second half of the movie started.

Chapter Fifteen

Ingrid's short dark hair was slicked down with gel, like a swimming cap with a fringe that skimmed the top of her eye sockets. Excitement radiated from her every movement. Pippi had been the same when I'd given her a small bit of salmon as a treat last night. She had tried to play it cool but her large eyes had given her away and she purred as she ate it. She was still purring as she jumped on to my lap afterwards. As I stroked her soft fur from her ear to where her tail started, which made her bump her lower back into my hand, I reminded myself that I should really call her American owners to let them know she was okay.

The memory and Ingrid's eagerness made me smile. It was mid-morning and I had suggested that we go to the office refurbishment where Frank Stapel had worked. She had immediately pushed aside the pages she was scanning through. She and Thomas had divided a stack of files between them, trying to find a missing man with a broken arm. Hopefully we'd get a DNA match for him too.

I'd looked at Mark Visser's website. I'd read that this building had at one point been three apartments and an office but now they were turning it back into one house. The photos showed how two of the three kitchens had been ripped out, one bathroom removed, dividing walls between rooms demolished and new walls put in.

When we got to the building itself, I showed my badge and we were let in by one of the workmen.

'Lotte Meerman,' he said. 'This must be important then. I saw the photos in the paper. After you'd been shot. How are you?'

'I'm fine.' It was odd that everybody thought they knew me. I told him I wanted to check if the skeleton could have come from here. The man opened the door and said that we could look around, of course, and just give him a shout if we needed anything. Mark Visser was luckily nowhere to be seen. His sister hadn't been out of my thoughts. She'd been my classmate, the same age as me.

I was conscious of Ingrid at my side, an observing but non-speaking presence who watched my every move as if she wanted to make a permanent record in her mind of everything I did.

On the floor above, I heard a man singing along to a radio, his voice high and squeaky as he tried and failed to hit the top notes. I went up the stairs, where dirty footprints on the naked steps showed how sensible it had been not to put carpet down until the other work was done. I walked into the room where the singing was coming from and saw the man himself. I recognized his gnarled leprechaun face from the funeral. 'I'll be with you in a second,' he said before turning back to the wall. He was applying plaster in large pink half-circles on a background of white. He evened it out, put more on and took more off. When he was happy, he turned around from the wall. He held out a hand with paint residue tattooed deep in the skin around his knuckles and said his name. Robbert Kloos. Tessa had mentioned him two days ago.

'You're the joker of the outfit,' I said.

He raised his eyebrows, plastering knife dangling from his left hand. 'Who said that?'

'Tessa Stapel. Frank's widow.'

'Ah, her. Yes, we talked.'

'At the funeral yesterday.'

'Yes, she kept grilling me. Wanted to know what I knew.' He put the plastering knife on the floor and stretched his shoulders up to his ears and back.

'She thought you'd put that skeleton in the locker.'

'Yeah, so she said. But it wasn't me.' He picked up a bottle of Gatorade and glugged down half of it in one.

'Could it have come from here?'

He nodded. 'Sure.'

My head shot up and I met his eyes.

'It could have done.' His gaze was steady and his voice deliberate. 'It's unlikely, but sure, there could've been a skeleton here. But I never saw it.'

'You didn't dig here?'

'No, we just changed the interior walls.'

The room looked nothing like it had done on the website. I should have expected a building site. Straight horizontal and vertical lines were cut through by the diagonal shape of a stepladder, which also blocked the view out of the window. That ladder was Frank's memorial; it showed how far he'd got in painting this room, and where work had been interrupted by his death. A large pale sheet with a set of multicoloured paint stains was tucked under the ladder. It had been used at previous jobs, as none of the walls here were magenta pink or sunflower yellow; this room was all about shades of beige, and pale browns. These could be Frank Stapel's paint rollers and brushes. His pots of paint were distributed around the base of the stepladder, still ready to be used but with the lids once again tightly on.

'You didn't put in any new foundations or anything like that?' I said.

'There was no external work at all.'

'We know our skeleton had been buried. It was covered in soil.'

'Then it didn't come from here and I don't know what Frank was up to. I've never found one of these war deaths. Never seen a skeleton. But if I did, I'd call the police. Most people would. He didn't. It's strange, and not like him. He was a good guy, just got married, liked to chat.'

'He worked for both Mark Visser and Kars van Wiel, didn't he?'

Robbert nodded.

'Just on those two sites?'

'He might have done some bits and pieces here and there.' He finished the rest of his drink, then screwed the top back on the bottle and wiped his mouth with his hand.

'Do you know where?'

'He was a good worker. There were always little projects coming his way.'

'Did he seem different on his last day? Excited?'

Robbert shrugged. 'No, not excited.'

'But not normal either, right?'

'He wasn't able to concentrate on anything. Had even more smoking breaks than usual.'

'Those glass panels,' I said. 'They're supposed to withstand a certain amount of force, right?'

'I don't know. I'm just a decorator. Me and Frank, we stayed well away from that stuff.'

'But he was out on that terrace.'

Robbert shook his head. 'I know. It doesn't make any sense.' He said it softly. I could tell he was finding it hard to talk about Frank.

'Did he get on with Kars?'

'I just kept my head down. Look, I don't want to get anybody in trouble.'

'If you know anything, you should tell me.'

'Frank's death, it was just an accident. A stupid accident.' He threw the empty Gatorade bottle into the corner, where it bounced and made a dent in the newly plastered wall.

As Ingrid and I walked back along the canal, I was still wondering what Frank Stapel had been distracted about. A removal van had stopped in the middle of the road and was blocking all traffic. A sofa jerked through the air, each upward movement caused by two men pulling the rope that made it fly. On the second floor, the windows had been removed. Three Chinese tourists stood behind the van, taking photos of the floating sofa. I stopped and watched the couch on its journey into the sky. Having windows as the only way to get your furniture into your flat was a good reason not to buy any. Ever. Behind the van, one of the cars beeped its horn. You could easily get stuck for half an hour on the canal. It was the risk of driving along here, where there was only enough room for one car. The van wasn't going to move until the sofa had gone through that second-floor window, and then they would have to unhook the rope from the pulley.

'That was very interesting,' Ingrid said.

'The sofa?'

She rubbed a hand through her short hair until it was bunched up in spikes. Everybody else pulled their hands through their hair to straighten or flatten it. Ingrid had a different motion, rubbing and twisting at the same time, which created chaos. 'No, to finally see you in action, I guess. I read so much about you even before . . . well, before I moved to Amsterdam. Watching you, observing you, it's really great. You know that I asked especially to work with you? Anyway. Is there anywhere else you want to go? Talk to Mark Visser?'

I shook my head and we went back to the police station.

Thomas greeted us from behind a desk covered with files. 'This is a needle in a haystack,' he said.

'We'll find this man, because nobody buries one arm,' I

said. 'So that means there are more bones in the ground somewhere. We can find the rest of the second skeleton.'

'It's not at either of the two building sites,' Ingrid said.

'No, right, so it's somewhere else.'

'A forest, a field – hey, how about a cemetery?' Thomas said. 'Had you thought about that? Maybe the bones have come from a cemetery.'

'No,' I shook my head, 'no, Francine said that her grandfather was never found.'

'Because his body had been buried anonymously. It's the simplest answer, isn't it?'

I looked at Ingrid. She stared at her monitor. A cemetery. Thomas's suggestion hooked itself in my mind. What if the body was one of the ones that Forensics had dug up to re-identify?

'The second body is too recent,' I said. 'We have a builder and we have a skeleton. The simplest answer isn't that the body came from a graveyard. The simplest answer is that a builder came across a skeleton as he was working on a building site. That's how most of these get found. Thousands of victims from the Second World War are still missing on Dutch soil.' I had known that spending an evening on Google would come in handy. There was nothing more effective in shutting Thomas up than some facts. 'They are finding them all the time. Either soldiers or civilians. So that's the simplest answer.' I took a breath.

Thomas took advantage of the gap to talk. 'But not on either of the two sites where Frank worked.'

'So he worked somewhere else as well. A third site. We find it and then we'll find the second body that's still buried.'

'Okay.' He tapped his pen on his desk. 'We identify the man whose arm bones we've got, and you locate this third site.'

'Why me?'

'You're the only one interested in that builder.'

I drew a circle on my notepad. 'Decorator.'

'Whatever. And that girl.'

'Thomas, can't you see it's all linked?' I'd promised Tessa I'd look into Frank's death. To investigate his accident properly, I needed to know where else he had worked. That would lead us to the second skeleton.

My thoughts were interrupted by the shrill ringing of my phone.

Chapter Sixteen

Francine Dutte frowned at me from across the table in Interview Room 1. 'How's the investigation going?' It was normal for a prosecutor to ask for progress reports on a case, but this wasn't Francine's case. It never would be, because of the family connection. She knew that as well as I did, which was why she wasn't wearing a suit but smart casuals. Jeans combined with a jacket and the same red scarf as yesterday.

'We're doing everything we can to—'

'Don't give me the official line. I know how things work.'

'Then you also know what I can and cannot tell you.'

When I'd picked up the phone and said, 'Hi, Francine,' Thomas had arced an eyebrow at me that said: I told you so.

'To you it's just a skeleton, but that was my grandfather,' Francine said. She folded her hands, put her elbows on the table and rested her chin on the hands. It made her look thoughtful but she also moved into my space.

I didn't sit back. 'Yes, I'm well aware of that.'

'You need to find where his remains came from.' With the index finger from the folded hands she pointed at me.

Francine had stipulated that she wanted to see me alone. When I told Thomas this, I could see something shift in his face, behind the obvious glee. It was one thing to feel that Francine was putting pressure on the weakest link; it was quite another to be excluded.

'If we know where his body was buried, maybe we can find out who killed him,' she said.

'As I was saying, we're doing all we can to do exactly that.' I drew a circle on my notepad. I filled it and added some straight lines from the bottom of the circle. It started to resemble a jellyfish. 'But Francine, it was during the war. We won't find out who killed him.'

'You don't think it's important?'

'I do, but you have to be realistic. It was over seventy years ago. There isn't much to find.' My stomach grumbled its desire for lunch. I pressed my hand on it to stop the sound.

'You don't want to look, you mean.'

'Trust me, we're desperate to find out where he'd been buried.'

'Desperate? Why?'

'The bones we found weren't all your grandfather's, so we're working very hard to find the rest of the other skeleton.'

She raised her eyebrows. 'Really? There are two war bodies?'

I didn't respond.

'Why did Frank Stapel have it anyway?' she said.

'We don't know.'

'What *do* you know?'

'Frank Stapel put the bag with your grandfather's remains in a locker at Amsterdam Centraal at 13.15 on Friday. He then had a fatal accident on Friday evening.'

She waited for more. There wasn't any more. 'That's it?'

'That's it.'

'Today's Wednesday. You haven't got very far.'

'We visited both building sites where Frank worked. It seems unlikely that the skeleton came from either one of those. Neither his colleagues nor his family know anything. Or so they claim.' I clammed up. I was already telling her too much.

'I don't think I need to tell you how important this is.' She was making notes. 'To me personally,' she said to the notepad in front of her.

'I understand.'

'I'm sure you do.' She clicked the top of her pen and placed it across the paper. 'Therefore I hope you understand that the prosecution service will keep a close eye on this. After all, it is your first case since you came back. We wouldn't want you to mess this one up.'

I pushed my teeth together to stop myself from responding to her.

She smiled at me, had probably seen that I'd reacted to her needling. A smile of victory. 'How are you anyway?'

As if she really cared about how I was. The fake pleasantries weren't fooling me; I knew she was trying to catch me out. 'I'm well.'

'My husband's very excited that you're working on this case. After that dramatic shooting. He's a big fan of yours.'

'Thanks.' I managed to keep the sarcasm out of my voice.

'But he doesn't know how either the police force or the prosecution service works. I'm not so happy. There are some within our department who question whether you should have come back at all. Your performance on the witness stand was . . . well, let's say that it was to the point.'

I'd come out of hospital three days before testifying and had still been full of medication. It had been after my second set of operations. There'd been a nagging suspicion in the back of my mind that the only reason I'd still been employed was that they needed me to testify. It had been hard to look at the murderer and officially identify him. That I'd slept with him made me feel sick. It had been difficult just to stand up, so keeping my answers as short as possible had been the best plan of action. Getting him imprisoned for murder had been one of the hardest things I'd ever done. Afterwards, I'd needed the painkillers that had taken the edge off reality for a few weeks.

'He was convicted,' I said.

'Yes, he was. I think the judge gave you some leeway.'

'He understood my circumstances.'

'I guess he did. I also understand your circumstances now. You're being watched. You're the one being judged.'

I smiled, as fake as the one she had shown me earlier. 'We're always judged.'

'Judged by us and judged by your own people, from what I hear.'

I knew who Francine had been talking to. 'You've heard wrong. I've been cleared.'

'Officially. But you know that's not how it works. What your colleagues think is important, what the top cadre think is important. Yes, you've been cleared, but you wouldn't want to go back to uniformed service, would you?'

I took a gulp of coffee. The caffeine hit the back of my tongue as bitter as bile. 'Who's talking about that?'

She folded her hands. Her eyes looked steadily into mine. 'Lotte, let's be honest with each other. You do this one right and you'll get a lot of credit within the prosecution service. That'll make your boss happy. It'll make the rest of your team happy. You know who I mean.'

For a second I considered biting the hook Francine was fishing with. I needed help with Thomas. His words came to mind, that Francine was good at applying pressure wherever the weak spot was. She was actually doing something smarter. She was offering me what I wanted. 'It's all in hand,' I said, however. 'We're doing a final check on the skeleton, taking ground samples so that we'll be able to make a positive match when we know where the remains came from, and we think we can release them for burial soon.'

'Don't make it too soon; better do it right. I'm not at all sure about you. I don't like what I've heard about your previous case.'

'Thanks for coming in, Francine, we'll talk again.'

'Lotte, if you mess up, I'll make sure it's the last time you do.'

'Francine, I promise you—' My mobile rang. 'Just hold on a second,' I said before picking up. I didn't recognize the number.

'This is the Slotervaart hospital,' a male voice said. 'Could you come and collect your mother?'

'Sorry, what?'

'Your mother. She's had an accident.'

My mother sat in the middle of a row of plastic seats. To her left was a man with his leg in plaster and another man holding his hand. She seemed as fragile as the petals on a parched rose. Her face was swollen. Her clouded blue eyes were set back in puffy sockets. She was staring ahead of her but wasn't actually watching anything. On the phone, the doctor had told me my mother had broken her wrist in a fall. They needed someone to look after her as she couldn't go home by herself. Even though Francine was threatening me and Tessa was counting on me, what else was I going to do? When I'd told the doctor that I would come straight over, Francine had looked at me as if I'd just proved to her that all her misgivings had been correct.

In the waiting area, the harsh scent of disinfectant failed to completely mask the sour odour of sweat coming from the man with the plastered leg. Even though I'd stayed in a different hospital, these smells brought back memories of the time after my shoulder operation. None of those memories were good. I moved forward to hug my mother. She raised her good hand slowly, as if it weighed ten kilos, and put it on my arm to stop me. A nurse walked by, the rubber soles of his shoes squeaking on the linoleum floor. That sound and the bright lights on the ceiling reminded me of lying on a stretcher and being pushed to the operating theatre. I covered my mother's hand with mine and together we slowly followed the blue line on the floor that would take us out of here.

My phone rang. It was Thomas. 'Where are you?' he said.

I'd completely forgotten to tell him. I explained the situation and heard the annoyance in his voice. I drove my mother to my flat, walked behind her up the stairs and settled her in the spare bedroom. 'I'll get some clothes from your place. Are you going to be all right on your own for half an hour or so?'

She closed her eyes. Blue veins intersected her eyelids. 'I know you have to do this.' Her voice was slurred, and there were spit bubbles on her lips. 'But please touch as little as possible.' The words floated away on the draught of the open door.

'I'll just get what's necessary.'

'No need to rush.' She rested against the pillow. 'I'd rather be alone.'

I drove over to her flat. She would hate that I had to go through her cupboards and drawers while she wasn't there. It worried me that she hadn't insisted on coming with me. My father had done the same for me after I'd been shot: taken my keys and packed a bag with underwear, pyjamas and toiletries.

My mother's front door was reluctant to respond to my attempts with the spare key that I hadn't used in years, but eventually it opened. At least all the boxes in the front room had gone. The room felt empty without her. Her presence had filled it and was as much a part of the furniture as the oak table. I rested my hand on the back of the chair where she always sat. She rotated them so that they wore out evenly. Every three months we would move the chairs one place anticlockwise round the table. So I had used this chair exactly one quarter of the time I lived here, but never at this place at the table. I pulled the chair back and sat down. It was as strange as drinking from her mug or eating from her plate would be. I had the view that my mother had for the last thirty-five years or so. A corner of the middle strip of wallpaper had peeled. Would my flat look like this after I'd lived there on my own for four decades?

We'd moved to this flat when I was eight. When we talked about that time, my mother always said that the move from Alkmaar to Amsterdam had been easy for both of us, that I was only going to primary school and that if you had to change schools, this was the perfect time to do so. It hadn't felt easy. We'd stayed with my grandparents for a couple of years and then moved to another part of Amsterdam. I wasn't sure if my mother needed her independence back, or if they'd argued, but the end result was that we had to move again. I didn't know anybody, and worse, everybody else knew each other. For me, it was all new: the school, the children and the neighbourhood; all new, all equally frightening. My mother said that it was this that had made me so fixated on Mark Visser's sister Agnes. After all, we'd only been at school together for six months before she disappeared. My mother had been wrong. What had made me obsessed was that Agnes had been my only friend.

She would suck the end of one of her blonde pigtails as she drew. They were always tied with purple ribbons. She loved purple. She even had a lilac pen. When I pictured her now, the few times when I didn't see her dead body, I imagined those blonde pigtails and those violet ribbons flying back from her head as she ran the kilometre home from school.

I shook my head to get rid of the memories, then got up and opened the door to my mother's bedroom. I'd slept in her bed when I'd been little and ill, but I had no memory of ever having been here on my own. She used to close this door behind her. I opened drawers and stared at the contents. It was a relief to see they were organized differently from mine. Putting some T-shirts, two pairs of trousers and seven pairs of socks in a bag, I pictured my father opening every cupboard in my bedroom to find what I needed.

I grabbed seven pairs of knickers and seven bras from her underwear drawer. I didn't check if they matched. I hesitated over the vests. I lifted one by my fingertips. It was made of pale-yellow cotton with spaghetti straps and lace trimming on the front. It was strange to think that this was what my mother wore under her jumpers. Something pretty that nobody would ever see. I stuffed two in the bag.

I heard a noise. I imagined that at any point my mother could open the door behind me and ask in a quiet but sharp voice what I thought I was doing. It was only the downstairs neighbours' toilet flushing. I slammed the drawer shut. It seemed that my whole life my mother had been at home, waiting patiently to check that I'd returned safely. She never went out. Even after I left home, she'd always been here. Had I ever rung the doorbell unanswered? I didn't think so.

A couple of shirts and a cardigan completed the packing. I went into the bedroom that used to be mine. Here was my single bed with the crocheted bedspread, the shelves with the rows of books, mainly detective novels, and the small desk that I'd used all the way through university. The room was all in white, with green curtains and green carpet, the only colour scheme that my mother and I had been able to agree on. I knew so many details about this small space: for example that the room was a perfect square, that the bed fitted tightly lengthways as well as widthways, and that if I opened the curtains, I'd see the silver birch trees at the back of the block of flats, the canal at the end of the street and the little park across the canal. With the curtains closed, everything was the same as it had been twenty years ago, when I'd moved out with little more than I'd just packed for my mother to start my first job as a police officer. I wondered if my ex-husband's child slept here when my mother was babysitting.

Chapter Seventeen

Francine noticed Michael Kraan coming towards her in the corridor of the Courts of Justice. For the last month, whenever she saw her fellow prosecutor's round face with the scarce baby curls surrounding it, she wasn't sure whether to speed up or slow down. Her black gown with the white collar was like armour, powerful enough to ward off whatever was coming her way. She held the files she was carrying in front of her as a paper shield.

'Francine, good afternoon. This has been an interesting time for you.' He took a step closer and lowered his voice. 'Apologies about Sam.'

He talked in a confidential whisper, as if Sam were a secret. All the people who walked past them, every paralegal and every defence lawyer, knew about Sam. There might be a couple of visitors to the Courts of Justice who didn't know who Francine was, but even they would know Sam. She raised her chin. 'You asked for the highest possible sentence and the judge agreed. No need to apologize.'

'I didn't see you in court for the trial.'

'No, I'd taken a couple of days off. Spent some time with

my father.' No need to tell him that she hadn't planned on coming this time anyway.

'It must be hard for him to see his son in court.'

'There's been something else. Did you read about the bones in the locker at Centraal station? It turns out those remains were his father. My grandfather. He was a resistance hero. Did you know that?'

'I had no idea.' He studied his fingernails. 'You've had lots of turmoil in your family this week.'

She shrugged. 'Sam's not turmoil. That's almost normality.' She tried not to let her annoyance show that he kept bringing Sam up. Couldn't they talk about her grandfather without mentioning the bad things? 'I've been meaning to ask you something. You worked with Lotte Meerman, didn't you?'

'Yes, I did.' He grinned. 'Someone must like me. I keep getting the high-profile ones.'

Francine had to swallow down the thought that her brother was one of them. 'What's your opinion of her?'

He pushed his lip together and spoke carefully, as if she'd asked him for his legal opinion rather than hallway gossip. 'She's clearly dedicated. She'd only been released from hospital a couple of days before her testimony.'

'I feel a "but" coming on.'

'No, she performed well. Without her we might have been in trouble. She was perfect. If she'd been really pretty, there might have been other questions about what she'd done to get him to confess, if you see what I mean.'

Francine thought of the woman she'd met. Not young, early forties. Could do more with her appearance. She needed a better haircut. As it was, the length was just over the shoulders, but it looked like a short cut that had grown out, and it was a pale brown that a quick dye job could easily turn into a more attractive blonde. More colour in her clothes would help. But presentable nonetheless.

'As it was, the defence claimed police brutality against the suspect,' Michael said. 'He was injured during the arrest.'

'She broke his cheekbone, didn't she?'

'Right. If it hadn't been her . . . I don't know. The judge might have been swayed by that. She's a woman, so it was easier to argue that it hadn't been excessive force. Did you ever meet the other guy in the team? Hans. He's left now, but he was a man-mountain. If he'd been the one accused of brutality, it would have been much harder for us.'

Lotte Meerman didn't strike her as someone with a short fuse. She'd been calm when Francine had met her by herself. Even when she had tried to put pressure on, the detective across the table had stuck to the rules. No flashes of anger. If she had been like that on the stand too, the judge would absolutely have bought the argument that the violence had been out of necessity. It did make Francine wonder what the guy had actually done. Resisted arrest probably. How much force would you need to break a cheekbone?

'But she was very gaunt and looked as if a small push would make her tumble over.'

'Really? That surprises me.' There was something about

Lotte that screamed determination. The long strides when she'd walked away when she got that phone call, for example. 'Must have been the surgery. She doesn't seem fragile at all now.'

'She was very skinny then and on a lot of meds. I had to keep my questioning brief, but that worked well.'

'So she's competent.'

'Oh, absolutely. She was word-perfect on the stand. Very diligent in her work, too. You should have seen the files.'

'But there have been rumours about irregularities.'

'Those were just rumours.' He smiled again. 'Maybe people were just jealous, I don't know. There were some colleagues who thought . . .' he straightened the black gown with a self-conscious gesture, 'who might have thought they should have been prosecuting this case instead. There was that thing with her father, of course, but nothing serious.'

'Thomas Jansen isn't a fan.'

'I talked to Thomas and for a while I was worried there was going to be a problem, but I was wrong, thankfully.'

'What kind of problem?'

'There was some talk of suspension and that would have looked bad. And Thomas . . .' He scratched his head under the small prosecutor's wig. 'Every time he came to see me, I worried that he was going to tell me something I didn't want to hear.'

'Did you ask?'

'No, I didn't ask any questions and neither did anybody else.' Michael grinned. 'I think there was just some bad blood between the two of them.'

'Thanks, Michael, this has been useful.'

'Francine, I just want to say that I am really sorry about Sam.' He put out a hand and rested it on her shoulder.

'Don't be. Seriously.' Somehow sympathy was the worst thing to deal with. Maybe her husband was right. Maybe it was time her colleagues heard about her grandfather instead of her brother.

Chapter Eighteen

As soon as I put my key in the door, Pippi greeted me noisily. It had been some time since anyone had been pleased to see me come home. She rubbed her body against my legs all the way on my walk to the kitchen. I put some food in her bowl. I opened the door to the spare bedroom carefully. My mother was asleep. I placed the bag with her clothes as quietly as I could into a corner of the room. The rhythm of her breathing through her mouth, which was slack and slightly open, didn't change. I put her toiletries in the bathroom.

I had my dinner, a cheese sandwich and an apple, and read the section about failing health in *Surviving Your Elderly Parents* again. This time I paid attention, especially with the pages about losing balance and osteoporosis. Pippi jumped on my lap, nestled against me and purred, so I ended up reading for longer than I normally would. Only when I'd finished the section did I put her on the floor. I went into my study and looked at the drawing I'd made of the case so far. Pippi joined me and sat under the table.

Frank Stapel's name was still in the middle of my drawing,

and I wasn't going to supplant him with Francine's grandfather. I wrote *Dutte* in pencil above the box with the word *skeleton* in it. Pippi whimpered softly with the start of a meow that she couldn't be bothered to finish, and I bent down to give her a little rub behind her ear, just at that really soft spot. She bumped her head into my hand for more stroking, which I did for five minutes, until she decided she'd had enough and ambled back to a spot closer to the door frame.

Frank Stapel never worked at a site when they were preparing the ground. He was a painter and decorator, brought in long after any digging had been finished. We knew the skeleton had been buried, so maybe someone else had unearthed it and stored it somewhere – perhaps in a cupboard – or left it lying around to be dealt with later. Alternatively, one of the property developers could have paid Frank to dispose of it. I drew two boxes, one for Mark Visser and one for Kars and Tony van Wiel. I added two straight lines to the box with Frank Stapel's name, to show that he'd worked for both men. I noticed I'd made the line from Mark's name lighter than the one from the Van Wiels. Was it because I found it hard to believe that he was caught up in this? Because I owed him something for abandoning him that day when we were kids? And now he wanted me to see his mother.

The day I had first seen her was when she had come to our school. We had been reading from *Pim, Frits en Ida*. I was bored; I'd already read the whole book three weeks ago, after I'd got it from the library. It was much better to read by myself anyway. Outside in the playground, a blackbird was hopping from paving stone to paving stone. Agnes wasn't in today; the chair across from me in our group of four was empty. She had been ill for a few days last week as well. My mum had said that measles was doing the rounds and she thought I might get it soon. I would have liked to have measles. Then I wouldn't have to go to school and could lie in bed and read my book all day. I didn't like school but I liked Agnes, and if she gave me the measles, I'd be happy.

If I had measles, Mum would stay home from work to look after me.

The classroom door opened and a woman walked in. I hadn't seen her before and I liked her dress. It had large flowers on it and was tucked in with a wide red belt around her waist. Her face was crumpled up the way Piet's had been when he was reading. He had stopped when the door opened and returned to normal. The woman walked to the front and spoke to Teacher. They talked softly and I couldn't hear them. Teacher's eyes went to the empty seat opposite me.

'Everybody,' he said, 'this is Agnes's mother. Has anybody seen Agnes today? Anybody? Lotte, Patrick, Piet?' He looked at me and the two others who were in our group of four desks.

I shook my head. 'Doesn't she have measles?' I asked.

Agnes's mother said, 'No, she's fine. She went to school this morning but didn't come home for lunch.'

'She hasn't been here,' Teacher said to Agnes's mother. 'We should call the police.'

That got my attention. Maybe my father would come to Amsterdam, if there was really important police work to do. He told me that policemen from different towns sometimes came together to work on big cases. That was why he once had to go away for a week. Agnes was my friend, and if my father had to work here, he might have a little bit of time to see me. If he knew I was in the same class as the missing girl, he might even interview me. If I had some information, I could call him to tell him. Then I wouldn't be bothering him, wasting his time, my mum called it; I would be helping the police.

How had I gone from being a child helping the police to now actually *being* the police? It seemed as if there hadn't been enough years in between. I drew circles and oblongs on a piece of scrap paper that I had lying in my study. The oblongs resembled bin bags. Bodies. Maybe Forensics would be able to tell me how long the body had been in that bag. Hadn't Edgar Ling mentioned that he'd found pollen in the soil sample he'd taken from the skull? Pollen didn't last for ever in a bin bag.

I looked at the box with Francine's grandfather's name. Was he important? Or was he just a pile of bones? Frank Stapel had put the bin bag in the locker. We knew that because his fingerprints had been all over the bag, as well as the locker, along with Tessa's from when she got the bin bag out. Frank had taken the ticket and put it in the inside pocket of his leather jacket. He went straight to work; he wouldn't have had time to go home. He worked late because he hadn't been on site that morning, and then, when everybody else had gone, he had his accident.

But the leather jacket somehow got back to their flat and Tessa found the ticket in the pocket three days later. That was odd. I wrote *leather jacket* below Frank's name and drew a circle around the word. I should talk to Tessa tomorrow.

I went to bed. In the night, I heard my mother rummaging around, heard her footsteps going from her bedroom to the bathroom. I listened to the sounds she made, listened to her brushing her teeth and gargling with mouthwash. I listened out for her steps returning to her room, the two of us only separated by one thin wall.

I thought I could hear my mother's breathing through that wall, and imagined her listening out for mine.

Chapter Nineteen

There was a noise in my flat. Someone was moving round. I listened to the sounds more closely. Something clattered on the floor of the bathroom. My mother was probably rearranging things, and had dropped them as she moved my toiletries to make way for hers. It didn't sound as if anything had broken. The bright red numbers on the alarm clock by the side of my bed read 7.03 a.m. It was time to get up anyway. The sound of teeth being brushed came from the bathroom. Running water. Gargling. Then a sound like heavy rain, water falling into water from a height. I hated the picture it created in my mind.

I pushed Pippi from my stomach and got out of bed. She meowed and followed my every movement with her big green eyes, as if she wanted to make sure that this human would continue to take care of her and not stick her in a pet carrier. I told her I would be there for her, then fed her and made a cup of tea. The bathroom door clicked, the door to my mother's room opened and closed. A cupboard was being pulled open. Stumbling behind the door.

Even as I made breakfast I kept listening out for her. She would call for my aid soon. I would have to help her and be tied to the flat all day. Ingrid and Thomas would have to do without me on the investigation. They would prefer that anyway. Could I get moved to another team while I was absent? I drank my tea too quickly and the hot liquid burnt away some of my anxiety along with the roof of my mouth.

My mother came in, fully dressed, with her arm in a sling. 'I thought you'd gone to work already. I thought I'd slept so soundly that I hadn't heard you leave.'

'Do you want me to stay home today?'

'Of course not, don't be silly.'

I smiled and offered her a cup of tea.

'You've got a cat, I see. I thought you didn't like cats.'

'I do.' I bent down to rub Mrs Pippi-puss's soft head, just in case she'd heard what my mother had said. 'It's you that doesn't.'

'How long have you had this one?'

'She's not mine.' I started to prepare my mother's breakfast. 'Maybe she will be. That would be nice, wouldn't it, puss?' I stroked Pippi's soft fur. She purred. 'I don't think her owners want her any more.' I'd pop into the bookshop that afternoon to get a book on cats, now that she was staying for longer.

The canal was like a floating garden. Every houseboat had been planted with a verdant roof terrace, the owners using plants in pots and raised beds to make a green outdoor room, additional space to sit in if the weather allowed. Nobody was sitting outside today; rain was falling steadily. The sofa that was still outside my front door was now completely sodden. I would call the council to make sure it was taken away. Two bicycles had fallen over, their wheels, handlebars and pedals entangled as in a lovers' embrace. Ahead of me, a woman in a dress that clung soaked to her legs cycled with her dog in the front basket. The white terrier didn't seem to mind that he was getting wet. His tongue was hanging out of his mouth as if he were drinking straight from the sky.

After I'd locked my bike, I went up the stairs to our office, newspaper under my arm. 'Sorry I had to leave yesterday afternoon. I had to look after my mother,' I said to Thomas.

'Lotte, I talked to the boss,' Thomas said. 'He's concerned about the extra bones.' He tapped the boxes of files, which had shrunk from a tower to a two-storey building.

'Can I help with those? I can go through some too.' I dropped the paper on my desk.

My phone rang. I threw my coat on the hook and dashed to pick up the call.

'I don't like what I just read about Mark Visser,' Francine said.

I sat down and picked up a pencil. 'What's that?'

'There are unusual things in his past.' Her voice was smooth as oil but also persistent, with the fluid power of water forcing through a small gap.

'Unusual?' I turned my chair round. The coat dripped water on the vinyl floor.

'You knew his sister died?'

'Yes, I knew that,' I said.

'He found her. His sister,' Francine said. 'Did you know that?'

Her emphasis on the word 'that' made me smile. If she was hoping that she knew something about Mark's sister that I didn't, she was wrong. 'Yes, I did.'

'You don't think that's interesting?'

'I think it's sad.'

'Okay. So what about the house?'

'Which house?'

'The one where he found her. Where she died. He's bought it. He's redeveloping it.'

My mouth filled with saliva and I couldn't talk.

'See, that's not normal,' Francine said after a few seconds' silence. 'Even you think that's not normal.'

I swallowed. 'Thanks, Francine.' I put the phone down and stared past Ingrid's empty seat out of the window.

Mark had bought the house. The first time I'd really talked to him had been in the park as he was walking to school.

'What do you want?' he'd said.

'I'm investigating—'

'That's the police's job. You're just a nosy girl with no friends and nothing better to do.' He walked faster.

I ran after him, to keep up. 'Agnes is my friend. And my father is a policeman,' I said to explain myself.

'But you're not. You're just strange.'

'I've walked all the paths in the park. She isn't here.'

He stopped. 'I know,' he said. 'I've done the same. Me and

my friends, we've searched the whole park. On our bikes.' His dark hair was so long that it nearly touched his eyes as he bent his head forward. He pushed it back with his hand. He squinted as if he were looking up into sunlight, but it was a cloudy day and there was no sun.

'When did you last see her?' I said.

'I should have walked with her to school.'

'Was that what your mother said?'

He carried on walking. 'I'm older than Agnes. I should have looked after her.'

'And be late for school every day?' I looked over at him to see if he smiled. He didn't. 'Sorry,' I said. 'I didn't want to be—'

'Didn't want to be mean about her? Don't worry, she was mean about you.'

I looked at the toes of my new shoes, two different shades of blue, suede and leather, which were not like the shoes the other girls wore but were bought from the shop that sold 'good' children's shoes, according to my mum. Of course 'good' was just a grown-up way of saying 'ugly'. I didn't like that Agnes could have been mean about my shoes, or any of my clothes, or about how I didn't join in with games, or that I liked books. She had a lot of things she could pick from. 'What did she say?'

Mark didn't answer and I was glad about that. Maybe she hadn't said anything. He was just being horrid, like most boys. How would he know who his sister's friends were? 'Why didn't you walk to school with her?' I said.

'I thought she was fine by herself.'

'Did anybody see her that morning?'

'No, nobody.'

'We should ask the neighbours, show her photo, we should—'

'The police did that the first day.'

'We should—'

'You shouldn't do anything. You shouldn't come here with your notebook.'

'I'm not coming anywhere, I'm walking to school.'

He snorted. 'You were waiting for me. To ask me questions.'

'I'm only trying to help.'

'Why?' he said, his voice angry. 'Why are you trying to help? Stop whatever it is you're doing.' He ran away to school.

I stood still on the path, then sat on a bench and wrote down what he had said: that nobody had seen her that morning, that he and his friends had gone through the whole park and hadn't found her. That had gone well, I thought. I had two bits of information that I hadn't had before. When I saw my dad, when I had all my information, I would ask him if this was what questioning was all about, that you needed to get new information, and that it didn't matter if the people you asked the questions liked you or not. It was much more likely that they didn't like you, because I'd already found out that nobody ever liked answering my questions. I was going to talk to all the neighbours next.

I hopped off the bench and walked to school, notepad

tucked under my arm, pen stuffed in the pocket of my trousers. I skipped over a puddle and kicked a small stone sideways into the grass to the side of the path. I hopped on one leg up to the first tree, then changed legs. I wondered if the police had looked for Agnes in the canal that ran around the park. I chewed the end of my pen.

It was the memory of the little boy that Mark had been that made me want to ask him if he was really redeveloping that house. Ingrid was out. Thomas was diagonally opposite me, at his desk by the window. He glared, probably wondering who'd called and what they'd said to silence me. I wasn't going to do anything that was going to get me suspended, not with Francine on my back. I was going to abide by the rules, and that meant being accompanied by a colleague when you were going to see a childhood friend, especially if you were starting to doubt him. What Francine had told me had nothing to do with the skeleton in the locker or with Frank Stapel's death, but I didn't like it. If Mark had bought that property, what did that say about his personality? Probably that he was willing to do a lot to make money. In the past, a child had died there. I remembered the feeling of Mark's hand in mine.

I looked at Thomas, who wished I'd joined another team. 'What can I do to help?'

'It's under control,' he said.

'There must be something—'

'The builder. You stick to the builder. Plus your childhood friend. And the builder's widow. You deal with that. That's enough to do.'

'Let's go for a coffee,' I said.

His mouth was halfway through forming 'no' when he closed it again. I braced myself for a more cutting refusal. 'Sure,' he said. 'I could do with one. Didn't get much sleep last night. We worked all hours.'

In the canteen, we got our coffee in brown plastic cups. I automatically sat at my favourite table by the window, on my seat, the one that let me see everybody. A few survivors of the night shift were winding down; a few colleagues who liked each other chatted about work.

'I'm sorry about yesterday,' I said.

'What do you want, Lotte?' Thomas said.

'What's your problem with me?' I picked at the corner of the lid of the small tub of coffee creamer.

Thomas raised his eyebrows. 'Now isn't a good time for this.'

'It is. We need to work together, and that's hard because you don't like me.' The corner tore off. I dropped the tub back on the table and sighed.

'It's irrelevant whether I like you or not.' He opened a sachet of sugar and sprinkled it into his coffee.

I sat back in my seat and made eye contact. 'No it isn't. As I said, I'm sorry I wasn't here yesterday. I'll make it up. But you need to let me take a part. What have I ever done to you?'

'To me? Nothing as far as I know. But I do know about the mistakes you made. The mistakes that got you shot. Bad mistakes. Remember?' He took a sip of his coffee. 'I listened to the tapes of your previous interviews. I know exactly what you did.'

I stabbed the top of the tub of creamer with the sharp edge of the plastic stirrer, shaped like a traffic light without its lamps. It went through the cover and spilled most of the creamy-beige liquid on the table. 'He was convicted, wasn't he?' I tried to block out the memory of the murderer's green eyes on mine as I had been giving my short testimony. 'I've learned. I'm trying to work on this case with you. Together with you. I've taken you to every interview, involved you in every call.' I took a sip of the coffee. Caffeine raced through my body, the first hit of the morning, so good, so invigorating.

Thomas flexed the thin white piece of plastic between index finger and thumb, judging how much stress he could put on it before it would break. 'The boss is interested in this case. I can't risk it, Lotte.' His voice sounded more tired than angry. 'Now more even than before.'

'Risk what?'

'You going it alone. Like you did last time. I know Ingrid will do as I say.'

'I'm doing everything by the book. I haven't excluded you,' I said, keeping my tone light. 'Not even when one of the dead man's employers turned out to be my childhood friend. Even then I made sure you came with me.'

'To protect yourself.'

I shrugged. 'No harm in covering my back.'

'And now we're having this lovely heart-to-heart.'

'I want to clear the air.'

'Clear the air.' He took another sip of coffee and put the plastic cup back on the table. 'You're trying to be charming. Unfortunately,' he pushed his chair back and tapped the table with both hands, 'you're failing. You're not very good at the charm.' He got up. 'And it wouldn't make any difference anyway.' He was half turned away from me, already on his way out of the canteen. He threw his plastic cup in the bin. It sounded heavy; it had still been half full.

I took a big gulp from mine then rushed after him. I caught up before he'd reached the stairs. 'I need you to work with me.' I was slightly out of breath.

He sighed and folded his arms. 'Lotte, it's you who's not working with me. Actually, you haven't done much work at all.' He tucked both hands more securely under his elbows, holding his ribcage. 'Just tell me one thing: why are you so interested in that builder's death?'

'His widow deserves to know what happened, and it's all linked. We find out where else he worked and it'll help us find where the skeleton was buried. Where that other body still is.'

'Sure, but his death was an accident. He fell. Tessa will never accept that.'

'She said she would believe me if I—' I bit back the rest of the words.

'If you told her so.' Thomas finished my sentence. 'She won't. You know the type: she'll still be here years later, trying to get us to investigate that accident.'

'I don't think so.' Her smile had told me she'd accept whatever outcome I presented to her. 'I think she trusts me.'

'For as long as you do what she wants.'

Over his shoulder I saw that Ingrid had come in. 'Never mind.' I hoisted my handbag higher up my shoulder. I smiled at Ingrid. I knew she would think I'd given her a birthday and St Nicolaas present all rolled into one. 'Want to come interview Mark Visser?'

'Oh yes please.' She didn't even think about it.

I grinned a smug smile at Thomas.

Chapter Twenty

I left my bike at the police station and Ingrid and I drove in her car through the relentless flatness of the polder. The rain had stopped, and where the sun peeked between the thick dark clouds, it gave them golden edges. I could see as far as I wanted; nothing interrupted my view for several kilometres. The long, straight road followed a small canal from field to field. It was a back road, with only enough room for one car. If another came from the opposite direction, both of us would have to drive with one wheel on the grassy verge. There were no other cars. It was just us this April morning.

The fields on either side were lower than the road, which made them seem like sponges that had filled up with groundwater over the years and descended below sea level. The cows that chewed the verdant grass were weights that submerged the meadows further. If it continued to rain, the puddles and cows combined would surely make the land sink.

I hadn't called ahead this time. This would be a surprise visit.

'Is there anything specific, anything in particular, that you want to question him about?' Ingrid said. 'Or is it something more . . .' She didn't finish the sentence.

'Something more what?'

'Personal. Something personal.'

I gripped the seat belt tightly. 'No, it isn't personal. It's about another property that Mark Visser is developing.'

'What's special about it?'

'His sister died there.'

'She died recently?'

'No, when she was eight. Mark found the body.'

'How old was he?'

'Ten.'

'That poor boy, that must have been terrible.'

'Yes, and now he's redeveloping the house.'

Ingrid was silent for a bit. I feasted my eyes on the long view to the horizon. In the distance, tulip fields were blankets of colour. It wasn't possible to see any of the individual flowers, they were too far away, but together they formed an army of petals that fought against the gloom of the grey sky. It was getting late in the season for them to still be flowering. Soon the farmers would cut their blooms off to allow all the energy to stay in the bulb. They removed the beauty to increase the strength and value of the product they wanted to sell. Were these the tulips that had shed their pollen on Francine's grandfather's skeleton? I didn't know how many acres of tulip fields there were in this area, let alone in the Netherlands as a whole.

Ingrid parked the car and we got out. I rang the doorbell.

It took a while before Mark opened the door. His eyes were puffy behind the glasses. This time he wasn't wearing a suit but a jumper over jeans. Stubble hugged his jawline and the plains below his cheekbones. You could spend hours tracing the hollows in his face with your fingertips.

'More questions?' he said.

'Always.' I introduced Ingrid. Mark smiled his salesman's smile. We followed him to his office at the back of the house. It was still quiet; the diggers weren't wrecking anything yet.

'Tell us about another property you're developing.'

'I gave you the files—'

'Tell us about Parkstraat 12.' Even just saying the address made my mouth feel odd, as if a dentist were about to stick a needle in my gum.

Mark twitched with a short jerk of his shoulders and arms. His eyes seemed to sink deep. 'What about it?'

'You're working on that one too.'

'I don't want to talk about it.'

'Unfortunately that's not an option. Why are you redeveloping that house?'

Mark scrunched up his face, then released it, trying to calm himself. 'I have no choice.'

'You don't?' Ingrid said. 'How come? Have you been contracted by someone else to develop it?'

'In a way, yes. He left my mother the house. When he died.'

'What?' The word left my mouth on a sudden exhalation.

'All the time when he was in jail the house was rented

out. Then he died and left it to my mother in his will. He must have known that my father passed away a couple of years ago. He said he was sorry and wanted to do something . . .' His mouth moved as if he found it hard to keep talking. 'To make up for killing Agnes. My mother doesn't want it, of course. She's been trying to sell it but nobody would buy it the way it was. She asked me for a favour. What could I do?' He looked at me. 'I don't go there. I let my guys run with that one. It makes me sick every time I think of it.'

I nodded. 'What did he see, Mark? Frank Stapel? What did he see?'

'I don't know. He didn't see anything working for me. Or at least he didn't tell me.'

'Was it at the house where your sister died? Did he find those bones while he was working there?'

'No.' He frowned. 'Is that why you're here?'

'But he worked there.' I scrutinized Mark's face. 'Frank Stapel worked at Parkstraat 12, didn't he?'

The hollows underneath his cheekbones seemed to deepen. His mouth became as thin as a line.

I nodded slowly. 'I see. He worked on the house where your sister died.'

Mark hung his head. 'Yes, he did. But he didn't find a skeleton.' He took off his glasses and pinched the marks they had left behind. 'It won't matter what I say. Do you want to check? Go over there now? Let's go, Lotte. I'll get the keys. You can check to your heart's content.'

'Yes,' Ingrid said before I had a chance to refuse. 'We'll come.'

We followed him out of the house. On the other side of the road two red and yellow rectangles of tulip fields were bright as the crayons that Agnes and I had shared, happy in their primary colours, unaware that they would only last for another couple of hours or so, that they were next to be destroyed and have their heads cut off.

Mark opened the car door.

'Coming?' he said.

'We'll follow you.'

He nodded and got in his car. He was looking at me. I gave him a thumbs-up to say that I was ready to go. Behind him, we drove to the house that had haunted my nightmares for so many years.

Chapter Twenty-one

'Tell me about your grandfather,' the journalist said.

Francine looked at the girl. She was different from the journalists who had chased her for comments about her brother. They had been a mob, a clump of people with microphones sticking out. They had followed her and hunted her to get her opinion on something she didn't want to talk about.

'My grandfather was a hero,' Francine said. 'When so many people just stood by, he did something.' Maybe the journalist seemed different because she was asking about a subject that Francine did want to talk about.

'So he was important to you?' The girl tipped her head sideways.

Francine could see that the girl's eyes were taking in her appearance, not staying on her face but also checking what she was wearing. It made sense; of course she had to give a description of Francine as part of the interview. Francine could imagine what it would say: *Successful prosecutor Francine Dutte, dressed in a stylish maroon dress, talked about her grandfather with* . . . With what? Delight? Obvious interest? 'My father told me stories about my grandfather. He talked about what he remembered. He was young at the time, of course, but he told me about the leaflets they were printing and that people came to their house to distribute the illegal papers.'

The journalist nodded. Ella was her name. She was young. She was pretty, even though Francine thought that twenty years ago she herself had been more attractive than this girl was now. But that was before decades of gravity had tugged on the skin around her jaws. Botox kept her forehead clear of wrinkles, but there was no substitute for young skin. Maybe Ella would write: *Successful prosecutor Francine Dutte had clearly made an effort for the interview, but her age showed in dark spots on her skin and the deep lines above her mouth. Her maroon dress was elegant but a bit too youthful.*

She wouldn't write that. Francine's husband had recommended Ella especially. Francine couldn't remember which paper she worked for, but Christiaan had said she would write a positive interview. He'd briefed the girl beforehand. He said she'd been very excited by the chance to write a lifestyle article about Francine.

'Which paper do you write for again?' Francine said. 'Sorry, I forgot.'

'I'm freelance,' Ella said. 'But this will go into the *Metro*.'

It was going in the free paper? Her husband must have had his reasons for suggesting this girl. After all, that was his job. This was what his international clients got from him: hints on what to say and tips on which journalists to use. The girl was wearing a very tight top. Deeply cut, even if it was covered by a jacket.

'Christiaan, your husband, will he be joining you later?' Ella smiled. It was a hopeful smile. As if seeing her husband would be a good thing.

'No, he's at work today.'

'That's a shame.'

Did the girl think she'd dressed up for nothing? Styled her long blonde hair straight for nothing? What was there behind her smile? Was that pity Francine was seeing? Ella reminded her of someone. She pushed that thought to the back of her mind. 'Why a shame?' Her voice was sharp.

'Just thought it might be nice to get some photographs of the two of you together. The power couple, so to speak.'

Prosecutor Francine Dutte and her successful husband, the PR guru Christiaan Dermezjia, at their elegant house in Amsterdam. 'No, just me in the photos.' She was overshadowed by him often enough; he didn't need to take this away as well. This was her chance to shine, Christiaan had said, her chance to make herself stand out from everybody else in the prosecution department.

'So, your grandfather, he was important to you?'

Hadn't they had that question already? Was this girl really that good, or did she just have perfect skin and pert tits? 'He has always been a role model to me. He was one of the reasons why, after law school, I became a prosecutor. Like my grandfather, I wanted to do the right thing, do something for society.' Why had she said that? Francine felt slightly sick. She thought she'd opened the door to a question about Sam; something like: if you felt that way, why didn't your brother? She imagined the pretty girl turning into one of the horde. But this was a journalist who'd been hand-picked by her husband. She forced a smile on to her face. Maybe she should keep talking before Ella could ask that inevitable follow-up question. 'My grandfather really influenced every choice I made in life. He and my grandmother, who died in a concentration camp. Even though both of them died long before I was born, they've had a huge impact on me.' Shut up, Francine, you're rambling.

'It must have been a shock how they found his skeleton.'

'Yes, it was a shock, but we never had anything to remember him by. It has been very important to me to find something of him. To at last be able to bury him, have a place to put flowers. Have some closure.' Francine felt how saccharine the words were on her lips. Her husband had helped her prepare for the interview. You have to give them sound bites, he'd said. He'd even written some of the sentences for her. Such as 'have closure' and 'at last be able to bury him'. Did Ella, the journalist, notice how fake the words were? The feelings were much deeper, much more fundamental than the platitudes made them sound.

'So your grandfather played a big part in the resistance?'

'Yes, he and my grandmother both. That's why she was arrested. My father told me that wasn't long after my grandfather disappeared. Someone must have betrayed them.'

'Do you know what they did? What they were involved in?'

'It was mainly the underground newspaper. The printing press was hidden away in the cellar, with whatever food they had left, and came out once a week.' Francine smiled.

'My father said he used to listen to the sound it made as he was lying in bed.'

'Tell me what happened to your father.'

'He was only seven when his mother was arrested. He got scared and ran away. He walked north, almost seventy kilometres, until he came to his aunt and uncle's farm. It took him a whole week.' Whenever she told the story, she pictured her father as that little boy, wearing socks that came up to his knees and short trousers, with a knitted vest over a buttoned shirt. She had no idea where the image came from. There were no photos of her father from those days, no childhood photos at all, and she had a suspicion that it was actually from a movie or a TV programme that she'd seen as a child. If it seemed like something from the TV to her, was it because it was too perfect a story? 'His mother had stitched the address inside the waistband of his trousers. She knew that the day would come when they'd come for her. She knew she had to give him at least a chance to get somewhere safe.' Was it now starting to sound unreal to her as well?

'But she was too late to save herself.'

'My father told me she rehearsed the route with him, the place names that he had to pass. Do you have children?'

'No, I don't.'

'She wanted to keep her son with her for as long as she could.'

'It's a great story. I can see why it was such an inspiration to you. Let's go back to why finding your grandfather's remains was so important. After all, you knew he had died, that wasn't news to you.'

How could she explain it, how could she tell Ella of the hero worship she had always felt for her grandfather even though she had never met him? How in her mind her grandfather was like one of those characters in the movies: fearless, fighting for his country, doing the right thing. And how that had informed the choices that Francine had made in her own life. After all, she was the granddaughter of a man who'd been in the resistance, a man who hadn't stood aside when the Germans had invaded the country. 'My father told me stories about my grandfather. It made me what I am today, trying to live up to his example.' Was she repeating herself? Keep to the story you want to tell, her husband had said.

'But now you know he was shot. How does that feel?'

'We knew he'd probably died a violent death. He died during the war. It's as we'd expected. I don't know, and will probably never know, who killed him: if he was caught at a drop of the underground newspaper, or if he was just rounded up with a group of other people and shot as a reprisal for the death of a German, this we'll never know. But we have his body. We can bury him.' She paused at the click of the camera shutter. 'We never found my grandmother's body either. As I said, she died in a concentration camp. We'll never have anything of hers, nothing to remember her by. But now we can at least bury my grandfather. I am truly grateful to the police for finding him. For identifying him. Even though I would have wished he was found somewhere else, in a different way, it's better than not having found him at all.'

'How did your father react?'

'He's confused these days. He lives in the past more and more.' It was the answer Francine and her husband had decided on.

She didn't want to tell the journalist about her father's reaction. As she and Christiaan had discussed, if she just said that her father was muddled and couldn't remember things very well any more, they wouldn't try to interview him. If she told the truth, said that her father was upset and angry, they might want to talk to him. She couldn't let them meet him at the nursing home. He had many more lucid days than she'd admitted to Ella, but she didn't want journalists or the police anywhere near him: he was an old man and deserved to be left in peace.

'And of course you have your work as a prosecutor. A high-profile role.'

'Yes, that's my way of doing something for society.' And this story was going to make her career. She smiled as the camera clicked again and hoped she didn't look too smug.

Chapter Twenty-two

Mark was parked two cars in front of us.

Here, Amsterdam was for living. Not for working or sight-seeing. The streets were empty and wide. The houses were squat. They gave a sense of dependability, with their wide bases and low ceilings. They seemed sturdy. Solid. Looking at this house, nobody would have thought a little girl had been murdered here. But all the muscles in my body were tensed. Because I knew. I knew what had happened here thirty-five years ago.

Mark's parents had moved out of Amsterdam almost immediately afterwards. At the age of eight, having a friend in another town was like having a long-distance relationship. I had no memories of meeting Mark after that moment when we'd seen his sister's body. I remembered that I ran. I remembered his mother's screams. Adults must have turned up at some point. Someone must have called the police. Those things must have happened but I had no memory of them. Looking back at early childhood was like that: a set of scenes, flashes into a past, not linked together, just horrible moments that shone brightly through the fog of history.

Mark got out of his car. He walked towards ours. I lowered the window.

'Have you changed your mind?' he said.

I shook my head but made no move to get out. For a moment it felt as if we were two children again.

'We can just drive back.' His eyes were pleading with me. The morning sunlight picked out the hair on his temples, more white than brown. 'There's nothing to see here. Can we turn back? Not go inside the house?'

I wanted to. Every fibre in my body shouted that I should go back. A brick in the middle of my stomach pushed its way towards my mouth. I don't know what I would have done if Ingrid hadn't been sitting beside me. 'You can stay here,' I told Mark.

Ingrid depressed the button on the handbrake and pulled it up. It complained with the sound of unwilling metal. 'As long as your workmen are there to let us in,' she said.

'They're not here today.' He sighed. 'No, I'll come.'

We walked up the path to the front door. It was smaller than I remembered. It had only seemed large compared to the flat we'd lived in. The front door had been dark brown before. Strange I remembered that detail but not so many other things about that day. Now it was painted blue. It was the same colour as the neighbours'. It still smelled of paint. Mark got his keys out, reached past me and opened the door.

Inside it was bright. The walls were painted bone white. The skirting board was one tint darker. The colour of old ivory. Light was reflected into all corners. The wood of the window frames was painted in a rusty-red primer. There was nowhere to hide. 'Did Frank Stapel do all the decorating?' I said.

'Most of it. He'd nearly finished when . . .' He glanced up to the ceiling and blinked. 'When he died.'

I nodded. There was no furniture in the rooms, and with plastic still covering the carpet against any building stains, it looked like a crime scene. Ingrid went up the stairs and I went into the kitchen. Mark followed me. Through the large window above the work surface, I saw that the garden was a forsaken wilderness of hawthorn and waist-high hogweed. There was still one large tree. I forced myself to look at the bottom right-hand corner. The shed was gone. 'Did you take the shed down?' Now that Ingrid was out of earshot, I could talk about Agnes.

Mark joined me but rested against a kitchen cabinet, his back towards the window. 'The police destroyed it. They were concerned that there were other children. Other girls.'

'I'm sorry, Mark. I'm sorry for putting you through this. Please go back to the car.'

'I've been avoiding coming here. Maybe this is good.'

'It's not. It'll just bring it back.'

He grimaced. 'You don't believe in closure?'

'The more you think about something, the clearer the memory becomes. I'll dream of her tonight.'

'Will you dream of me?'

I didn't respond, even though I knew that in my dream I would feel his hand in mine as I saw his sister's body. I would see the purple hair ribbon flutter in the wind, stuck at one end of a branch. That tree was still there. I could tell exactly where the purple ribbon had been. Frank could have seen something here.

In the garden next door, the garden of the house where Mark had lived, two children were playing on a slide. I could hear them through the double glazing. They wore raincoats and wellies. They were laughing. They climbed up to the top of the slide again. Screamed high-pitched screams as they skidded down. A little boy and a slightly bigger girl. Siblings maybe, one or two years apart. The garden looked so much smaller than I'd remembered. At the bottom of the slide the girl waited, whispered something in the boy's ear, looked over to the fence between their garden and that of the neighbour, the garden at the back of the house I was in. The girl climbed the steps to the top of the slide. Stood there staring over the fence. She looked down at the boy. He shook his head. His hair flew out to the side with the force of his denial. She slid down. Walked to the fence. Stood on tiptoes but still couldn't see over it. She jumped up and down but didn't get anywhere near the top. I was rooted to the spot, could only watch the two children. The girl had a couple more goes, looked for something higher to climb. Then a woman's voice shouted to them that there were biscuits. Treats were more compelling than a look into a forbidden garden. The children went inside and I was released from my trance.

I could hear Ingrid's footsteps above my head as she walked around the upstairs rooms. 'When your sister died,' I said to Mark, 'when she disappeared, I had no friends any more. She was my only friend and she went away. I lost her, as I'd lost my father before. Then you became my friend and you left too.'

He turned to face me. 'I'm here now,' he said. 'I'm not planning on going anywhere.'

I put my hand on his chest, right on the place where mine felt tight. His heart thumped rapidly.

He covered my hand with his. I measured the hollows under his cheekbones with my thumb as I'd wanted to do from the first time I'd seen him again. He was so close that I could see his pupils expand in desire until his eyes were more black than blue. When he exhaled, his breath tickled my lips.

His mouth found mine. I opened my lips and welcomed his tongue. Pleasure ran like electricity over my skin. His fingers mingled with my hair. His thumb ran over the base of my skull. My legs could no longer carry me and I stumbled against him. Desire made me almost forget about dead girls.

My mobile rang and I pulled a few centimetres back. I shook my head in disbelief, both at the kiss and the interruption. 'Sorry,' I said. I was breathing hard. I answered the phone.

It was Thomas. 'Where are you guys?' he said.

For a minute I'd forgotten I was here with Ingrid. She was upstairs while I was kissing Mark. 'We're at Parkstraat 12. With Mark Visser.' I looked at Mark. His hand covered his mouth. 'But we're pretty much done here.'

There were a few seconds of silence on the other end of the line. I stepped further away from Mark. 'He's got nothing to do with it,' I said to Thomas.

'Like hell he doesn't,' Thomas said and disconnected the call.

I went out into the garden to wait for Ingrid. I knew Mark wouldn't follow me. He would stay inside and watch me through the window, safe behind the glass.

Like next door, there was a patch of grass in the middle of the garden. Here there was no slide. The grass reached my knees. I couldn't see any footsteps other than the ones I'd left behind. Where next door's borders had been filled with roses and colourful bedding plants, here there were only weeds. They didn't look new. How long did it take for giant hogweed to get this big? The leaves spread wider than my umbrella. Cow parsley flowered in small parasols. Bindweed was tying other plants together, its white trumpets shouting that there was much further still for it to grow. It also shouted that it had been there for a while. There wasn't a single spot that wasn't covered by a plant that looked as if it had been growing for more than a month. These were the weeds I used to fight when I still lived in a house with a garden.

I'd avoided the back right corner of the garden so far. The same tree was still there. It was big and bushy and its branches dominated a quarter of the garden. Two giant hogweeds were standing guard. I skirted around them, making sure I didn't touch their poisonous leaves, and got so close to the tree that I could touch its trunk. Which branch had held the ribbon? In the thirty-five years that had passed, that particular branch must have grown far up, so that it now had a view of the garden next door and could see the children playing on the slide.

The back door opened. I turned around at the sound of footsteps. I stepped back, wanted to get back on to the grass, out in the open, no longer under the shadow of the tree.

'Nothing upstairs,' Ingrid said. 'And there's been no digging here, has there?'

'No, this all looks pretty well-established.'

'Coming?' Ingrid said.

I nodded and went back indoors.

Mark was still standing where I'd left him, rooted to the spot, just like the tree. 'So am I cleared then, Lotte?' His voice sounded tired. Resigned. As if he knew that if I answered, I'd say that no, he wasn't.

'My mother said you still hadn't visited. Could you go and see her?' He bit his bottom lip. 'You can check out the story about the house, if you still doubt me.'

'I was going to, but my mother's had an accident. It's been rather hectic.' My excuse sounded feeble even to myself. He'd said she didn't have much time left and I hadn't bothered to go round.

'Is she all right?' Mark said.

I nodded. 'Yeah, not too bad. She's fractured her wrist.'

'Give her my regards.'

'Will do.'

He followed us out of the house, closed the door behind him and drove off.

Ingrid and I got back in the car.

'His mother knows you?' Ingrid said.

'Yes.'

'You know him well, then? You avoided the question last time.'

I didn't respond. Behind us were the thick clouds that had been hanging threateningly close. They overtook us as we reached the ring road, and the change in visibility together with the falling light levels made it seem that golden sunshine was banned from our capital city these days.

Ingrid parked the car in the basement garage at the police station. She looked at me. More than ever she reminded me of that high-jumper eyeing up how high the bar was. 'What's between you and Mark?' she said.

'We held hands once. When we were children.' I wanted to take her mind off what could be between me and Mark. I wanted to take my own mind off it as well. 'When we found his little sister, Agnes, dead.'

I thought it had been a good move to tell her that until two hours later, when she passed behind me. She put her hand on the back of my chair as if there wasn't enough space for her to squeeze past. I moved my chair forward and rolled away from her touch. 'I've asked for the files from the archives,' she said.

'Which files?' Thomas said.

'On Mark Visser's sister. On her murder.'

I shouldn't have mentioned it.

'That's so amazing,' she said. 'You solved your first case at eight years old. You're like the police version of Mozart: a child prodigy.'

'It was nothing like that. I didn't solve anything.'

'But it shows something, doesn't it? I can tell you're not comfortable talking about this, but it shows how your mind has always worked like this. How you've always been, I don't know. Tenacious? Brave?' Her skinny form was bent forward over the desk and to the right, to get as close to me as she could, as if she wanted to share a secret with me. She took a half-eaten chocolate bar, milk with nuts, and put the last few squares in her mouth. She left the empty wrapper, paper and foil, in the middle of her desk, which was already completely covered with folders and notes.

'I'm not brave.'

'Four months ago you stepped out in front of that bullet. You knew that man had a gun. You got shot.'

I looked over at Thomas. I couldn't tell what he was thinking about this misguided adoration. I shook my head. 'It wasn't like that.' I thought I'd said that three times already.

'But still, locating Agnes Visser's body when you were only eight, that's amazing.'

She couldn't stop talking about the little girl whose body I'd found. She thought it was the most thrilling thing that had happened since she'd joined the team: finding something I'd worked on as a child. But I'd been nothing like Mozart. This wasn't my early masterpiece.

It was my early failure.

The thought that those files from the archive would be

sitting on the desk next to mine made my lunch jump around in my stomach.

A knock on the door frame behind me made me turn round.

It was Edgar Ling. There was a small smile around the forensic scientist's lips that he was trying to suppress. His eyelids were half closed over his bulging eyes, as if he were tasting his favourite food. 'Your extra bones,' he said. 'They might be rather important.'

'DNA match?' Thomas said.

'Yes. I double-checked it.' He looked at the printout in his hand and shook his head.

'Who is it?' Ingrid said.

'It's . . .' Edgar paused. 'It's Tim Dollander.'

'You're fucking kidding me.' Thomas jumped up from his desk.

At the start of my career, I would not have said Tim Dollander's name out loud without looking behind me. Then he was in jail for the best part of a decade. After his release he'd seemed to pick up where he'd left off and there had been the years during which we'd failed to prove him guilty of human trafficking and drug dealing. Everything he did, all the money he'd made, was hidden behind seemingly legitimate property deals. A reformed man, he'd called himself, but we'd suspected different. Six years ago, he disappeared, his property firm closed down and we thought he'd moved his main business somewhere more conducive to what he was trying to do. Somewhere like South America had been the most often voiced theory. I knew these facts. Everybody in the Amsterdam police force did.

'That's why I reran the test.' Edgar Ling's smile was so broad, it split his features. It sat uncomfortably on his face, in contrast to the melancholy of his bulging eyes.

Ingrid's face was like Munch's scream, but with an O of delight. 'Wasn't he seen in Portugal? Or on the Costa Brava somewhere?'

'Yeah, well,' Edgar said, 'that's why I checked.'

'How do a gangster's arm bones get mixed in with a Second World War skeleton?'

'That's for you to figure out.' Edgar held out the printout to me, but Thomas reached over and grabbed it.

He scanned the page. 'Fucking hell. Tim Dollander.' As if he only believed it now that he'd read it. 'Think he's dead?'

'Unless someone just cut off his arm,' I said.

'With him, that's possible,' Thomas said.

Edgar shook his head. 'No, it's too high up. They would have had to cut it above the shoulder joint. There aren't any knife marks on the bones. He's most probably dead.'

Thomas punched the air. 'Oh man, this is unbelievable. Lotte, I'm suddenly loving this case.'

'This is insane,' I said.

'It's fantastic.' Thomas picked up the phone and called the boss.

'This is the best day of my career,' Edgar said. 'When I was working on old skeletons all day, I dreamed of one day finding something like this and being the person who makes the breakthrough in a case.'

'Dollander,' Thomas said to the boss. 'Yes. Tim Dollander. Yes. Yes, I know. DNA evidence. It's him for sure. Yes. Yes, we'll come right over.' As if it were impossible for the boss to come to us.

'You'll let me know, won't you? How you get on?' Edgar said.

'Of course we will. Thanks for this magic trick.' Thomas shepherded Edgar out of our office with a kind hand on his back.

We walked down the corridor like a group of excited schoolchildren. The smile never left Thomas's pretty face. Ingrid rubbed the short hair at the back of his neck in a playful gesture. Even my cheeks were hurting. It was how unexpected it was. I wanted to skip down the blue carpet, even though I realized that finding Dollander's bones mixed up with a Second World War skeleton raised more questions than it answered.

Chapter Twenty-three

The door to the CI's office was wide open. He stopped looking at his PC screen and pulled his reading glasses from his nose. His thin face didn't mirror our smiles. Instead it was set in a frown.

Thomas and Ingrid took the two seats opposite the desk. As there was nowhere else to sit, I leaned against the bookshelves in the back, careful not to disturb the rows that indicated the correct legal response to every situation. I was curious to see what advice the books gave on how to deal with finding the arm bones of a serious criminal.

'This changes everything.' The boss dangled his reading glasses, let them swing back and forth, stopped them at the highest point then allowed them to fall down.

'Right, that's why I wanted to bring it to your attention straight away,' Thomas said.

'Yes, thanks, Thomas.' Some of the CI's running gear was hanging over the radiators in front of the window. From where Thomas and Ingrid were sitting, it was hidden from view. He probably wouldn't like that I could see his sky-blue Nike top and a pair of dark-blue shorts. His running shoes were standing side by side, waiting to be worn again, waiting to be pounded on the pavement. 'Fill me in. Where are we with this?' He grabbed a notepad and clicked his pen.

I was silent. What did 'this' even mean in this case? Was he asking about Dollander? We hadn't even had time to look into him yet.

'We were looking at missing men,' Thomas said.

'And we now know who it was. Yes, I get that. But do we know where these bones came from?'

'Lotte's looking into that.' Thomas glanced over his shoulder at me. The giddiness of earlier had disappeared.

'Lotte. Where have you got so far?' Still the pen was suspended in mid-air, waiting for one of us to say something noteworthy.

'Can we take a step back?' I gripped the shelf that I was leaning against, dug my nails into the wood. 'It started with Frank Stapel's death.' This was my chance to convince the boss of what had been a certainty in my mind only.

Thomas sighed. 'Not this again.' He turned in his chair. 'Lotte, can you drop it?'

'Seriously, Thomas, you still don't see the importance?' I said.

The boss was writing something down. I waited until he looked at me again.

'Whoever killed Dollander is obviously a dangerous individual,' I said.

'We don't know what he died of,' Thomas said.

'Yeah, with someone like Dollander, and his body buried somewhere, hidden, there's a really good chance it was natural causes,' I said.

'You two, stop arguing. Lotte, make your point.'

Thomas turned back to look at the boss and folded his arms. The muscles of his shoulders were tensed, and two thick cords of stress ran from his ears to his collarbones.

'The guy who had those bones in a bin bag died by falling off the seventh floor of a building. Makes you think, doesn't it?' I said.

'Yes, it does.' The boss nodded and made some more notes. 'So do we know where these bones came from?'

'It's a tricky one. According to the books, and I assume his tax records, Frank Stapel officially worked on two sites, the one where he died, and another in the centre.' I moved my right shoulder round in its socket a couple of times and gave it a rub. 'Thomas, Ingrid and I checked both sites. The problem is that Edgar Ling said the bones had been buried, and on neither site had there been any digging recently.'

'Right.' Ingrid nodded at me. 'So apart from those building sites, he seems to have worked on a few things here and there, but nobody wants to confirm that.'

'Okay, so what I'm hearing is that you, Thomas, hadn't been able to figure out who the dead guy was until DNA showed it was Dollander, and you, Lotte, haven't found out where the body came from. So we're nowhere. You've done exactly nothing in a week.'

'We identified the bones,' Thomas said. He crossed his legs. One foot bounced in the air.

'You did?' The CI put his pen down. 'I think Edgar Ling did that. He's done a great job. I was talking about what *you* had done.'

'Dollander wasn't on the missing persons list, so we couldn't have—'

'I'm not asking for excuses. I'm not accusing anybody of anything. I'm just stating the facts. And now that this is Dollander's body, those facts are going to have to change. Maybe less bitching, no bickering and some more cooperation.' His eyes went from Thomas to me. 'That would be a good start.'

'Yes, boss,' Thomas said.

'Lotte.' His gaze turned to me. 'What have you got on the builder?'

'The key question is how his jacket got back to his flat.'

'His wife knew about the skeleton, I bet,' Thomas said.

'She seemed genuinely upset when she opened the locker.'

'Maybe she's a good actress? Why did she call you in the first place?' Thomas grinned at me over his shoulder. 'Maybe she played you. Knew you'd just come back. Not on your A game yet.'

'Didn't I say something about bickering?' The boss put his glasses back on. 'I'm starting to feel like a school teacher here.'

'Sorry. Yes.' He paused. 'I think Tessa was with her husband when he put that bin bag in the locker at the station. It is probably her jacket. She wears it constantly.'

'Let's look at Frank Stapel's death again,' the boss said before I could respond to Thomas. 'You're right, Lotte. If Dollander was killed, whoever did it is dangerous. We don't know how Dollander died, and we should trace that.'

'He was seen a year ago in Portugal,' Ingrid said.

'And that was clearly wrong. What do we have that's certain? Let's see.' He moved the mouse rapidly back and forth to wake his PC up again and read from the screen. 'Released from prison in 2008. Lived in Amsterdam for a couple of years. Was interviewed in 2010 about the murder of a Moroccan in the Bijlmer. Drug related.' He looked at Thomas. 'If we want one hundred per cent certainty, that's it. That's the last confirmed sighting.'

I narrowed my eyes against the glare from the sun that burst through the window behind the CI. For the first time in weeks, the sky was uniformly blue. The light brought the backdrop into sharp relief.

'He could have died soon after,' the boss said, 'from what Forensics thought. Does that make his death drugs related? Is there anything in Frank Stapel's past that could link him to that?'

'Tessa Stapel crashed a car in a drink-driving accident.' Thomas thumbed through a stack of papers. He read from one, held the rest aloft. 'She has a history of alcohol abuse and depression. Two known suicide attempts that required a hospital stay.' He put the papers down and looked at the boss again. 'Frank's brother Eelke had a few close shaves: hung out with a group of football hooligans. Minor player.'

I tapped Thomas on his shoulder. 'Can I see those?'

'Sure, yes. Here.' He handed them to me. 'Seems to have cleaned up. They both have.'

I could kick myself for not having checked into Eelke and Tessa's pasts. 'What about Frank?' I didn't see his name listed here at all.

'Completely clean. Not a single offence, not even a parking ticket. Nothing.'

'Any known links between Dollander and any of the guys that Frank worked for?' The boss held out his hand for the papers and I passed them on.

'I'll look into that,' Thomas said.

'What did Dollander go to prison for?' Ingrid said.

'He cleaned out squats with a group of his mates,' Thomas said. 'The violent route. Beating up the squatters until they decided that leaving was definitely the best course of action. That was a roaring trade. With one of them, it got out of hand and he beat a guy to death. Was sentenced to ten years in prison in 2002, got early release in '08.'

'When he got out, he seemed to do more of the same plus a bit of drug dealing, some GBH where the other party never pressed charges,' I said.

'Then the murder of that Moroccan in 2010,' the boss added.

'Yes, and before that, two working girls, both heroin addicts, in 2009. Nothing proven in either case.'

'Two girls that he brought into the country, right?'

'Yes, with three others girls who decided it was in their best interest not to testify.' I remembered that case. One of the ones that had driven the previous CI to distraction. Sure, we all understood that sometimes it was hard for someone without legal papers to come forward, but if only one of them had been willing to be a witness, we could have locked Dollander up for a long time.

'Okay,' the boss said, 'then he gets killed in . . . let's call it 2010. Was buried somewhere next to a Second World War resistance hero. How did that happen?'

Thomas and I looked at each other. This was the area where neither one of us had a clue. I shook my head.

'Okay,' the boss said. 'You don't know. I get it. What are the next steps?'

I pushed myself away from the bookshelf. 'Do you want to go back through Dollander's known acquaintances?'

'Makes sense,' Thomas said. 'We're mainly focusing on two property developers: Kars van Wiel and Mark Visser. We'll have a look to see if their paths crossed with Dollander at any point.'

The boss nodded. 'It's a plan. That prosecutor called again this morning. Francine Dutte. Does she have anything to do with this?'

'I don't think so,' I said. 'Of course it's her grandfather—'

'Yes, I know that. She was complaining about you, Lotte, but I shut that down.'

'Thanks, boss.'

'Just don't take any more time off to do personal stuff.'

I nodded. I couldn't believe she'd called the boss to complain about me.

'But there's a story with her brother, right?' Thomas asked.

'Another football hooligan. He's the guy who attacked that AZ player in the Ajax stadium last year.'

'Got a good kicking. Tried that on the wrong guy. Never mess with defenders,' Thomas said.

'The player got a red card,' Ingrid said. 'Can you believe it? How that wasn't self-defence . . .'

'It was violent conduct on the pitch. Automatic red,' the boss said.

'The brother was convicted the other day,' I said.

'Of course. Sam Dutte. Yes. Hooligans, squatters, is that the link? Did he know Eelke?'

'Maybe.'

'Okay. Check that out too.' The CI's phone rang. He looked at the display. 'The burgemeester. Heard about Dollander. I've got to take this.'

We left. On the way back to our office, Thomas said he'd make some calls to old colleagues. To get something on the Moroccan that Dollander had allegedly killed. He remembered that they'd made an arrest for that.

Ingrid put a hand on my arm and stopped me in the corridor. 'And there's Mark Visser.' She waited until Thomas had gone into our office. 'We know Frank worked on a development Tessa hadn't told us about.'

Even though I felt guilty about it, I knew I should meet Mark's mother to verify his story about the house. Suddenly everything had become important.

Chapter Twenty-four

I cycled along a long, straight road defended by poplars on either side. The wind was gusting against me, driving me back as if to remind me that this was a bad idea. I pushed the pedals as hard as I could, but it was heavy work and it was difficult to breathe with the wind blowing each of my exhalations back into my mouth.

I stopped next to the nearest poplar, kept my bike between my legs, and rested my head on the handlebars. A car came from the other direction and blew its horn. I dragged my bike off the road and stood it against the thin trunk of the tree. As a child I had been fascinated by how you could tell the prevailing wind direction from the shape in which a group of poplars grew. The ones that got most of the wind were most stunted in their growth.

I thought about Tessa. According to Thomas's theory, she and Frank had met at the station, either one of them with the bin bag full of bones. They'd gone to the stored luggage area, put the bag in a locker and Tessa left with the ticket. So far it was all entirely plausible. But then, when Frank has the accident, she needs to get rid of the ticket because moving human remains is a crime. She decides not to shred it, but to keep it in the inside pocket of his leather jacket. That was where this theory fell apart. She had screamed when she found that skeleton in the locker.

It didn't fit. It didn't make sense at all. I must have stood by the side of the road for at least ten minutes. Then I got back on my bike and continued the battle along the road against the wind to the nursing home where Mark Visser's mother lived.

I hadn't thought I'd ever meet her again. She was one of those people who belonged to my childhood. Now she was the husk of a person, a thin layer of skin and bones with a mind inside. Her eyes were the only part of her face with any colour in them: blue with smudged brown circles underneath. 'Thank you so much for coming, Lotte.'

'Mark mentioned that you'd like to see me.'

'I've been thinking about you a lot recently. After Mark told me you called him.'

I managed to keep the smile on my face.

'I remember you coming by with your green notebook and your pencil, straight after school, asking questions.'

She must hate me. I was responsible for her daughter's death. Why was she smiling at me? She poured me tea in a delicate porcelain cup with pink flowers painted around the rim. Her hand shook and I wanted to take the teapot from her to stop her from dropping it and spilling tea all over the pale yellow carpet.

'I must have been a right pain,' I said. What had I been thinking? Going round to those people's house, bothering them in their time of grief. Looking back, I couldn't understand why my mother hadn't put a stop to my obsession with my classmate's disappearance.

I had continued what I'd thought was an investigation for months, until my green notebook had been full. I had made a number of drawings: of the house and the garden, of all the paths in the park, of the houses next door and the street. I had asked my questions and written down the answers. I had lots of information. But I still didn't know where Agnes was. Agnes's father had been home twice; I'd seen him when I went round for a cup of tea. He was a big man, tanned, with dark hair. He didn't seem to fit in the front room, with the small chairs and the thin teacups. When he saw me come in, he asked me when I was going to stop coming round. When was I going to stop asking questions, like the police had already done a few months ago? They've stopped? I asked. But she hasn't been found yet. Her father's voice got loud. Yes, they've stopped. They've stopped looking. They think they'll never find her. He looked angry, Agnes's mother looked sad. I guess that for him it was difficult. He had been away for months, and when he came back, there were no policemen around the house any more and no photographers in the street. She was old news. Agnes's mother had seen them leave one by one and day by day. It would be easier that way, more like a little bit of pain all the time, like a bruise or a blister, instead of a huge pain suddenly, like a knife wound or an operation.

'You were helping,' she said now. 'Do you know that you were still looking even though the police had given up? That was a complete shambles.'

'I was looking because I hadn't found her yet.' What was still clear in my mind was that desire to trace her. It had been a need that had driven me, more important than going to school. Going to school was something my mother told me I had to do. Going round with my paper and pencil, asking questions, making drawings, taking notes, had been a compulsion. Even if I hadn't got anywhere.

Mrs Visser smiled, and her thin skin pulled together like crumpled paper. 'You were driving my son crazy with your questions. I remember it clearly.'

'I'm so sorry, I don't know what I was thinking.'

She reached out a hand and touched mine, as if I was the one who needed comforting. She bent over. Now she would hiss out her spite. Instead she smiled again. 'You didn't give up. Even though . . . Never mind. Has Mark helped you? With that skeleton?'

'I'm not sure how much he can help.'

'If there's anything I can do, let me know. I haven't got much time. I've set an end date, but I'd like to think that . . .'

I imagined that I could see her mind working through the paper-thin skin of her brow. I didn't want to think of my mother in Mrs Visser's situation, but I was.

'. . . I'd like to think that I've repaid my debt to you.'

There was pressure on the back of my eyes. 'There's no debt. I was only a child. I didn't do much. We were too late.'

I had been too late. I couldn't bear the thought that Mrs Visser felt she owed me.

We finished our tea.

'Do you know who has the room next time?' She pointed at the wall. 'Gerard Dutte. I read about his story in the paper this afternoon, how when he was seven, he walked seventy kilometres to his aunt and uncle's.' She laughed. 'That story wasn't news to us. Everybody here has heard it at least thirty times.'

She handed me one of the free newspapers. Francine Dutte's face smiled at me from the front page. Next to her was a smaller photo of her grandfather's skeleton as we'd found it at Centraal. The photos accompanied an interview with her.

I scanned it. 'I would love to meet him.' I had wanted to from when I first talked to Francine. Here was my opportunity. 'Would you introduce me?'

Chapter Twenty-five

I knocked three times. Once normal, twice loud. No reply. I raised my hand to knock again.

'Not here,' a voice said behind me. I turned to see an old man with a wooden walking stick standing just on the other side of the hallway. He was a similar age to Mrs Visser but his upright posture screamed that he wasn't at death's door yet. His bald head reflected the glare of the spotlights in the hallway.

'This is Detective Meerman,' Mrs Visser said to the man.

'Finally going to check his story, are you?' he said. He pointed with his thumb towards the door I'd been knocking on.

'What about his story?' I said.

'That war hero story. That story about his father.' He turned abruptly, then marched off, swinging the walking stick as if it was an accessory rather than a necessity. After about ten steps, he slowed down and began to put more weight on the stick. Halfway down the corridor, the march turned into a slow stroll. He thought we'd stopped watching him. He joined an elderly woman and two men built like bulldozers. They occupied the table closest to the TV. I recognized their silhouettes from the back. 'Kars van Wiel. And Tony.'

'Yes,' Mrs Visser said. 'They come every week to visit.'

The old man put his hand on the old woman's head. He tucked a strand of hair behind her ear. Her hair was pure white and hung loose down her back. The young girl's hairstyle lined an ancient face. She looked up, then pulled her head back and shuffled closer to her son. Kars van Wiel covered his mother's hand with his own. She put her head on his shoulder. The old man looked away, grimaced, and rubbed his hand over his bald head. The woman smiled at her son, cupped his jaw with a crooked hand and kissed him on the mouth.

'Have his parents been here long?' I had to look away as the kiss lingered.

'Just his father. Not his mother. He's recovering from a hip replacement. I try to avoid the mother when she's visiting and her sons are here too. Kars especially. With Tony she isn't too bad.'

'How long has his father been here?'

Laughter broke out from the table. The woman's voice made a noise like a cracked church bell. She threw her head back and shook her hair. Her hand was on her son's thigh.

'Over a month. Due to stay another week or so.'

The woman got up. Shook her husband's hand. Only when she moved away from the table did I see she was wearing a miniskirt and high heels. Her legs were slim. As they say: eighteen from the back, eighty-one from the front.

She hooked her arms through her sons', and thus entwined, like an ageing star with two bodyguards, they left the nursing home. The father's gaze followed them for a while, then he buried his head in his hands.

'What does he know about Gerard Dutte's past?' I said.

'Everybody here has war stories. Everybody did the right thing, you must remember.' Mrs Visser winked at me.

'So what's Father van Wiel's war story?' A woman dressed in a cardigan with a string of pearls around her neck and her white hair neatly permed took the seat next to Kars's father. She put one hand on his shoulder and poured him a cup of tea with the other.

'Job van Wiel's story isn't that different from Gerard Dutte's. His father was in the resistance, hid Jews in his shed and printed illegal newspapers. To be fair,' her eyes were on the two people at the small table, 'his father did get a medal, so in his case the story is indisputably true.'

'You don't think Gerard Dutte's is?' To my mind, Francine definitely thought it was. She wouldn't have given that interview if she had any doubts. 'I guess it's true, because the mother died in a concentration camp, didn't she?'

That's what Francine had said, but the old man had asked if I was finally going to check it. I should not have taken Francine's word for it. I made a note of it, to do later. 'What about you?' I said. 'Do you have any heroic tales?'

'Me? During the war, nothing happened to me. Nothing happened to my parents. I can remember being hungry, but we got through it. Had an uneventful war, I guess.'

I noticed she looked tired. It was long after the war that Mrs Visser's life became eventful in a way that nobody would have wanted. 'Let's go back,' I said. 'I can talk to Francine's father some other time.'

She nodded and put her arm through mine. She leant on me. I could feel the bone of her arm through the papery skin and the thin layer of her cardigan. The cancer had eaten all the flesh away.

We waited for the lift. 'So what did his father get a medal for?' The lift arrived and we got in. The doors closed unhurriedly behind us. Even a geriatric patient with a Zimmer frame could have got in with time to spare.

'He saved three Jewish people who'd been hidden in his shed. Killed some Nazis to protect them.'

The lift crawled to the next floor down. 'I guess you've heard everybody's stories quite a few times by now.'

'Job van Wiel's stories at least were new, but he's going home soon.'

'One less person to tell you his war stories.'

'I'll miss Kars. He came to see me the other day, without his mother that time, so kind. He and Mark know each other, of course.'

'They do?'

'They were friends at school. They both . . . they felt they had a lot in common.'

'Like what?'

'After Agnes . . . after Agnes died . . .' She closed her eyes. 'I thought this would be easier. That I could talk about her. But it's still . . .' tears ran down the gullies that wrinkles cut in her cheeks, 'it's still so hard. Anyway, Mark recommended this place to Kars. For his father to stay in when he was recovering from his hip replacement.'

After I'd escorted Mrs Visser back to her room, I cycled towards the band of canal rings that had Centraal station at their centre and I thought about the different generations. Francine Dutte said her grandfather had been a resistance hero and gave interviews in the papers about how important he'd been to her. The war threw long shadows. Not so long ago, an eighty-year-old woman had confessed to the murder of a man in 1946, the year after the war. She'd thought he'd been a Nazi sympathizer, but in reality he'd been in the resistance. His cover had been so good that even other resistance members hadn't known about it. She shot him on his own doorstep.

My father once told me that when he had just joined the police – that must have been the early sixties, only fifteen years after the end of the war – when Germans asked him for directions, he sent them the wrong way. Ten years before that, someone like Kars van Wiel's grandfather got a medal for shooting Germans during the war. Today we were all friendly, didn't even ask them to give our bikes back but politely pointed them the right way if they wanted to visit the Anne Frank house. When I'd been in uniform, we were happier with the German tourists than with the English ones. Less drinking and more sightseeing. I'd read somewhere that Amsterdam had the highest ratio of tourists to inhabitants in Europe. Less than a million people lived here and more than two million visited every year.

I was so close to Centraal station that I might as well talk to the security guard again to check if he had seen Frank Stapel when he'd put the bin bag in the locker.

The same guard was on duty in the stored luggage area. His uniform was still immaculate. He smiled when he recognized me. 'I knew you'd want to know,' he said. 'I talked to my boss, asked if I should call you, but she said you'd come back.'

'What did you want to call me about?'

'The tapes,' he said. 'The CCTV footage. I've got it lined up to when Frank Stapel gets here. I found it for you,' he said. 'I found the exact spot.'

I looked up at the CCTV camera, trained on me like a gun. 'Show me,' I said, and stepped into the office where Tessa had sat less than a week ago.

The security guard gave me his chair. The edge was damaged and some of the stuffing was coming out. He stood behind me, reached over my shoulder and pressed play. He smelt of cigarettes and coffee. The screen flashed to life.

'There he is, can you see?' he said.

I nodded. The images were jerky but clear. A man walked into the stored luggage area. He had his back to the camera. He wore a leather jacket and carried a bin bag in one hand.

'You have one down every corridor?'

'Yes, we've got footage of him coming in, too.'

'Nice.'

The man stopped by the lockers. He looked for one that was still free. He stepped back a row, and that was when he turned towards the security camera. I recognized that face with the snub nose from the photo in Tessa's bedroom and from when we'd seen his body lying on the pavement. It was Frank. He opened a locker, C7, and lifted the bin bag in. He closed the door, walked up to the pay point and inserted a card. The machine spat out a ticket. He undid the front of his leather jacket and put the slip of paper in the inside pocket. Then he walked out of the field of vision of the camera.

'Nice job. Well done finding it.'

He showed me a wide grin. 'Thanks. My mum said I shouldn't take this job, that it would be boring. It's been anything but.'

'I can imagine,' I said. 'Is this your first week?'

He grinned again. 'Is it that obvious?'

'Just how new your uniform is.'

'Fair enough.'

'Sorry, I never asked your name.'

'Carl. Carl Renburg.'

'Can you show me again, Carl?'

'Sure.'

I watched it five times. Saw Frank come in all alone, lift the bin bag and put the ticket in the pocket of his leather jacket.

'How's the girl?' Carl said. 'Tessa? How's she doing?'

'It's tough for her, but I think she'll be okay.'

'Good, that's good.'

'Can I see it once more?'

Frank held the bin bag by the top as he walked in, keeping it away from his body, as if he were putting the garbage out on bin night. But when he positioned it in the locker, he placed his hand under the bottom. He didn't just shove it in. After he'd closed the door, he stood there for a second. Dipped his head before setting off to pay. As if he'd said a little prayer.

I cycled home. The sofa was still by my front door. I really needed to get that taken away tomorrow. My mother was in the spare room with the door closed. It was quiet inside. I went into my study. Pen in hand, I stared at my drawing. Frank Stapel had been wearing his leather jacket when he'd put the skeleton in the locker. He hadn't been wearing it when he'd fallen from the terrace. How had the jacket come back to Tessa? That was the key to this. Had she been with him on the terrace? I imagined the scene. Tessa had come to the building site and they'd had a few drinks on the deserted seventh floor. Could have been romantic enough for a recently married couple. Had a few drinks, then he'd persuaded her to come out on the terrace with him to have a look at the view, because it had been a lovely evening. They'd joked around, maybe kissed; he lost his balance and fell. She got scared, grabbed the drinks, the picnic, his jacket, and ran back home. Waited until the call from the police came. Distraught, partly because of guilt, partly because of grief. Or maybe they'd had a plan concerning the skeleton. It went wrong. He died. She kept the jacket and the ticket. No. She would have just thrown the ticket away.

It couldn't have been her.

I crossed her name out. Someone else had taken the jacket back to Tessa's flat. Someone else had been with Frank at the time of his death. Someone who'd watched him fall, or maybe someone who'd pushed him, as Tessa had said at his funeral. Then that person met Tessa to give her the jacket back. She would know who it was. I would call her in for questioning at the police station tomorrow, or interview her with Thomas. That would remind her of the day that Frank had died, and she would tell us what had happened. What it had to do with Dollander, I wasn't sure. I wrote his name in a different colour pen, right in the centre of the paper.

Chapter Twenty-six

The next morning, I was sitting at my desk with my first cup of coffee, reading through the specs for glass panels to check how much force they were supposed to hold, when the boss came in.

'I wanted to tell you guys this in person,' he began.

Thomas looked up.

I couldn't tell from the CI's thin face if this was going to be good or bad news. He seemed poised between concern and excitement.

'I talked to the burgemeester at length last night,' he continued, 'and we've decided to completely change the scale of this operation. Now that we're looking for Dollander.' He pulled back the chair at the desk opposite mine and joined Thomas, Ingrid and me. For a second I thought he was planning on personally working with us on this case. Even though that was clearly not his plan, having him here was unusual enough to make me worried. Did this mean we were no longer on the case? Had it gone to a different department? I needed to use the bathroom but couldn't walk out while the boss was still talking. I felt as if I was back in kindergarten, when I'd needed to ask for permission to go. These meetings were never long; I could wait it out.

'I wanted to give you all a chance to voice what part you want to play in the investigation. It was yours to begin with and I wouldn't want you to feel sidelined now that we've got more resources coming in.' He looked at me specifically, as if he particularly wanted me to speak up.

I listened to the CI tell us his tactics and I thought he was all wrong. Ten years ago I would have said something, but you get to the point in your career when you know that nobody wants to hear it. However outspoken they say they want you to be, those in power prefer people to agree with them; people such as Ingrid, who was nodding enthusiastically at every word the CI said.

What was the best way of solving a crime? That was really what this meeting was about. Was it to throw a lot of resources at the problem and then plough your way through the input you got? That was never the way I did it. I knew the boss would probably listen to me, would accept what I said, but wouldn't act on my suggestions. And was there anything more annoying than someone who knew you were right but who would do something else anyway? For political reasons mostly. How stupid would he look if he didn't use all the resources at his disposal to find the body of the most wanted criminal of the past ten years or so. Sometimes you had to be seen to do the right thing, I fully understood that. That was another reason why I kept quiet.

The CI's suggestion was that they were going to pull all other teams from whatever they were working on to help us find Dollander's body and his killer. I drew some circles on my notepad as they discussed how best to use those groups. From circles I moved on to curly lines.

'Lotte,' the boss said, 'maybe it's best if you work on some of the drug smuggling.'

Here it was. This was the moment to say that of course I was going to do whatever he wanted me to. After all, he'd made it sound like a suggestion rather than an order. But there were too many interesting loose ends dangling in front of me. 'No,' I said.

Thomas laughed in astonishment but managed to turn it into a cough.

'No?' the boss said, his eyebrows raised in a genuine query. Surely he must be used to people disagreeing with him? Maybe normally people didn't voice it quite this openly.

'I still think we need to look at Frank Stapel's death. There are many questions surrounding that and I would like to follow up on them.'

'Right.'

More explanation was needed, I could see that in the boss's face. 'It's like knitting,' I said. 'You have a loose thread somewhere and you keep pulling at it and it unravels until you can see what's behind it.' I looked over at Ingrid next to me. I expected her to agree and nod, but instead she was frowning.

'If you're sure,' the boss said. 'There are a lot of angles to explore. There's Dollander's work as a property developer, which we think he used purely as a front to cover his drug dealing and people trafficking. You don't want to trace that?'

'No.' I shook my head. 'I'll stick with Frank Stapel. Find out how his leather jacket got back to Tessa.'

'Okay, you and one other person can do that. You'll need someone.'

I looked at Ingrid, but she kept quiet.

As soon as the boss had left, I dashed to use the bathroom. When I came out of the cubicle, I saw Ingrid waiting for me at the washbasins.

'Knitting?' She spat the word out. 'You had to use knitting?'

I turned on the tap. 'What's wrong?'

'This is the biggest case in years. Dollander. And you keep going on about Frank Stapel and his leather jacket. You think so small.'

The soap dispenser failed to dispense any foam, no matter how often I pressed the button. 'That's what's going to get this case solved.'

'And knitting? God, you couldn't have picked a more stereotypically female word. Could you not at least have said that you were going to take a wall down with a sledge-hammer? Knitting and sticking with the small stuff. The domestic stuff. You know they'll bundle me in with you.'

I looked at her via the mirror. Her inverted face was oddly lopsided, but what was obvious was that she was angry. 'What's the problem?' I rinsed my hands under the cold tap.

'Because of what you said, they'll make me work with you. Give the big stuff, the drugs, the trafficking, to the men. Leave you and me with the part that will unravel your knitting.' Her voice lingered on the last words with heavy sarcasm.

'You don't have to work with me.' I turned off the tap and shook water from my hands.

'You know that's what will happen. And the boss kept saying you could do another part. But you had to turn it down. Didn't you see what he was offering you? You could have led this investigation. Now it will be Thomas, because you want to focus on a leather jacket.' Anger radiated from her.

'He wouldn't have given the lead to me.'

'Don't be stupid. You're his favourite.'

I laughed, even though I knew I shouldn't. I grabbed a paper towel. I suspected that deeply hidden under CI Moerdijk's aesthete's exterior, there might once even have been something like friendship towards me. But after the last case, I was sure that whatever there had been was eroded away. Still, he didn't dislike me. A cynic might say that was because I had made him look good two cases in a row.

I judged how people perceived me by the way they acted towards me. The boss had ignored Francine's complaints without even checking why I had been out of the office. The implied statement was that if I hadn't been doing my job, hadn't been at work, he trusted that I had a good reason for it and didn't need to check. So yes, he had my best interests at heart, for as long as they didn't clash with his own.

Ingrid's anger only seemed to increase at the thought that I might be laughing at her.

'I'm sorry,' I said, 'but I'm far from the boss's favourite.'

'You've been a role model for so many of us. It makes me fume to see you throw your chances away.'

'I've always been good with the details,' I said.

'You care about this girl Tessa and it makes you blinkered to what's really going on. Why didn't you grab it? The big stuff?'

'Because that's not going to solve this case.' I had once been young and ambitious like Ingrid, and what had happened to that? I wasn't interested in my career as such. I wanted to get answers and that was enough. No need for promotions, and if that was what Ingrid was after, she was welcome to it.

Ingrid sighed, pushed open the door to the hallway and left.

I wanted to find where Frank Stapel had got the bones from. That would lead us to where the rest of Dollander's remains were still buried, and then probably to his killer. I would work it from that angle, and at the same time, Thomas could look into Dollander's past and come up with reasons and motives. I understood what Ingrid was saying, I hadn't chosen the most high-profile part of the investigation, but it was what was going to get this case solved, I was sure of that. I couldn't be a role model for every female officer in the force. I couldn't make decisions based on what would be best for the image of women. I had to do what was best for the investigation, and I knew that if I didn't, then nobody else would. It was too important to let drop.

I went back to the office, but Ingrid wasn't there. 'Can I ask you something?' I said to Thomas.

'Sure.' He looked at his watch as if he had to make sure I wasn't going over the ten seconds that he had decided to assign as my allotted time.

'You remember when we first saw Tessa Stapel?' I said. 'We went to her flat.'

'Sure.'

'That leather jacket. Was it at her place? Do you remember seeing it?'

'You really are obsessed with this jacket,' he said, but he hesitated. His eyes focused on the ceiling, whether to try to call up the image or to avoid looking at me, I wasn't sure. 'I don't think I saw it. At least it wasn't hanging over one of the chairs.'

I nodded. 'I agree. It wasn't there, was it? That means someone brought it round later that evening or the next day.' I handed him the tape from the security camera at the station. 'Frank was wearing that jacket when he put the skeleton in the locker. Someone was on that roof terrace with him.'

'Yes, you said.'

'I just can't imagine it was Tessa.'

'Are you okay with . . .' He paused. 'I don't know. With that part of the investigation?'

'Yes, that's what I want to cover. The rest,' I shrugged, 'I trust you. I know you'll do a good job.'

'Thanks, Lotte.' A surprised smile shot across his face. 'You know, I never told anybody about what I heard on those tapes. You know the ones I mean.' He looked down the corridor to make sure nobody could overhear him. 'The ones of you and that murderer.'

'I know.' I grimaced, because I didn't like being reminded of that. 'I also know that nobody else would have discovered what you did.'

He stared at me and was about to say something when his mobile rang. He swore, then picked it up.

Chapter Twenty-seven

Francine called Thomas as she crossed the road to the police station.

'Hi, Francine.'

She could hear she'd caught him in the middle of something. 'I'd like to talk about my grandfather's case.'

'Sorry, Francine, now's really not convenient.'

She grimaced at his tone. Yesterday she would not have doubted that he'd want to see her. Of course he had bigger fish to fry now. When he and Lotte Meerman had first talked to her, three days ago, she had been priority number one. Now she wasn't any more, and she knew why. Michael Kraan had been only too happy to fill her in. How he had another high-profile case now. She knew he hadn't been interested in her grandfather before, even though of course he had made all the right noises. And then everything had changed this morning, when he cornered her in the office and asked if her brother had ever been involved in organized crime, because otherwise it was a very strange coincidence . . . He'd looked at her in a meaningful way and she had only just managed to bluff that yes, it was a strange coincidence, wasn't it? But no, no organized crime in Sam's past.

Michael Kraan needed to learn to keep his mouth shut. She hadn't had to push him hard before he told her about Dollander's bones found next to her grandfather's. His bones mixed up with her grandfather's in a bin bag. He wouldn't say any more, so she still didn't know which bones or how many. She'd heard in his voice how for him the case had suddenly become important. Just like for Thomas, she didn't matter at all any more.

'You need to talk to Lotte,' Thomas said. 'She's dealing with that.'

'I don't want to talk to Lotte. I want to talk to you.'

'She knows you've complained about her, of course, but I'm pretty sure she's not holding it against you.' There was a hint of sarcasm in his voice.

'Is she there?' She said it through clenched teeth. So that was what it was like. Now that she'd complained, he was choosing sides with his colleague and against her.

'She is. Hold on a second.' There was noise in the background, muffled by his hand on the mouthpiece. 'Can you be here in about half an hour?'

'I'm downstairs now.'

A sigh. 'I'll let her know.'

'Now, Thomas.' When Lotte showed up would be a sign of how important Francine still was to this investigation.

Lotte came down in five minutes. Was that the same suit she'd worn a few days ago? A non-descript navy-blue trouser suit over a cream V-neck top. Francine would have worn some jewellery with it, a necklace and definitely earrings. Lotte chose not to. There weren't any rings on her fingers either.

'Thanks for coming in, Francine,' Lotte said. 'I've been meaning to talk to you.'

As if she'd set up the interview. Francine followed her to a room marked Interview Room 3. A different room from last time. A camera hung in the corner and a microphone rested in the middle of the table. Lotte didn't switch any of them on, and Francine didn't feel the need to have their conversation recorded either.

'Have you made any progress?' She put an emphasis on the word 'any'.

'A lot has happened since we last talked,' Lotte said.

'I sincerely hope so.'

'But it's thrown up more questions than answers, I'm afraid.'

'Why am I not surprised?'

'I can't tell you much because—'

'I know about Dollander.'

Lotte blinked a few times. 'You do?'

Francine kept a straight face at having landed such an excellent blow. 'Word is getting round.'

'Who told you?'

Francine smiled. 'What does it matter?'

'So that's why you're here?'

'Yes, what the hell's going on?' Her smile suddenly felt fake to her. This had been her big moment. She had loved all the attention her grandfather had been getting her, and now that was being taken away. As if anybody would care about a Second World War hero now that the carcass of a major criminal had been found as well. Thomas's attitude had told her that loud and clear.

'I have a couple of questions for you.' The fact that Lotte's voice stayed calm was only more annoying.

'About Dollander, I guess. No, I don't think my brother was involved with him in any way.'

'No, not about Dollander, even though that's an interesting angle. Thomas and Ingrid are looking into ways Dollander might be linked to either of our property developers. They've got that covered. Or at least they were going to until everything changed this morning. We still don't know where your grandfather's remains came from. That's going to be key in solving this.'

'Solving what exactly?' Only a few days ago Lotte had told her that they wouldn't be able to find out how her grandfather had been killed. 'The only reason you're interested is because you hope my grandfather will lead you to Dollander's killer.'

'Whoever killed Dollander is clearly a dangerous individual, and of course we're anxious to know who that is. However, I'm really interested in what happened with your grandfather. When we first spoke, you were in a rush to go. I've had to read his story in the newspaper.' Lotte smiled to take the sting out of her words.

Francine leant back on her chair. 'Yes, I had to go to the airport. I'm sorry I complained about you.' Even though it was hard to believe, it seemed that Lotte was going to be her only ally. The worst ally she could possibly have, of course, and definitely not who she would have chosen, but the only one who was still interested in what had happened in her grandfather's past.

'And I'm sorry I walked out of our conversation the other day. I had to look after my mother. She had an accident.'

'Is she okay?' For the first time since Michael Kraan had told her about Dollander, Francine felt the muscles in her shoulders relax. Was there something about other people's misfortune that made hers look less important? Maybe it was the fact that Lotte was sharing something about her personal difficulties that made the situation easier.

'She's fine. Only broke her wrist. It could have been worse at that age. If it had been her hip, we would have been in real trouble.'

'At least my father is being looked after.' Francine tapped on the table. 'Touch wood, he's still healthy physically, even though he is getting more forgetful every day.'

'What has he said about his father's remains being found? It must have been a big shock to him.'

'Yes, it has. And especially that they were stuffed in a bin bag.'

'I understand. Of course I do. Has he read the article in the paper? Your big interview?'

'I don't know. I haven't spoken to him since it came out.'

'Did you talk to him beforehand?'

'No, not really.' Her husband had set up the interview and she had just gone along with it. 'Why do you ask? There's another one tomorrow.'

'Maybe you wanted to check your facts with him before giving that interview?'

'No,' Francine laughed, 'that really wasn't necessary. He's told me the story so often, I know it by heart.'

'He didn't try to stop you?'

'Giving the interview?' At Lotte's nod, she continued. 'No, why should he?'

'In case he wanted to change part of the story?'

'What are you implying?' Francine frowned. This interview room should have warned her that this wasn't a friendly chat, however much Lotte was talking about her mother and however much she was smiling. She leant forward and rested her elbows on the table. 'Why are you saying that?'

'Someone asked me when I was going to check your story. Your father's story. They indicated that . . . that maybe there was something else going on.'

'Are you calling me a liar?'

'Not at all. It could just be that your father . . . embellished his story.'

'My grandfather was shot, my grandmother died in a concentration camp.' Francine could feel her pulse racing. 'What more do you want? What other proof?' She hissed the words across the table. Amazing how it was actually worse to have her grandfather doubted. Questions about Sam were almost par for the course. This was new. This was raw.

Still Lotte sat there with that infuriating calmness. Francine felt as if she were pushing her words against a foam wall. She had never felt like hitting someone more. And suddenly it popped into the back of her mind that it was clearly all a facade. This woman had broken a suspect's cheekbone. The calmness was a front. Break it and she would see Lotte's mistakes. How dare she doubt her grandfather? How dare she ask those questions?

'Your father was very young at the time,' Lotte said. 'He was what? Seven years old?'

'Yes.'

'It was a very confusing time. All I'm saying is that seven-year-old boys, they might want to tell stories that are more interesting than what happened in reality.'

'No.' Francine shook her head. 'There's no way. It all happened.'

'Do you have your grandmother's death certificate?'

Francine laughed, even though it seemed to grate in her throat. 'Are you insane? As if the concentration camps handed out nice bits of paper for the people they killed.'

Lotte nodded. 'I understand. However, if your father says anything when you see him next, can you let me know? The person who mentioned it to me, let's just say that I have reason to believe he knows what he's talking about.'

'Another war hero? Everybody is one these days.'

'Exactly.' Lotte gave the word a meaning that Francine really didn't like.

She wished she had talked to her father before doing all those interviews. Her life had this amazing ability to blow up in her face. Why did the story feel unreal to her all of a sudden, like something made up? She hadn't told her father she was doing these interviews. That felt like a mistake suddenly. Francine felt how the smile around her mouth had turned into a rictus grin. As she walked out of the police station, she was happy that the sunshine forced her to hide her eyes behind her large sunglasses. She had to see her dad. Tomorrow. She would do it tomorrow.

Chapter Twenty-eight

When I came back from the meeting with Francine, wondering if I'd made even more of an enemy of the woman, our office was empty. I'd missed the CI's briefing and now I wasn't entirely sure what everybody was working on. That I hadn't needed to be there was a clear enough message: all the focus was going to be on Dollander, and Frank Stapel was only of minor importance now. How could they not see that it was Frank's death that was the key to unlocking this puzzle?

'Hi, Lotte, are you the only one left here?' Edgar Ling sounded amused.

'It appears so. What's up? Have a seat.' Keep me company, I thought, but didn't say.

'Did Thomas tell you? About the phone call?'

'Yeah.' I pulled my hair back from my face. It really needed a cut. 'I just met with Francine.'

Edgar frowned, which looked odd because of his lack of eyebrows. 'Francine? No, the guy from the glass panel manufacturer. The ones that were installed on the roof terrace where Frank Stapel died.'

I blinked and shook my head. 'What guy? No, he didn't tell me about that.'

'This guy called because of the bad publicity. Of course it's been all over the papers that those panels fell after him.'

'Sure.'

'The make of the panels was named and now they've had a few orders cancelled. He claims those panels should never have fallen down just because someone leant against them.'

'Perfect. This is just what we need.' Those panels had been bothering me from the beginning. Now we might finally get some answers. I pulled my notepad from my handbag.

'Funny, that,' Edgar said. 'Thomas said the same words but in a very different tone of voice.'

I laughed. 'I can just imagine. No, all Thomas cares about now is Dollander, and I can't blame him for that. I think he's pretty much got every police officer in Amsterdam and the surroundings helping him out. Do you mind liaising with this panel guy? Maybe take him to the site where Frank died? If there's anything wrong with those panels, that would be worth knowing.'

'Sure, I can do that.'

'So, Dollander. How do you think his arm got mixed up with the other skeleton? And just his arm?'

'The simplest explanation is this.' Edgar got a piece of paper out and made a quick drawing of two stick men lying side by side. 'We found the main bones of Dollander's right arm. If he was buried on his back, then he was on the left of Francine Dutte's grandfather. Maybe his hand was on his stomach.'

'And someone picked up those bones by mistake? They wouldn't have noticed the rest of the skeleton?'

Edgar sucked his lower lip between his teeth in thought. 'Well, bones do move during decomposition. As flesh and ligaments disappear, the skeleton shifts.' He redrew his leftmost stick man and put the arm into a triangle shape. 'These bones move here.' He added two arrows to show that they'd shifted towards his other stick man. 'The hand stays behind and those bones fall into what used to be the stomach cavity.'

'Makes sense,' I said.

When Edgar had left, I stuck his stick men to the whiteboard. Ingrid came into the office and threw her handbag on her desk. 'What did I tell you?' she said. 'I'm working with you. We were all in a briefing with the CI while you were away.'

'I was talking to Francine Dutte,' I said.

Ingrid shrugged. 'I looked at those files on Mark Visser's sister. I found something interesting.'

'What's that?' My voice had been sharper than I'd intended.

Ingrid looked at me with a frown.

I rubbed my face with my hand. 'Okay, tell me.'

'You're not in the files. You don't get a single mention. There was this, though.' She held out a notebook. 'It's Mark Visser's.'

'Give me that.' I wondered why I'd never looked at it. It was mine, of course, not Mark's. The evidence of my first failure. Mark had figured out what I had missed. He'd come over to our flat to tell me. I could have rescued Agnes. The first time I'd rung the doorbell at Parkstraat 12, she'd still been alive.

'They dug up the entire garden. They took down the shed, cut down the tree.'

'No, that's not right. The tree is still there.'

'No it isn't.' She took a photo from one of the files and handed it to me.

It was of the garden as I remembered it. From before the digging, before the destruction. The garden still intact. The shed still there.

'They thought,' Ingrid said, 'well, that there could be more children, more girls, so they dug it all up.' She handed me a second photo.

They hadn't just taken down the shed. They'd been thorough. The garden had been turned into a barren patch of earth. Not a single plant had been left standing. Even the tree had gone. Only the wall at the back and the shape of the fences between the houses showed that it was the garden we had been in a couple of days ago.

'Who replanted the garden?'

'It's been more than thirty years, Lotte.'

'Thirty-five,' I said automatically. 'We need to start this from scratch. We never looked at it as a murder investigation. We wrote it off too quickly as an accident, so we never even did the basics.'

'You mean Frank Stapel's death? You want to redo it as a murder investigation?'

'Yes.'

'It *was* an accident.'

'Humour me. Think of our questioning as a sledgehammer to take a wall down.'

She closed her eyes and shook her head but didn't argue when I suggested we meet with Tessa Stapel again to check her alibi.

'Tell me about the day Frank died,' I said. Tessa's flat was a lot tidier than it had been last week.

'What do you want to know?' she said.

'Where were you that afternoon, that evening?'

'I worked late. I was at work until about nine p.m. and—'

'Is there someone who can confirm that?' Ingrid interrupted. She had reluctantly come along, telling me on the way over what Thomas was working on and how talking to Tessa would be a waste of time.

'Yes, my boss.' Tessa gave the man's name. 'I'd been home for about ten minutes when you and that other guy arrived.'

'Tessa, what was going on between Frank and Kars van Wiel? Was there any trouble?'

'Well, there are a lot of foreigners on the site. Eastern Europeans. Polish, Bulgarian. Frank didn't have anything against them, don't get me wrong, but they don't speak any Dutch. And Frank thought that maybe it was dangerous. Couple of months ago, there was almost an accident.'

'So were you on a late shift? Were you at home in the morning?' I said.

'No, we were doing month-end work and I was working overtime.'

'Did Frank leave the flat before you?'

Tessa pulled her eyebrows together. 'No, I left first.' She was dressed in the same jumper she'd worn at Centraal station. She pulled the too-long sleeves over her hands and made her fingers disappear. Her face was pale and gaunt, as if her skin had been stretched too tightly over her cheekbones.

'Frank was still in bed when you left?' I asked. I hoped my voice was encouraging her to think.

Tessa started to cry. 'He made me breakfast. It was the last time I saw him alive.'

'Do you know what he had planned for the morning?'

'Go to work?'

'But not at the building site. Was he working for anybody else?'

'No, just the two of them. But they were always getting him to do stuff. Their house, a bedroom here, a bathroom there, their kids' houses, their parents' houses. He worked hard, did a good job. It was cash in hand.' She stopped. 'I shouldn't tell you this, should I?'

'It's okay. I'm not looking to do anybody for tax evasion. His colleagues must know more than they're saying. They've been paid cash. They're reluctant to say where they worked. I get it. But I don't care if none of it was declared to the taxman. I want to know where Frank could have found the skeleton.'

'He didn't tell me all the addresses. But someone at the funeral said something about a house they're working on that was . . . What word did he use? Creepy, I think.'

I might have thought that was the house where Mark's

sister had died, only we now knew it couldn't have been. 'But you don't know the address?' I asked.

'No. Sorry.' Tessa chewed her thumb. The nails on her other hand were bitten to the quick.

Ingrid and I drove back to the office through beautiful spring weather. The wind had blown three different seasons across the sky in half an hour. The sun warmed the tulips that were out in people's front gardens. The daffodils planted on the roundabout were already past their best, their yellow trumpets drooping as if silenced.

'She's lying,' Ingrid said.

We overtook a kid on a scooter, his helmet hanging from his handlebars and pushing a girl on a bicycle, his foot on the luggage carrier of her bike. They were only a few years younger than Tessa, but carefree, school kids, not a widow with a job and bills to pay. Widows were women my mother's age.

Tessa's smile came to mind. I thought of the way she had run across the grass outside her flat to talk to me at the tram stop. She had called me from the station. She could have called Thomas, but she'd called me. She trusted me.

'Did we check the ticket for fingerprints?' Ingrid said.

'Yes, only mine and Tessa's were clear. Otherwise there were partials, but they couldn't lift any other full prints.'

'So Tessa, then,' Ingrid said. 'She had the ticket.'

I remembered Tessa's cries when she'd opened that bin bag, and how small she'd looked when she'd asked me to investigate her husband's death properly. 'There were partials,' I repeated, 'so other hands touched it before Tessa's. Plus she can't have been on the terrace, because she's got an alibi.'

'For the time of his death. But what about earlier? She could have met with him any time in the afternoon. We'd better check that and her alibi.'

'Didn't you see what the girl looked like? Her husband just died, for God's sake. If you had seen how she looked when she opened that bin bag . . .'

'No need to shout. I know you like her.'

'It's got nothing to do with liking her. She was truly upset.'

'Good actress?'

I swallowed the angry retort and ground my teeth together so that I wouldn't react. When you were accused of defending someone, every angry response was seen as proof that you felt you were in the wrong. Ingrid had said she wanted to learn from me. It hadn't taken her long to start doubting me.

We drove back to the office in silence. It gave me time to think and to figure out how the jacket had got back to Tessa's flat. As soon as I'd hung up my coat in the office, I grabbed a blue marker pen to write on the whiteboard. 'There was someone with Frank Stapel on the roof terrace,' I said. 'There must have been.' I wrote names down: Frank's brother Eelke, Mark Visser, Kars van Wiel. 'Someone gave that jacket with the ticket in it back to Tessa.'

'Tessa was probably in cahoots with that person,' Ingrid said, 'and stirred up trouble at the station so you'd turn up and witness her retrieving the bin bag. She argued with the guard and called you.' She drew an arrow that linked Tessa and Frank. 'She knew what he had planned.'

'You weren't there.' Someone walked past the open door to our office and turned his head. I was talking too loudly. I pushed my chair back and rushed to the canteen.

I sat in my favourite seat, drinking coffee in silence, and sent Edgar Ling a text to ask him to join me when he came back from his investigation on the roof terrace. He turned up half an hour later.

'How did things go with the glass-panel manufacturer?' I said.

'We went to the terrace, as you suggested. The guy was mortified: it seemed they'd installed those panels all wrong. Upside down. That meant,' he took out a notepad, 'that where there should have been a ridge to hold them together, now they slid out of the groove.' He looked at me. 'The bevelled edge that should have been at the top of the panels was at the bottom. The panels pivoted and Frank Stapel fell through the gap. There were a lot of foreigners there. Nobody spoke any Dutch. If they misunderstood the instructions . . .' He shrugged. 'Maybe this was just an accident.'

That was what Robbert Kloos had said the other day when he angrily chucked his Gatorade bottle against the newly plastered wall. Tessa had mentioned a previous incident. So we'd found Dollander's bones due to something that could have been an accident?

* * *

It was late when I finally went home. From outside the building I could see that the lights were on behind the windows of the top floor. I hadn't asked my mother when she was going back to her own flat. The doctor said it would take six weeks for the broken bone to heal but she could probably leave sooner if she wanted to. I could help her with the shopping and the washing. I locked up the bike in the storage area under the stairs and went up.

When I got close to my front door, I heard voices. I froze with my keys in my hand. I tried to breathe without making a sound. My heart was pumping fast, partially from walking up the stairs but partially from the concern of who might be behind that door. I covered my eyes with my hand and rested my forehead carefully on the door. My mother was talking. I couldn't make out the words. I crouched. I pressed my ear against the keyhole. A man's voice, no more than a deep rumble. I stood up. My mother had visitors in my flat. The idea that it could be my ex-husband Arjen and his new family made me turn and flee down both flights of stairs to the communal hallway.

Standing on the black and white tiled floor, underneath the chandelier, I wondered where I could go. Back to work? I didn't want to. It was my flat. Why was I standing here with nowhere to go while she was entertaining people in my home? I dashed back up the stairs, taking them two at a time, and put the key in the lock. I uncurled and extended my fingers. I'd been holding the keys so tightly that a locksmith could have made a spare from the imprint in my palm. I turned the key and pushed the door open before I could change my mind. There was no sound of another woman and also no sound of a child. My breathing became easier. My mother wasn't babysitting, then.

'There you are,' my mother said. 'We've been waiting for you.'

Opposite her was the owner of the man's voice. Mark Visser.

'Why are you here?' I said.

'I wanted to thank you for visiting my mother,' he said. 'It meant a lot to her.'

I liked that he'd made up an excuse to see me again, but had he been in my study? Had he seen my drawing? He didn't know about Dollander. Nobody did apart from our team, the CI and the burgemeester. And of course Francine and wherever she had heard it. Mark didn't know that there was still a body in the ground that we were desperate to find. I stared into his eyes, noticed his black polo-neck jumper under the charcoal-grey suit, the same one he'd worn when we first interviewed him. 'Okay,' I said, 'you've thanked me. Now you'd better go.'

'Lotte,' my mother said. So much disappointment in one word.

'You need to leave now.'

'I made tea,' my mother said.

Mark stared at me. His eyebrows pulled together in a frown. He put both hands flat on the table and got up slowly. 'You think I have something to do with—'

'I don't think anything,' I said quickly, because I wanted to say that I was worried that he could have.

He shook my mother's hand, said it had been nice to meet her again after all these years. He said he'd see himself out, but I followed him down the stairs.

He stopped under the chandelier and stood where I'd paused earlier. I tipped my head back to look at him.

'How can you possibly think I'm involved in this?' he said. 'You've known me for so long.'

I shook my head. 'I knew you when we were kids. I haven't talked to you for thirty-five years. I don't know you.'

'I don't understand why you're so angry.'

'I'm not angry.'

'Why did you just throw me out of your flat, then?'

'We're still investigating . . .'

He frowned again. 'I thought Frank's death was an accident. I thought you'd identified the skeleton.'

I thought of Dollander. 'We haven't concluded the investigation. That's all I can say.'

'Two of your colleagues came to see me today. They were asking about Tim Dollander.'

'What?' As if he'd read my mind.

'That wasn't related to this, was it? It was that same man who came with you the first time. Thomas Jansen? With a colleague.'

'Sorry.' I brought my hand to my forehead. 'They came to see you and talked about Dollander?'

'Yes, they said they had some information about his whereabouts. It didn't make any sense to me at all. I've never met him. But now I'm wondering . . .'

'I'm sure it has nothing to do with that,' I lied in a

soothing voice. Inside I was fuming. What were they thinking, talking so openly about Dollander? If they were trying to stir things up, they were taking a massive risk. I should have attended the team briefing. 'He was probably involved in a property development deal,' I said.

'But what has it got to do with me?'

'Nothing. Probably nothing.'

'Neither does Frank Stapel's death.'

'You employed him.'

'Sure, I employed him. He worked at one of my sites. He was a good worker. God, I even used him to decorate my own house.'

'You did what?'

'Ages ago. What I meant was that there is nothing wrong with employing someone, is there? He didn't die at my building site. It was at Kars's.' He reached out and touched my arm.

I pulled back.

He stuffed his hand in his pocket and turned towards the external door. 'I was going to ask if you wanted to go for a drink, but I guess I shouldn't.'

'I'm sorry.'

'Well, thanks for seeing my mother anyway.' He took a step towards the door, then turned back to me. 'How do you do it, Lotte? How do you keep sane in your job?' He put his hand against the door frame ten centimetres away from my face. I would only have to lean in a little to have those fingers touch me.

To stop thinking of him caressing me, I laughed. 'I don't think I do. I don't think I stay sane.'

'But you weren't really sane to begin with. You were a scary crazy girl from the start. Remember? You were going round asking all those questions, ringing doorbells, talking to the neighbours.'

'Was that crazy?'

'It wasn't normal. You were tenacious. You just wanted to find Agnes.'

'No I didn't.' I moved a hand through my hair. 'It wasn't only about that. It was also about finding information to get my father to come and see me.' I shook my head. 'You're right, I was crazy, or naïve, or just blind. I thought that if I discovered something, he would come to Amsterdam.'

'And did he?'

'My mother never told him what I was doing.' I laughed again, a single exhalation. 'I'm sure he would have put a stop to it straight away. He would have known how dangerous it was. My classmate had gone missing, and I was out in the park trying to find her, talking to everybody.'

He pushed away from the door frame and I could breathe more easily. 'Yes, my mother didn't like it. Even when I was with my friends, she didn't want me combing through the park.'

'But they never stopped us going that way to school. If it had happened today, there would have been a blockade. There would have been a mothers' protest.'

'Or they would have teamed up to make sure we were always accompanied to and from school.'

'Why didn't they?'

'It wasn't the park, though, Lotte, was it? We were perfectly safe in the park.'

'Still, parents today . . .'

'True. There's no way I would let my kids do what you and I did. I've never been the same since.' His face was baggy, especially around the jawline. The skin drooped, but somewhere in that man in his mid-forties, I could still see the child with eyes full of tears. His hair had been long then, but now, as he bent forward and stared at his feet, I could see his scalp shining through the stubble on the crown of his head.

'No, nor me.' I said it softly. 'And it still didn't get me what I wanted.' I grimaced. 'My only friend was gone. Then you were gone. My father never came to see me. My mother refused to take his calls.' I offered up something that was still deeply painful to distract Mark from his memories. To drag the conversation away from his little sister. To no longer talk about what had happened over thirty-five years ago.

'Sometimes I wished I'd never asked you for your notebook.' Mark brushed his fingers over mine.

It was as if he'd pushed all the air from my lungs. I leant against the wall and closed my eyes. I hadn't wanted to give him the notebook with my drawings in it, and the notes I'd made in large, looping writing after I'd talked to the neighbours. If I hadn't given it to him, we wouldn't have found Agnes. And now we were standing here together in my hallway. 'What happened after we found her?' I said. 'I can't remember.'

'My mother came running out of the house. She was screaming.'

'She called the police?'

'Yes. She hugged me. Turned my face away from the shed.'

That moment was a blur to me. 'I can't remember,' I said again.

'Then the police came. They sat me down, asked me why we . . . why I was in the garden.'

I rested my hand on the wall, even though I wanted to put it on his chest. 'Did you tell them I was there?'

'I don't know.'

'Maybe they talked to my mother.'

'Maybe,' he said. He was close. I only had to stretch my hand out slightly and I could hold his as I had done that day.

'I better get going. Goodbye, Lotte.'

I stayed glued to the black-and-white-tiled floor until he had left the hallway, to stop myself from calling out to him, asking him to come back. I shut the front door behind him. I didn't want to go back upstairs. I waited for five minutes until I was sure he'd gone, then I followed him out of the front door, unlocked my bike and cycled along the canal in the falling darkness.

I followed the route I had cycled so often. Along and across canals, the houses getting newer the further I went from my flat. I liked to think of the map of the city as the dissection of a tree, where the canal rings were like year rings, building up as the city kept growing. It held true for a few centuries. The centre of the city was full of seventeenth-century idiosyncrasy, with houses as tall and narrow as they could build in those days. Then, like a river that had burst its banks, Amsterdam had outgrown its canal rings and, no longer restricted for space, spread more widely. Roads now had enough space for cars to pass each other. The houses had gardens and weren't split up into shops, businesses and flats. The space didn't last. Further out, the flats came back. Sixties and seventies blocks this time, apartments that looked as if the architect had designed them with a toddler's colourful bricks. To the left I saw the familiar shape of the church at the edge of the park. Its steeple was sharp as a knife, ready to cut a patch of grey out of the low-hanging sky and clear the way to heaven. It was made from bronze that had oxidized to match the pale green of the willows that grew along the canal on the outside of the park. The park that bordered my mother's flat.

I turned and cycled through the entrance. It had been so big when I was a child. I'd walked every possible route through it. It had taken me weeks to search every metre of it for clues. Now it took me just a few minutes to cross it. At the exit, I didn't turn right, as I normally did, to go to my mother's. After all, she was at my place and it was to avoid her that I was out on my bike. Instead I turned left and headed for Tessa's.

Chapter Twenty-nine

'How are you?' I said.

'Okay.' In front of Tessa was a stack of black-rimmed cards and envelopes.

'You're having trouble sleeping.' It wasn't a question; I recognized the telltale signs.

'In the beginning,' she said, 'I'd get his clothes, hold them tight, and sleep. I can't do that any more. I still want to, make the hours pass quicker, but I can't.'

'I used to go for a drive in the middle of the night when I couldn't sleep.'

She nodded. 'If it gets bad, I need to get out of the flat. I walk. Try to get some exercise too.'

'It hasn't been great weather for walking at night.'

She shrugged. 'A bit of rain is the least of my problems.'

She was probably right.

'Your family must help you,' I said. Someone had tidied up. The carpet was visible and there was somewhere to sit. Edges of the chaos were still there, but more under control.

'They help make my life more difficult. Told me I should send cards to everybody who came to the funeral. I was going to put something on Facebook, but apparently that won't do.' She wrote her name on three of the cards and stuffed them in unaddressed envelopes. 'You came to the funeral. Would you like one of these?'

'Tessa—'

'It doesn't matter. To be fair, my mother did bring the cards and she's coming back later to put the names on the envelopes. She can choose who to send them to. Anybody who cared about Frank was his Facebook friend anyway. Not my mother, though. Frank always thought she didn't like him.'

'That's tough.'

'He was wrong. I think she knew how important he was to me.' She took the next card from the stack. 'He was the strong one. She saw that.'

I wouldn't have written them, those death-edged cards that nobody wanted to get through their mailbox. I didn't know anybody still sent them. Tessa wrote her name on the next card. She looked like a schoolchild writing her lines. Punishment.

'But she would have liked someone else for me. She's an intellectual snob. He wasn't as smart as me. He didn't have a proper education.' Each of the sentences was accompanied by the swish of stuffing a card into an anonymous envelope. She stopped halfway through her name and lifted her pen off the paper. She stared at the letters. 'But brains aren't everything, are they?' The pen went back down and finished her name. *Tessa Stapel*. 'Maybe if I'd been a bit more stupid.

Thought a bit less about everything. Frank could do that: just enjoy life.'

Outside, rain had started to fall again. The sky was only a little lighter than the rims of the envelopes. A mourning sky, crying for something. The grey was the perfect backdrop for the leaves of a tree, bright green, just arrived, young, not yet damaged.

'How many of those do you have to write?'

'My mother said seventy-three.'

'I don't even know that many people.'

Tessa looked up and smiled. 'Nor me.'

'Her friends?'

'The only generation that still cares about this stuff.'

'Got another pen? I'll give you a hand. Sign some for you.'

The grin widened. 'Isn't that falsifying my signature?'

'Only if your mother's friends find out.'

She pushed some cards my way and I picked up a pen. I wrote Tessa Stapel on a card. I looked at the writing; spikier than hers, more idiosyncratic. Memories came back of a time when I'd seen stacks of cards like these. Who had they been for? My grandfather maybe. I took the next card from the pile. Wrote my own name on it.

Tessa looked at me.

'I'm sorry,' I said. 'I've ruined it.'

She took both the cards I'd signed, the one with my name and the one with hers, and tore them into small pieces. 'I should keep writing them.'

'Sure. I'll put them in the envelopes.' We worked in silence and did ten in quick succession.

'Shall I seal them?' I didn't want to bring those envelopes of doom close to my face, let alone lick them.

'No, just leave them open. We'll do that later, when my mother gets here. She's bringing a sponge.'

'So what about Eelke, does she like him?'

'I used to go out with him, you know that? But she knew that was never serious, so she could like him for himself. It's odd. He's just as much a fuck-up as I am.'

'Did Frank care?'

'He always tried to prove he was good enough for me.' She passed me another card. 'He was worth ten of me.'

I pretended to concentrate on sliding the card into the envelope.

She put her pen down and evened up the stack of cards in front of her until all the black edges aligned. 'He thought that if he just earned enough money, she would change her mind. It was stupid. That's why he was working so many hours, in so many places. My mother didn't care about the money. She only cares about education.'

'So many places?'

'Little jobs here and there. He painted Mark Visser's house.'

'Yes, Mark told me.'

'Did a great job.' Her voice shot up in enthusiasm. 'Oh my God, have you seen his house?'

'Where is it?'

'Oud-Zuid. One of the big houses.'

Oud-Zuid. Expensive. Walking distance from Station Zuid. Walking distance to where Frank had died. 'How long ago was this?' I said.

'We weren't engaged yet, so it must have been eighteen months, two years ago.' Tessa kept talking. Vowels and consonants glued together until they were no longer individual words but a stream of speech. 'It's wonderful. A nineteenth-century house but all modern on the inside. When you go through the front door, it's meant to feel as if you're going forward in time. From past to future. That's what Frank said. He made sure the paintwork took pride of place. He had to be very careful with the plastering, to make it really smooth. There were no pictures yet to hide any mistakes or bumps. He showed me, when it was nearly done. I was . . .' She rested both her hands on the cards, the hand with the double wedding ring on top. Suddenly she looked like a widow, even if she wasn't dressed in black. Her eyes filled with tears. 'Last night I slept with Eelke.'

I put a few more cards into envelopes. I felt more like an agony aunt than a detective, and made an encouraging sound to keep her talking.

'He looks so much like Frank,' she said. 'You must have seen that. And I . . .' She sighed and turned the wedding rings round and round on her finger. 'I was sad and lonely.'

'I understand.' I remembered Eelke hugging her at the funeral, holding her tight.

'I needed . . . some comfort, I guess. It was either Eelke or alcohol. I'm not sure I made the right choice.'

'You know you can call me if you need help or company.'

She signed a few more cards.

'There's one other thing I want to ask you about,' I said. 'Frank's jacket. When he fell, he wasn't wearing a coat.'

'It was a warm evening.'

'But how did it get back here? Did you meet him earlier?'

'I was at work all day. What does the jacket matter anyway?'

'Come on, you're a smart girl, Tessa.' I reached out and touched her arm. 'Frank was wearing this jacket when he put the skeleton in the locker.'

'He wouldn't have done.'

'He did. We've got it on CCTV. He went back to work immediately afterwards, as far as we know. That evening he fell to his death. And somehow, as if by magic, the jacket found its way back to your flat. If Frank was with someone else that evening, if he met someone, that person would have a lot of information that we'd want to know. Did you see something that scared you? Were you at the building site?'

'I've only been there a couple of times. I don't have a head for heights and I don't like the inside of buildings when they're not finished yet. So fragile without the walls. As if they could fall over at any time. Or crumble. Frank always said I had too much imagination.' She whispered the last words. There were tears in her eyes. She lifted her head and looked at me. 'The jacket. You think he was wearing it when . . .'

'When he fell? No, he can't have been, because then he would still have been wearing it when we found him. Even if someone had taken it afterwards, we would have seen the marks. Like we did—' I was going to say *like we did on his skin*, but bit the words back just in time.

She sucked her lips between her teeth.

'Tessa, if you were there, if you saw anything, if you held his jacket while he was working on something, doing something, you have to tell me. If it really was an accident and if someone gave you the jacket back, tell me. We won't think badly of him. Or of you.'

'Maybe he came home, from Centraal? Before he went back to work.'

'We checked the time on the ticket and when he arrived at the building site. He wouldn't have had enough time. He couldn't have come back here.'

Tessa dropped her shoulders on a short exhalation. 'My mother's coming soon. Thanks for helping me with these.'

'Here's my card again,' I said. 'If anything happens, call me.'

She took it. 'I've got your number stored in my mobile. From when you first gave it to me. When you came to tell me that Frank had died. Remember?'

That seemed ages ago. 'Of course.' I scanned through the history of received calls. 'This one, is that you?' I showed her my mobile.

She handed the card back. 'Yes, it is.'

I stored it under her name.

Tessa opened the door. She stood close. On impulse, I gave her a hug. Her arms went tight around me. Her shoulders shook. The wetness of her tears soaked through in the nook of my shoulder, just above my collarbone.

'It'll be all right,' I said, and wiped a tear from her cheek with my thumb.

She showed the gap between her teeth in a watery smile.

As I left the building, I came face to face with a woman my age whom I recognized from the funeral. Tessa's mother. She had similar wrinkles to mine: the small vertical lines above her top lip, the lines that radiated out from the corners of her eyes into an age-defining fan, and that paper-cut-thin line between her eyebrows.

'Detective Meerman?' she said.

I nodded.

'I'm Vanessa Koning. Can we talk?'

Chapter Thirty

I shouldn't have taken her to my mother's flat, but it was empty, and the closest place where we could speak in privacy. Vanessa hadn't wanted to chat in the corridor as she was worried that either Tessa or Eelke would overhear.

'That's where Eelke and Tessa met, you know. At an AA meeting. Tessa was difficult as a teenager. First anorexia, then she self-harmed. Always such an unhappy girl. Then she started drinking.' Vanessa lifted the glass of water to her lips. When she put it back down, her eyes glanced over the table with the scratches where I'd tried to mark my initials in the wood. The white crocheted tablecloth was stained yellow at the edges. Seeing it through Vanessa Koning's eyes made me feel embarrassed all over again.

'First she was just drinking every weekend,' she said. 'Normal teenage stuff, smoked a bit of pot. Nothing we hadn't done ourselves. You must have done too.' She smiled at me.

'Sure.' I remembered that I'd sat in the same chair I was sitting in now, swaying but trying to keep still, wanting to giggle but articulating as carefully as possible to avoid slurring my words. My mother's hurt eyes had shown me that I wasn't fooling anybody. I knew she would pray for me six hours later, when she'd be at the early church service. She wouldn't reproach me. Instead I'd get the silent treatment for the next two days, which would tell me louder than words how wicked I'd been.

'When she left home, it got really bad. Soon she was drinking every night, all night. Took a lot of pills, we later heard. Tried to commit suicide one night, or it was a binge gone wrong, we never knew. That call, that rush to the hospital.' Her mouth contorted as if she'd bitten into a sour apple. She pinched the corners of her eyes against the bridge of her nose. 'We were just grateful her friends got her there in time. We didn't ask too many questions.'

Tessa had cut herself with that knife when Thomas and I interviewed her. 'Was she continuing to self-harm?'

Vanessa nodded. 'Her arms looked awful. She never wore short-sleeved tops. Tried to hide the marks. She said she couldn't deal with the pressure of university. The exams. Those big lecture halls. She told me she felt as if she was anonymous for most of the time, then suddenly had to perform at the end of term.'

I had liked the anonymity, how you could sit at the back and nobody would ever know you. I didn't think most of my professors had ever known my name. 'Is that when you got her help?'

'No, not at that point. I should have done, I guess.' She tucked some of her blonde shoulder-length hair behind her ear. The grey was carefully blended in. 'Instead we let her move back home. She got a job as a secretary. It seemed fine. Then, one evening, she'd been out drinking and got in her car. She lost control and crashed it into a tree. They had to cut her free. It was a miracle she wasn't hurt. She could have killed someone. She was four times over the limit and they took away her licence for three years. I set her an ultimatum: if she wanted to stay living with us, she needed to dry out.'

'And she agreed?'

Vanessa nodded. 'She was badly shaken up. Also by how difficult she found it not to drink. I hadn't realized, you see, that she was having a couple before going to work.'

'So she went to the AA and met Eelke.'

'I like Eelke, I really do. He used to be at our place all the time. But all the same, I was happy when Tessa and Frank got together.'

'And Eelke? Was he happy too?'

'It's funny.' She looked at her watch. 'Even though Frank was younger than Eelke, I think Eelke looked up to him. Recognized that he was the stronger of the two.'

'Thanks for telling me. That's useful background.'

'What I really wanted to tell you is that I'm worried about her. She seems to be coping, but I'm not sure.' She met my eyes.

'I understand.'

'I'm worried she's going to snap.' She reached out and put a hand on my arm. 'Don't put too much pressure on her.'

'We just had a chat.' I smiled. 'I helped her with the cards.'

'Sure. But just be careful. Because if she cracks this time,

I don't think she's going to bounce back.' She looked at her watch again. 'I'd better go see her.'

I closed the door behind her. My mobile beeped. It was a text from Mark. *One final offer of that drink?* Phone in hand, I sank down on my mother's chair.

Mark had come to this flat all those years ago. He'd stood on the doorstep with my notebook, the one that I'd given him two days before, in his hand.

He looked around him to see if anybody was listening. 'Someone lied,' he said. 'I've read through all the questions and answers. Mr Korenaar at number twelve, you wrote here that he said he was on holiday the week that Agnes went missing. But he can't have been because he always asks us to look after his cat when he goes on holiday and I fed his cat two weeks earlier. I'm sure because Agnes helped me. She loves that cat.'

I wanted to run back upstairs. I finally had a reason to call my dad.

'We should see him again. We should ask him your questions again. Maybe he just got the week wrong. Maybe he didn't want to talk to you.'

We went to the neighbour's house together. How could I have ever thought Mark had had anything to do with Frank's death? I could meet him or I could sit with my mother in my flat. I could be desired or I could be lonely. Was I worried about liking him too much? About wanting him? I needed to make up for my suspicions. And nobody would find out anyway.

I texted back: *Where do u want to meet?*

Chapter Thirty-one

He was back at home, he said, at the house in Amsterdam Zuid that Tessa had so admired and that her husband had decorated. He gave me the address. I cycled there. I loved the wide streets and the houses with their stately grandeur and silent dignity. I smiled as I thought how my hair would be a mess, the wind playing havoc with it, blowing it forward, then back. A weight lifted from my stomach as soon as I turned away from my mother's flat and towards Mark's house.

I chained my bike to the nearest lamp post and rang the doorbell. I slicked my hair back, tried to massage it into its side parting and smoothed it down. If I'd had a lipstick in my bag, I might have used it in the thirty seconds that it took Mark to open the front door.

'Hi,' he said.

'Hi.' My stomach turned somersaults.

'Come in.' He didn't kiss me.

The result of Frank's paintwork was amazing. From the front door, through the hallway, into the lounge, it seemed as if you were a time traveller, going from the exterior – which was firmly nineteenth century – through the more baroque hall, into the entirely modern sitting room. Spotlights were sunk into the ceiling, a dark-wood floor seemed to stretch for ever and the walls were painted into a smooth pale continuum. I loved the art displayed there, bold, modern, full of reds and blues, swirls of broad brushstrokes. Then I came to a long white canvas, a few dark lines creating the sense of a house, some water. A tree. Pointed trunk, pointed branches, green swirls to indicate leaves. Two swallows in the top left corner. An indication of summer. They mirrored my hope.

'Chinese,' Mark said. 'Not that familiar in the West, but I love his work. It's after Wu Guanzhong. There's no way I could afford the real thing.'

I'd never heard of Guanzhong, but I couldn't take my eyes off the painting, enjoying the space that it created, room for my mind to fill in the parts that the artist had left out. I saw an entire house. A lake. Reflections. And the two swallows promising something good to come. 'I love it,' I said.

'Come through,' Mark said.

I followed him to the kitchen. He opened a bottle of wine. Filled two large glasses. I brought mine to my lips, enjoyed the feeling and savoured the flinty crispness of a good Chablis. I sighed deeply. A relaxed sigh. Pleased to be here, where there was space and light.

He smiled. 'I wasn't sure you'd come.'

I drank some more. The sound of my breathing and swallowing was the only thing I could hear. Peaceful. I didn't want to spoil it, but there was something I needed to know.

'When we found your sister . . .' I kept my eyes on his face, scanned it to see if he didn't want to talk about it, but he was still smiling at me. 'Sorry to bring this up.'

'You're not "bringing it up". I haven't thought of anything else for the last few weeks. Ever since you came to my door that first time. With your colleague. Ask what you want.'

'It's just . . . I was there, wasn't I? I'm not misremembering that?'

He ran the back of his fingers along my arm. 'You were there. You and me both. We climbed that fence.'

Under my shirt, my skin tingled where he'd touched me. Talking became harder. Still I couldn't stop asking about the past. 'Then what happened? What happened after?'

'You left. Remember? Through the door in the fence. Into the back alley. As soon as my mother came.'

'I abandoned you.'

'You didn't abandon me. I asked you to go. I was screaming, I told you to run. To run away.' He shrugged. 'You were a little girl, I didn't think you should be there, in case he came back. I never mentioned it to my mother. I didn't tell the police. I said it was just me.'

'You wanted to sound brave.' I smiled to hide my discomfort. I couldn't believe I had left him there, but I also remembered that door. I remembered looking for it to make sure I had an escape plan. Get out before the grown-ups come.

'Something like that.'

'I'm sorry.'

'You can't apologize for something you did thirty-five

years ago. It's done. It was fine. You were kept out of it. Even me; the police didn't talk that much to me either.'

I shook my head. 'I guess it was only too obvious what had happened. I was too late.'

'No,' he said, 'there was nothing you could have done.' Over my shoulder, he looked at the clock. I turned round too. Half past eight.

He reached out and took my hand. He rubbed his thumb over the inside of my wrist and the nerves that ran just under the skin drew goose bumps all over my arms. I put my glass down. He unbuttoned my shirt and eased it from my shoulders. I raised my left arm, not to cover my breasts but to hide my scar. He took my hand and kissed every finger as he eased them away from my body. Then he lowered his head, pressed his lips to the scar and caressed with his tongue that ugly taint where a bullet had entered my body.

Rain was falling so hard that the drops bounced off the road surface. Puddles the size of lakes made my journey back more difficult. I'd dozed a little bit before I put my clothes back on and left Mark's house. Now the water running towards the drain holes formed rivers along the tarmac. Before I'd even got through the park, my trousers were saturated and my legs cold. I pushed as hard as I could, head tilted forward to keep the rain out of my eyes. I moved the gears up, put them on the highest setting, so that each circle of my legs would cover as much distance as possible. Luckily there was no wind. The rain drew vertical lines in the beams of the street lights. On the other side of the park, partially protected by the porch of the church, another cyclist had stopped to find shelter. I exchanged a wry smile with him. There comes a point when you cannot get any wetter and you might as well keep going. I reached that point when I crossed the next bridge and felt the water seep through my socks.

Two cyclists in full rain gear came from the other side. As I passed them, I caught the smell of wet rubber. It instantly took me back to secondary school, where, on a rainy day, everybody would hang their wet-weather gear all over the communal areas and corridors. The whole school would smell. A few kids, always the first-year ones, would keep their wet dark-blue rubber trousers in their lockers, afraid that someone might steal them. There was nothing worse than having to put your damp rain trousers over your normal clothes if it was still raining when it was time to go home. The older kids would be cool and cycle with umbrellas, not as effective but definitely preferable. Cycling in plastic over-trousers made you sweat. Another thing to add to the school stink. It had given me a lifelong preference for getting wet over wearing waterproofs. I'd had a poncho for a while; the front would drape over the handlebars, which kept your legs dry but also created a miniature lake between your arms that was difficult to dispose of without soaking yourself.

I wiped the rain from my face. A small trickle of water dripped from my hair down my back, between my shoulder blades. It should have been annoying but instead it struck me as amusing. The fabric of my trousers was now glued to my skin. Two more canals to cross before I was home. I turned along the road to the opposite side of the canal from where I lived. I looked over to my side of the canal, saw how much my flat was lit up. My mother's silhouette was clear. She waved. She had waited up for me.

On the steps, I wrung as much water out of my trousers as I could and took my saturated jacket off. My feet squelched in my shoes as I walked up the stairs, leaving a trail of drops behind. All I wanted was a hot bath to drive the cold away from my bones. The chill had seeped deep into my shoulder.

'Oh, you're soaked,' my mother said. She handed me a towel. 'Did you have a nice evening? Did you have dinner?'

I dried my face and rubbed the towel over my hair. 'Don't let him in again unless I'm here,' I said. I went to my bedroom, peeled the wet clothes off, dried myself and got changed. When I went back into the front room, my mother was in exactly the same place I'd left her.

She tipped her head and looked at me. 'How can you say that? He's such a nice man.'

I sighed. 'I know.' Her words mirrored my thoughts. 'But Mum, a man's dead, there's a body still buried somewhere and if anybody knew that Mark had been here . . .' I tried to push to the back of my mind that there were other things that Mark and I had done that nobody should know about. The memory of his hands on my body made me smile. 'In future, don't let anybody in.'

'Mark's not involved. I talked to his mother.'

'I know he's not, but you can't talk about anything I've

told you. Not to anybody, but especially not to Mark or his mother.'

'You didn't say that.'

'You know that. You were a policeman's wife.' I rubbed my hands over my face. 'What did you tell them?'

'Nothing.' She held her plastered arm.

'Don't lie to me.'

'I'm not.'

'Did Mark see anything?'

'Like what? There's nothing here to see. You know, I recognized him straight away. It reminded me of the first time he came to the house. Do you remember?' My mother hadn't known that Mark was Agnes's brother. But then she hadn't known about my notebook and my questions either.

Even now she didn't know much about what I'd done. 'Did he look through any of my stuff?' I said.

'No, he didn't. Lotte, you're being ridiculous. I wanted to keep you away from this.' She pointed at the closed door of the study. 'From this life. From always seeing the bad in everything. I just wanted to protect you.'

I shook my head. If she wanted to protect me from seeing the bad in the world, she was decades too late. I'd seen it the afternoon we found Agnes.

'You have all these books about how to deal with life,' my mother said. 'You have this one.' She held up *Surviving Your Elderly Parents*.

'I'm sorry.' I picked it up and put it on the bookshelf next to *Cooking the Healthy Way*.

'But you're not learning from the books, are you? You're behaving as if we're all criminals, because that's who you see around you all the time.'

'Or victims,' I said.

'Lotte, the world isn't like that. I saw it in your father. He was the same. And I didn't want it for you: to learn about the world through the prism of dealing with violent crime all the time.'

They had definitely taught me what human beings were capable of. My mother only saw the good in people because she didn't know what they could do.

She used to hide the paper when I was a child to keep bad stories from me. She had done that when Agnes first went missing, but I had seen Agnes's photo on the front page anyway. Afterwards my mother had kept all the papers away so that I wouldn't read what had happened to my schoolmate. All pointless, because I'd seen it.

'Do you still have your scrapbook?' my mother asked. Her clothes showed her age more than they did in winter, when the loose folds around her neck were hidden under the tight turtlenecks of cold-weather garments. The skin on her breastbone looked like seersucker cloth and was on show in the V-necked T-shirt she was wearing.

I nodded. My scrapbook with the newspaper clippings of all the cases I'd ever worked on.

'Can I see it?' she said.

I hesitated. 'Why?'

'I don't know you any more.' My mother's face was a mirror of what was to come for me. The pattern of wrinkles would one day be chiselled into my own skin: the folds that started just below her cheekbones, a set of deep vertical lines, already stayed behind on my face when I finished a smile, and the frown that was deeply edged between her eyebrows was a razor cut between mine.

I took my scrapbook down from the shelf and put it in front of her on the table. She flipped it over, then opened it from the back and read the clippings that my father had cut out when I was in hospital. It had been on the front page, that photo. It showed me lying face up on the steps outside a canal house, blood pooling under my right shoulder, my eyes fixed on the rain falling from the sky, my face as gaunt as it had ever been.

She was silent for a long time, staring at the photo. 'You think I've been bad to you,' she said. She looked at me. The lines in her face were even deeper than usual, as if her skin was suddenly two sizes too big for her. 'That I've kept you away from your father. But I only ever wanted the best for you. Where is he, anyway?'

'Holiday. He's in Thailand. Would you like some tea?'

She shook her head. 'They finally took that sofa away,' she said.

I hadn't even noticed it had gone. 'Who did?'

'I called the council. They picked it up. It was awful having it sitting outside your front door like that.'

'Thanks,' I said. I left her paging through my work history and ran a bath. It took a good ten minutes before I was warm again.

Chapter Thirty-two

Half asleep, I waved my arm above the duvet to chase the fly away. The buzzing didn't stop. I sat up. It wasn't a fly; my phone was ringing. The display light was flashing. The display said *Tessa*. It was 0.36 a.m. I'd only gone to bed half an hour ago.

I picked it up. 'What's up?' I rubbed my eyes to chase the sleep away.

'Help!' It was a scream. A screech. 'Help me!' I could hear the panic in her voice.

The surge of extra blood through my veins pushed the hair on my arms upright. 'Tessa, where are you?'

'I'm at—' The call cut off.

My skin crawled. I kicked the duvet to the floor and swung my body out of bed. I forced my legs into my jeans, pressed the button to call her back whilst my good shoulder held my phone to my ear. 'Tessa?'

Nothing.

I rang again. This time it went to voicemail. 'Tessa, where are you? Call me back?' I got dressed, then grabbed my car keys and handbag and ran down the stairs. I tore the door of my car open. I shoved the phone in the hands-free holder. Through the dark, I raced to her flat. Street lights flew by, hurling their circles of light on ashen asphalt. Traffic lights flashed their danger signs on amber. All other cars had bled away throughout the evening until now in the dead of night there were only empty roads.

I made it to her block of flats. I slowed down but I didn't see her. I came to a stop. It was now 0.53 a.m. Had Tessa's mother been right? Had Tessa cracked and gone off the rails? Had I pushed her too hard as her mother had warned me? I rang her doorbell but there was no response. I rang again, held my finger on the buzzer for over five seconds, but deep down inside I knew it was pointless. I was just about to ring Eelke's doorbell in case Tessa was at his place when, through the window in the front door, I saw a tall man with dark curls walking towards me. He was zipping up his coat as he left the building. I caught the door as he came through.

'Police,' I said, to justify myself, but he just shrugged and put his collar up with a sheepish grin on his face. I considered asking him for his name, but my worry about Tessa and his total unconcern when I announced that I was police told me not to bother.

I ran down the corridor to Tessa's flat. I banged on her front door with a fist. There was no answer. It would be worse if I was too late.

'Tessa!' I shouted. 'Tessa, are you there?' Nothing.

I knew she wasn't going to open. I went to Eelke's flat. 'Police, open up!' I screamed at the top of my voice. My fist connected with the door. I heard stumbling inside.

Then footsteps approaching. I stopped the banging and stood aside.

Eelke opened the door wearing just pyjama bottoms. He was more muscular than he'd seemed in the tracksuit.

'Is Tessa with you?' I said.

He scratched his head. Sleep was hanging from his eyes. 'What?'

'Have you seen her? She called me, screaming for help. I'm worried about her.'

'Hold on.' He grabbed a T-shirt that was on the arm of the sofa. Why would anybody get undressed in their front room? He picked up his mobile. 'I've got no messages from her.'

'Do you have her keys?'

He hesitated.

'Eelke, I'm worried she's . . .' I swallowed. 'That's she's done something stupid.'

'Oh shit.' He suddenly seemed more awake. He opened a drawer and got a set of keys out. He didn't put any shoes on but walked out in bare feet. I let him open Tessa's front door, then pushed past him. Where to look first? Bathroom. Empty. Bedroom. Empty.

'She's not here,' Eelke said. I could hear concern in his voice. He looked at the coat rack. 'The jacket isn't here. She's been wearing it constantly.'

'Frank's jacket?'

'Yeah. She must have gone out.'

'Do you know where she could be?'

He paused, then made a decision. 'Yes. Let me get dressed. I'll come with you.'

Eelke and I drove back to the centre. The streets were still eerily quiet. 'Where are we going?' I said. I thought about calling for backup, but didn't want to spook Eelke. He seemed on edge. He held his mobile phone tightly. Every now and then he threw a glance at it.

'Take a left here,' he said. His mobile pinged. He read the text and slumped down as far as his seat belt would allow him.

'What's up?'

'I'd just hoped . . . Her mother hasn't seen her either.' He rubbed a hand over his eyes. 'Next right, and then left at the lights.' His voice was determined suddenly. As if he'd been re-energized by whatever he'd read in that text. 'The last time she went through a bad patch, I found her there. On the floor of the toilets. Covered in puke.'

'When was this?'

'Before she met Frank. I've been worried about her too.'

'She told me.' The traffic light went red. I considered jumping it, but instead I stopped. 'She mentioned you got back together.'

'Is that what she said?' His voice was bitter and I threw a quick glance at him, but he was looking straight ahead.

'You haven't?'

'It's not so great when someone shouts out your brother's name. I guess I look enough like him.'

I grimaced. 'I'm sorry.' The lights changed and I turned where Eelke indicated.

'It was stupid.'

What had Tessa's words been? *Either Eelke or alcohol.* What if the sex had made her feel so bad she'd gone for the second alternative tonight? 'When did you see her last?'

'She came for a coffee after her mother had left. A pick-me-up to calm her down, she called it.' He shrugged. 'Her mother can have that effect on people.'

'I can imagine.'

'Here. Stop here.' It was a dive of a pub, not the kind of place I'd normally go or where I would be comfortable having a drink. The windows were plastered with posters of heavy metal bands.

At the door, Eelke paused. The green light of the pub's sign made his face look pale under the red hair. With the dark shadows, his eyes were sunken like the holes in a skull. 'Are you still investigating Frank's death?'

'We are,' I said.

'Frank shouldn't have died. Those panels should have held his weight.'

I narrowed my eyes and looked at him. He was right, but how did he know that? 'If his death was an accident and you know what happened, you should tell me.'

He took a couple of deep breaths. Whether it was because he was deciding to give me more or because he needed courage to step inside, I couldn't tell.

I waited, but he didn't say anything else. I would push him

later, but for now Tessa was my priority. I needed to get inside. 'You don't have to come,' I said.

He shook his head, then opened the door to a still-crowded bar.

I checked my watch. 1.32 a.m. The noise level inside was deafening, as people shouted to make themselves heard above everyone else. The clientele here was mainly young. It made me feel ancient and also terribly conspicuous. About half of them seemed to have tattoos, both the men and the women. I scanned the area for any sign of Tessa. Nothing. I tapped Eelke on the shoulder. 'I'll check the toilets.'

He nodded and moved towards the bar.

In the ladies', a dark-skinned girl was applying fire-engine-red lipstick. Her blonde-haired companion was rubbing her nose. Her pinprick pupils screamed that she hadn't just been drinking.

'Have you seen a brown-haired girl? Early twenties?'

'Who are you? Her mother?' The blonde moved towards me.

I fished my badge from my handbag. The girl backed off.

'She's called Tessa Stapel,' I said.

The girl shrugged. 'Never heard of her.'

'Have seen so many brown-haired girls,' her companion said.

I pulled up Tessa's Facebook profile on my phone and showed it to the girls. 'That's her.'

'Sorry,' the blonde girl said, 'haven't seen her.' They both left, pretending not to rush.

I pushed open the doors to all three stalls, but Tessa wasn't there. When I got back to the bar, Eelke was holding a pint of beer in his hand. He had been absorbed by a group of men of his age.

Two of them had shaved heads, including the one talking, with his back towards me. 'I made this stupid woman jump into the canal the other day,' he said.

I recognized the tattoo. Coming here had been a seriously bad idea.

Eelke was looking at the beer glass in his hand as if unsure how it came to be there. I took a deep breath, then joined the group and snatched the glass from him. I put it on the bar. 'She's not here,' I said. 'Let's go.'

His eyes went from me to his drink.

'Come on, Eelke. Please. We need to keep looking.'

The man with the tattoo grabbed hold of my arm. 'I recognize you. You look a lot cuter in your pyjamas.'

'Shut up.' I pulled my arm free. 'Eelke, let's go.'

Tattoo took a firmer hold of my wrist. 'I don't care who you are, but my friend is staying here.'

My heart was racing. With my free hand I got my badge out, hoping it would work as well with him as it had done with the girls in the toilet.

Tattoo released me. 'He doesn't want to go.'

People were pushing against my back, making room for a woman with a round of drinks elbowing her way from the bar to where her friends were standing.

'You should leave,' Eelke said calmly. His voice was clear over the background noise. He took his glass from the bar.

'If Tessa wanted to be found, she would have come here.' He drank half the pint in one gulp. It was as definite as if he'd stepped off a roof terrace on the seventh floor of a building. 'We'll get through it together again. You'll see. Her problems are my problems.'

'This is stupid. Don't do this.'

'This is what I want. Just go. There's no point any more,' he said. He took the jenever chaser that stood ready for him and downed it in one. 'I was with him.'

Tattoo laughed loudly, just as he'd done when he'd thrown Pippi into the canal. I wanted to get to Eelke, but Tattoo stepped in front of me and blocked my route. He pushed his face in my space. 'What are you going to do? He wants to stay here and get drunk. There are no laws against that, are there?'

I felt sick, because he was right. There were no laws against an alcoholic deliberately getting drunk. 'Who were you with, Eelke? With your brother?'

Tattoo pushed me out of the bar and I didn't resist. It was better to leave now and get someone to come and help me. Through the window, I saw Eelke pick up another pint, as though he was on autopilot, while he stared at his phone in the other hand. Reading another text. I remembered that he had opened the door to Tessa's flat. He had the keys. He could easily have put that leather jacket back. He knew about the glass panels and he'd possibly admitted he was with his brother.

I called Thomas. Even though it was after 2 a.m., he answered his mobile at the second ring. I apologized for calling at this time but he replied that he was still working anyway.

'Can you come here with some backup?' I said. I gave him the name of the bar. Inside, Eelke was texting, then he picked up another jenever chaser and downed it. 'We need to arrest Eelke Stapel on suspicion of the murder of his brother.'

Chapter Thirty-three

Tessa's mother came to the police station around eight o'clock the next morning. I'd called her. We were still waiting for Eelke's lawyer to turn up. He probably wouldn't be here until nine, and then he would need some time to talk to his client. I hadn't been surprised that Eelke had demanded a lawyer as soon as Thomas and I dragged him out of that bar. The main surprise had been that his friends hadn't put up much of a fight. He had also mysteriously lost his phone.

The leather strap of Vanessa Koning's handbag folded double under the pressure of her now white fingers.

'Thanks for coming in. Come through.'

'Tessa sent me a text last night.' Her eyes closed for a second. 'I'm worried. It said she was going to sort it all out.'

I frowned. 'Sort what out?'

'Who knows. I've just come from Eelke's flat. He didn't answer. I'm afraid.' She rubbed the line between her eyebrows with the palm of her hand, as if that would smooth it out. 'I'm afraid he's drinking again.'

I didn't say that I knew where he was. 'And Tessa?'

Vanessa put her handbag on the table. The logo was

pointing towards me. I didn't recognize it but I understood that I was supposed to. It was understated, a small picture of a tree stamped into the leather. 'Eelke was probably out all night looking for her.'

'Did he say how he knew she was missing?'

'No, but he texted me to ask if I knew where she was.'

Those must have been the texts he was sending from my car. 'She called me last night. In distress.'

Vanessa closed her eyes. 'Was she drunk?' She sounded resigned.

I shook my head. 'It didn't sound as if she was.' When she'd screamed 'Help! Help me!' it had been the voice of someone in trouble, not the sound of someone who was drunk.

'She wrote on Facebook last night,' her mother said. 'She wrote: *I just want to die.*' She covered her mouth with her hand. Her eyes glistened with tears. 'Can you look out for her? I'm so worried that she's tried to kill herself again.'

'Have you tried the hospitals?'

'Yes, she's nowhere. Her flat is empty too.'

'Show me the text she sent you.'

She held her mobile out. The text had come in at 00.12. That was almost half an hour before she'd called me. *Gonna sort it all out.*

'Maybe something to do with Frank's death?' I said.

Vanessa shook her head. 'He just had an accident.'

'Did she talk to you? About the skeleton?'

'She didn't talk to me at all. But that's what she had you for. To come round and talk to her.'

'I interviewed her.'

'You helped her with the cards, were so supportive, but really you missed that she couldn't cope.'

'Vanessa—'

'I tried to call her all night. I think she's killed herself. That's her way of sorting things out.' She closed her eyes. 'After Frank died, I worried this was going to happen. That she was going to end it.' Her voice was soft. 'We'll keep trying the bars. But when you find her . . . somewhere else . . . can you call me? Straight away?'

'Of course.' Sometimes people took an overdose and changed their minds. Called us, called for an ambulance. Realized they'd made a mistake. But Tessa's call last night had not been like that. She'd been about to tell me where she was when the call had cut off. So unless she'd dropped the phone, there had been someone else with her.

Ingrid and Thomas were looking at me as I stepped through the door. The sudden silence told me what the topic of conversation had been.

I sat at my desk. I started up my PC.

'Lotte,' Ingrid said.

I looked up.

'She . . .' Ingrid's voice trailed off. She looked at Thomas. He remained silent, didn't answer her plea. 'She wrote on her Facebook page. Look here.' She turned the screen towards me. Tessa's smiling face. The last posting: *I've been wrong about everything. I just want to die.*

'Remember when we interviewed her?' Thomas said. 'She cut herself with that Stanley knife. She was self-harming.'

Tessa, at the table, cutting her thumb, looking at the blood that welled up. I shook my head against the memory. 'How come you can see her page?' I asked Ingrid.

'It's on her timeline.'

'We've put her description out to all cars,' Thomas said.

My eyes were burning. My throat was swollen; it felt so thick I could hardly swallow. Thomas put an arm around my shoulder. My instinct was to recoil, but his proximity was unexpectedly calming. 'She screamed, Thomas.'

'You're a mess,' he said, but his voice was gentle. 'I know you like the girl.'

'I'm worried I pushed her too hard.'

'She could just have drunk herself into a stupor.' His eyes looked straight into mine.

I shook my head. 'I went to see her last night. Yesterday evening really. We talked.'

'About . . . ?'

'About the leather jacket.'

'How was she when you left?'

'Not suicidal.'

'You could judge that?' Ingrid said.

'I'm not an expert, but yes, I can tell if someone is about to kill themselves. She was fine when I left. Her mother came.'

'After you'd gone?'

'Yes.'

'So maybe it's the mother who drove her to it.'

'The first time I talked to her, at Centraal station, she said, "It's so unfair." Now she's saying, "I just want to die." It's teenage talk.'

'She wasn't a teenager.'

'You know what I mean. Whatever they call it when you've moved into your twenties. It's just how young women speak. It doesn't mean she's killed herself.'

I left to get some coffee. Halfway down the corridor, the boss called me into his office.

'What happened, Lotte? What happened with this girl?' He was standing at the window, staring at the raindrops that were falling again. He had his hands in his pockets.

'She's missing,' I said. 'I'm concerned.'

'The parents are voicing some very strong allegations.' The grey of the clouds was only a little lighter than the dark grey of the CI's suit. He scratched the back of his head.

'All I did was talk to her yesterday evening. She knew something.'

'You pushed her too far. Why didn't you take Ingrid with you?'

'It was evening. It was on an impulse. To have a chat.'

'Not an interview?'

'It was very low-key. I didn't bully her, if that's what you're afraid of.'

'We've got nobody to back your story up. That's what worries me.'

'We'll find her,' I said. His running gear was hanging to dry over the radiator again.

'She did say she wanted to die.' He followed my eyes. 'Sorry, it got rather wet. In the rain.'

'She didn't mean it literally. It was just an expression.'

'The parents—'

'She knew something. Something about her husband's death. Remembered something. There's the leather jacket.'

'The parents think that Frank Stapel's death was an accident. That you're needlessly going on about it. They claim that you made Tessa snap, were bringing it all back to her.' He rolled his chair back, pushed it until he was beside the radiator. He lifted the running top. Fingered it. Turned it over. Touched the back.

'When I got there last night,' I said, 'she was writing thank-you cards to the people who'd gone to the funeral. Her mother had asked her to do that. I don't know how that wasn't reminding her of her dead husband.'

His running top must have passed the test, as he folded it in two, and again, and stuffed it in a sports bag with a flame drawn on it in white, the symbol of the police force. 'You're convinced the husband was murdered?' He picked up the shorts. Tested the wetness of the waistband. Stretched the material. 'You arrested the brother.'

'It's all connected.'

The boss looked over his shoulder, half bent over his sports bag. Behind him, the rain continued to wash the windows. I was tired. I got my notepad out and started to draw circles. I didn't want to draw the path of the raindrops, didn't want to register how they started at the top of the window and slowly slid to the bottom. Circles were neutral.

Beginnings and endings all rolled into one, never stopping, never starting. Not just going down but also coming up again. My pen kept going round, making the circle's outline thick. It spun off to a new circle, next to the old one but attached by the pen's line. The circles were thick like wedding rings. I filled them in so that they were coins instead.

'She called you twice.' He put the shorts back over the radiator. 'Maybe it was a cry for help.'

'Twice? Not yesterday. She called me from Centraal station, of course. Then she called me last night. The cry for help, as you call it.'

'Why did she call you?'

I thought of the sounds I'd heard. 'She sounded panicked. Really upset.'

'So that's why—'

'Why I went out looking for her. Yes.'

The boss nodded. 'I'm concerned about you, Lotte.'

'You don't need to be.'

'Are you sleeping? Are you eating?'

'My mother's staying with me. She had an accident.'

The boss raised his eyebrows. 'Is she at least cooking for you?'

'She's broken her arm. She can't.'

'If you need to take some time off—'

'I don't.'

'Ingrid said she's got some spare time to work with Thomas, if you need time off.'

'She told you that?' She was saying anything to get to the other part of the investigation.

'She's concerned about you too.'

'All those people concerned about me. How nice. But I'm fine. Nothing to worry about.'

I was about to leave when Thomas popped his head around the door.

'Eelke and his lawyer are ready for us,' he said.

Chapter Thirty-four

It had been seven hours since we'd arrested Eelke, but I could still smell alcohol coming from his every pore. He'd had another four or five drinks before Thomas had turned up. He'd drunk as if he'd found water after ten days in the desert. Maybe that was what being dry for years did to you. His lawyer, a well-dressed Moroccan man, sat next to him.

'You were with your brother on that roof terrace.' Thomas said. We'd agreed he'd take the lead. 'Tell us what happened.'

'No comment.' Eelke's voice was soft.

'That's not what you said last night. You told my colleague here that you were with him.'

'I don't know what I said.'

'There's no point denying it now,' Thomas said. 'You were with him on the roof terrace, you have the keys to Tessa's flat, you put the jacket back the next day. You're the only one who could have done that. Did you kill your brother?'

'Frank's death was an accident.' Eelke's voice was calm. Resigned.

'So tell us what happened.'

'We had an argument,' Eelke said softly. 'I pushed him. He

fell back against those glass panels and they just gave way. They pivoted and he fell through. Then they collapsed after him. I took our stuff, ran and left the building.'

'How is that an accident?' Thomas asked.

'Those panels should have held him. It was just a soft punch.'

'Which was it? A push or a punch?'

Eelke shrugged.

'A push or a punch, Eelke?' Thomas repeated.

'What does it matter? He fell back and those panels collapsed.'

'He fell and you ran away.'

Eelke laughed, a bitter laugh like the one in the car early this morning. Was that what this had all been about? Just two brothers fighting over a woman? Like the man who'd killed Agnes Visser, maybe living next door to temptation had been too much.

'Did you argue about Tessa?' I asked

Thomas looked at me as if to say: not everything is about this girl.

'Tessa?' Eelke looked genuinely puzzled. 'No, it was about his stupid plan.'

'To do with the skeleton?' Thomas asked.

Eelke looked at his lawyer, who nodded as if to give him permission to continue. 'Yes, he'd seen the boss dig it up that morning.' He dropped his head and stared down at the table.

I was ready at that point to stop the interview and send a car out to arrest Kars van Wiel. I could just imagine the bulldozer digging up a skeleton and somebody putting it in a bin bag to dispose of at the building site. Where had the skeleton been? At Kars's house?

'He saw it that morning?' Thomas calmly continued his line of questioning, as if Eelke hadn't just given us what we wanted. 'But Frank hadn't been on site.'

'No, he was doing another little job.'

'Where?'

'I don't know. At some house somewhere. He told me he'd seen the boss dig up a skeleton in the garden. Frank had been painting one of the upstairs rooms and had a perfect view of it.'

'His boss didn't know your brother was there?'

'No, Frank told him he'd already finished but he had to touch up here and there.'

'So then he sees the guy dig up bones in his garden.'

'Right, and stuff them in a bin bag. Then he put the bag in the kitchen and headed out. He didn't know there was anybody else in the house. Frank grabbed the bag and stored it at Centraal.'

Thomas pulled up his eyebrows as if this was the dumbest idea ever. 'But why?'

'Frank had this stupid plan. He thought we should do something with the skeleton. Put pressure on his boss. I don't know.'

'You mean blackmail?' Thomas said.

Eelke shrugged. 'Most ridiculous blackmail plan ever then, because his boss didn't want the skeleton back. He told me that over the phone, but Frank wouldn't believe me. The guy didn't come. He didn't bother turning up.'

Of course, Kars must have thought it was just a Second World War skeleton and didn't know he'd dug up some of Dollander's bones as well. Did he even know the second skeleton was there?

'Which guy?' Thomas said. It was the first time I remembered there was more than one boss. My heart rate sped up and my mouth felt dry. Another boss doing work on the kind of creepy house that Tessa had mentioned.

'And then Frank got angry with me. We'd waited over an hour. He said I'd messed up. Hadn't set up the meeting properly. He said I'd only had to do one thing and I'd managed to screw that up. He shoved me and then I punched him. He should have just left those bones where he found them.'

'Which guy?' Thomas said again.

'We didn't even want that much money to give him the bones back. I told the guy to bring the money to the site. We watched from the roof terrace so we could see him coming. But he didn't even bother to turn up.'

'Eelke.' Thomas's voice was loud and Eelke raised his head suddenly, as if he'd snapped out of reminiscing. 'Eelke, which guy were you trying to blackmail?'

'What's in it for me if I tell you?'

'If you cooperate, it will make a difference. I know your brother's death was an accident. We know you didn't mean to kill him. All of this matters.'

Eelke swallowed. 'It was Mark,' he said. 'Mark Visser.'

So this was how much it hurt when all your hopes were destroyed. Thomas looked at me. Maybe I'd made a noise. In his eyes I could see only pity.

Chapter Thirty-five

In the little garden outside the police station, a few bees were feeding from the small blue flowers of the forget-me-nots. They flowed from flower to flower, perpetually in motion, only pausing to collect pollen to bring back to their community. Their movement was hypnotic and graceful. They weren't something to be frightened of but something to be admired, with their work rate and community spirit. I straightened up from observing them only when some of my colleagues entered the garden and the beep that the door made when they swiped their cards through the reader pulled me out of my reverie.

The sound reminded me of my first day back at work. I'd arrived in Amsterdam the evening before, but it was only when I'd swiped my entry card through the reader at the police station and had seen the lights flash up green that I felt like I'd come home. Before I'd been forced to take four months off, I had never been away from work for more than a week. The need of my fellow colleagues to sit in a caravan for three or more weeks every summer never ceased to amaze me. For me, work had been much more fascinating than any holiday could possibly be. When I was married, neither my husband nor I had wanted to be away from our jobs for any length of time, and after the divorce, the thought of leaving home and employment to sit somewhere with a group of strangers became even less appealing. No, it was when I got to work that I felt I was finally back where I belonged. How wrong I had been.

Now one of my colleagues asked me if I was coming, holding the door open for me.

What could I do other than go through? Only a few weeks ago I'd been happy to be back inside the station. Now I was already lingering in the garden.

I went through the door and faked a smile at my colleague who'd held it open.

I went for a very early lunch and sat at my usual table. Ingrid joined me. I would have preferred to be alone but didn't have the energy to tell her to go away. She stared at me from over her salad. She picked at a few lettuce leaves with a fork. Missed most of them and ended up with one rocket leaf speared on the fork's teeth. Her shoulders were hunched forward. 'This isn't what I expected from working with you,' she said

'What did you expect?'

'That I'd learn from you.' She brought the fork to her mouth. Chewed the leaf. Slowly. 'That you'd show me how it's really done.' She pushed some sweetcorn to the side, moved a few pieces of beetroot to the centre.

'You're coming with me to my interviews. You're part of all the team discussions. What more do you want?'

'I thought, from reading your case studies, that it would be different.'

'Different how?'

'More . . . I don't know. You're clearly committed to work.'

'Right.'

'The work you did before, that seemed more alive.'

'Alive. What does that mean? It took a long time. Many meetings. Many interviews. What you read about, what you saw, that was only part of it.'

'I listened to the tapes.'

'What tapes?'

'The ones where you talked to that murderer. The tapes of the interviews. I studied your technique. I learned so much from that. How you got to the answers. How you talked to him for hours. Got close to him until you found the truth.'

I put my sandwich down. The last bite seemed to jump up through my throat and back into my mouth. I swallowed. Thomas had let her listen to the tapes. I guessed they were part of the archives now.

Ingrid continued pushing parts of her salad from one side of the plate to the other. Equal-sized dice of vegetables covered by an orange dressing. Rocket leaves ended up on a small pile. Another type of lettuce, which looked more like seaweed than something you should have for lunch, was collected in the centre of the plate. 'Now you were wrong all along, weren't you? You never thought it could be your childhood friend,' Ingrid said when she was finally happy with her food arrangement. 'You've given up so much for your job. That is so exciting. That's what I want to be like. I wanted to see how to become like that.'

'You're crazy.' I pushed my plate away.

'You lost your husband, you got shot—'

'Yes, I got shot. How's that good? How's that something you want to imitate?'

'You've been . . .' She swallowed. Paused. 'You were my hero. I wanted to be like you.'

'Like me? Why would you want to be like me?'

'You're a role model. When we studied your cases, we all wanted to be like you. Now it's just work.'

I shook my head. 'That's insane. Why would you want to be like me?' I knew I was repeating myself. 'My husband left me and I live alone in a flat; apart from that, I've got a cat and my mother staying. Yes, I've been shot and so I'm still in pain every day.' I had to stop myself from rubbing my shoulder. 'You've got some stupid romantic notion about what I'm like. But if you think that this is "just work", you're so wrong. Filling in endless reports and paperwork is "just work".'

'I thought you and I . . .'

'That you and I what? Would have cosy chats about my fucked-up life?'

'But it's just all lies anyway, isn't it, Lotte? You told me you found Mark Visser's sister's body. Well, I read the files and you're not in there. You're not even mentioned. You made it all up.' She got up. 'It's all lies.'

All lies. If only. Then I would not have seen my classmate's dead body.

She rested her tray on the back of the chair. 'Why did you do that? To sound more interesting?' She pushed away.

I deserved her anger, but not for the reason she thought. I took my old notebook out of my handbag and looked at the drawings I had made as a child. 'This wasn't Mark's,' I said. 'It was mine.'

In her face I saw the desire to believe me fighting with her suspicions. I knew exactly how that felt.

'It was mine,' I said, 'and I was too late to save her.'

'What do you mean?'

I closed my eyes. What did it all matter now anyway? After Mark had figured out that the neighbour had lied, he and I had gone to confront the man. We rang the doorbell in vain.

'He's not here,' Mark had said. 'Perfect. Let's check his garden.'

Even as I helped Mark carry the ladder, I didn't want to go over the fence. But when Mark had gone to the top and held his hand out for me to follow him, I climbed up anyway.

Mark stood still and stared at something in the garden, close to the shed.

He turned to look at me. His face had crumpled in on itself, like Piet's did when he was reading. 'That's her hair ribbon,' he said. The bright purple strands fluttered from a bare branch of the tree.

'Let's go,' I said. 'Let's call my dad.'

Mark didn't listen. He walked up to the ribbon. I was

close behind him. We stopped at the shed. I held his hand. It was shaking in mine. I wanted to look at the cat and I wanted to look at the sky and I wanted to look anywhere else, but together we looked through the window of the shed. And saw Agnes's dead body.

The memory of seeing her in that shed would haunt me for ever. 'When I first questioned the neighbour,' I said now, 'she was still alive. If I'd known then that he'd lied to me, I could,' I shrugged, 'I could have called the police, I guess, and they could have rescued her.'

Ingrid frowned. 'Are you sure? Let me check the files, but that's not what it seemed like to me.'

'I wish it wasn't. But when I saw her . . . she'd only just died.'

Thomas arrested Mark, and that evening I went home and played cards with my mother. Whatever hope I'd had that her lonely life wasn't going to be mine had been cruelly destroyed. I tried not to think about him.

The next morning Thomas passed a message on. Mark had asked if I could visit his mother.

Chapter Thirty-six

As I went up to Mark's mother's room, I tried not to think about why he had asked me to go. I was shocked when I saw her. I hadn't thought that two days could make such a difference. She had already been thin, but now the cancer showed in her face, the disease eating her up from inside until there was nothing to protect the skin from rubbing against the bone. The skin of her face hung loose around her skull. The arms of her chair were a necessity to keep her upright and in shape, like an exoskeleton.

'I'm glad you're here,' she said. 'I'm sorry I can't get up.' She had opened the door with the buzzer that was within reach of her claw of a hand.

'Have you eaten at all? Since I saw you last? Is there anything I can get you?'

She shook her head, pulled her lips into a macabre grin. 'I can't keep anything down. We had set an end date, that doctor and I. I was going to die on Tuesday. Now I need to wait. To see what's going to happen to Mark. I couldn't die while he was in prison.'

I could see the shape of her teeth through the skin of her cheeks. 'I'm sorry.'

'Don't be. He didn't do this. I know you'll sort it out. I know you believe in him, otherwise you wouldn't have come here.'

I sat down close to her, didn't know what to say other than sorry again.

'Your mother called, did you know that?'

'Yes, she said.'

'It was funny, just like the old days.' She coughed and took a sip from a glass of water standing next to the buzzer. A buzzer with two buttons, one to open the door, the other to call for help. 'The first time your mother and I talked was after you'd come to see me with your notepad, to ask questions about Agnes.'

'I didn't know you talked to my mother.'

'Of course I did. She needed to know where you were. She would get worried otherwise. She worried so much about you anyway, running around all by yourself, that you didn't have many friends. Just like that boy.'

'Like Mark?'

'No, not Mark, he always had lots of friends, always a houseful. He was a good boy. Like he's a good man now, but you know that. You know he didn't do this, that's why you're here. I know that.'

I swallowed. I wanted to believe that so badly. I couldn't get my hopes up again.

'No, I mean that other boy. Kars. Kars van Wiel,' Mrs

Visser continued. 'He was running wild, especially after his older sister left.'

'When did she leave?' I was surprised that my voice sounded so normal.

'She went to study in the States, I think. Nobody was doing that in those days. Kars, he missed her terribly. His father called, asked if Kars could come over to play with Mark. He used to work with my husband, you know, in the oil industry. They were both away a lot.'

'What was he like? Kars?'

'So angry. So upset. He really missed Barbara. He and his brother were alone with his mother, and his father away for months at a time.' She looked down at the floor. 'Like my husband, I guess.' She coughed again and drank the last of the water from her glass. 'Would you mind getting me some more?'

I got up, filled the glass in the tiny kitchen. It had a sink and a fridge but no hob or oven. It was just a space to store goods, tea and coffee. All meals were taken together, so there was no need to cook. This was a good place, it was clean, everybody had their own space, but still, I hated that this was the inevitable end. I hoped I'd die before I needed to go somewhere like this.

'Tell me about Barbara,' I said after I'd put the glass on the table next to the buzzer.

'I never met her. She didn't come back. Made a life in the States for herself, I guess.'

'Older than Kars, you said. How much older?'

'Kars was ten at the time, same age as Mark. She must

have been a good ten years older. Kars was always in trouble, always so angry. He had a real temper on him, but he's calmed down a lot. Both brothers have.' Her eyes fell closed, the eyelids swollen but still creased, the skin under her eyebrows sagging as if to form a second eyelid.

I moved slowly to let her sleep. I must have made a noise, as she opened her eyes and stretched her hand out to me. It was trembling 'Your mother said that you've been lonely.'

'She's one to talk.'

'She doesn't want her life for you. That's what she said.'

The sudden pain in my chest took my breath away. I wanted to forget that it was my worry about my life turning into my mother's that had made me sleep with Mark in the first place. It's better not to have any hope. It's much better not to take these chances in life so that you don't get hurt. 'Can I get you anything else? Another glass of water before I go?'

Her eyes closed again. 'Thank you for coming,' she murmured, more out of habit than because she even knew I was still there.

I placed my hand carefully over hers. The knuckles felt sharp. Bones like glass under my touch. I didn't dare put the full weight of my hand on hers, afraid I would shatter her fingers. I touched them carefully, like you would touch precious china. Maybe this was goodbye. Tears were close to my eyes as I walked down the stairs.

I was halfway down when I saw Job van Wiel, Kars's father, standing by the exit. He was leaning heavily on his walking stick. A small suitcase rested next to his feet. He was staring out of the window in the direction of the manicured garden that lined the path from the road to the entrance of the nursing home. His phone rang. He dug it out of the pocket of his corduroy trousers with one hand and placed his reading glasses on his nose with the other. He stared at the display before pressing a button with a careful index finger. 'Hi, Kars, what's up?' A long silence. 'Sure, that's not a problem.' He disconnected the call and took two careful steps from the exit to a large chair, dragging his suitcase behind him like a recalcitrant dog. He rubbed a hand over the smooth egg of his head, then rested both hands on his knees.

'Can I can help you with anything?' I said.

'My son was supposed to pick me up. He can't make it. Problems with his mother.' He ran a hand over his head again, as if the egg needed polishing. 'There are always problems with his mother.' The bags under his eyes looked so deep that they could hold an espresso cup full of tears.

'I can give you a lift. Where do you live?'

'There's no need,' he said, but he picked up the suitcase.

'Give me that.' I held out my hand. 'Most people take more luggage on a week's holiday. How long have you been here?'

'Five weeks. But I don't need much.'

The automatic exit doors whooshed open. We walked to my car and he gave me the address. I waited until he'd clicked the seat belt in place before I started my questions. 'I was chatting to Mrs Visser just now. She told me about your daughter.' I kept my eyes on the path behind me as I reversed towards the road.

'Barbara. Yes, that was such a long time ago. She went to the States.'

I put my indicator out and joined the traffic. 'Is she enjoying herself there?'

'I think so. I don't know.' His voice was soft. He had his head turned away from me, as if the other lane of traffic was holding his interest.

'You're no longer in touch?'

'Oh, we are. Just not as much as I'd like. She calls us once a month and is always in a hurry.'

'That's a shame.'

'She and my wife argued. She left. I was in Kuwait at the time. I travelled a lot. Worked with Mrs Visser's husband. Middle East mainly. Wherever there was oil.' His voice took on the tone of a storyteller recounting an oft-told tale. 'We had a big party planned, with all her friends. I was going to come back for it, then drive her to the airport the next day.'

'But she'd already left.'

'Yes. My wife called, three weeks early. She said she and Barbara had had an argument and she'd gone.'

'They didn't get on?'

'Always rowing, those two. We never really managed to make up. I wanted to fly out to see her. We've never been.' Job pointed to the next crossroads. 'It's a right here at the traffic lights.'

We turned into a residential street.

I knew which house was his as soon as I saw it. The street was ordinary, but one house differed from the rest, and that was the one we parked outside. All the other houses were identical, sets of two tied together by a single roof. This house didn't have a twinned neighbour. It stood alone. The other houses were 1950s or '60s. This one was older. Pre-war. I was reminded of the one house that caused the kink in the road when we went to see Mark Visser that first time. The house of Old Karel who'd refused to sell.

I undid my seat belt and rested both arms on the steering wheel. I remembered Tessa mentioning a creepy house. Not the house where Agnes Visser had died, but this one. Someone hadn't sold here either, but I doubted it had been to hold out for more money.

I got out and held the car door open. I helped the old man with his suitcase. As we walked up the path, Tony van Wiel opened the door. His body filled the frame. 'Detective Meerman. To what do we owe the pleasure?' His arm barred my entrance as effectively as a traffic barrier.

'I was at the nursing home and gave your father a lift.'

'Do you want to come in?' Job said. 'The least I can do is make you a cup of tea.'

Tony stepped slowly aside. I hesitated. The last time I'd seen him, he'd smiled. Now his face was tense. I held my hand on the holster of my gun as I stepped over the threshold. The long, dark hallway led to a perfectly preserved 1970s kitchen. The wallpaper had a pattern of brown and orange swirls. Low-hanging metal lamps lit up a wood-veneer table and grey linoleum covered the floor. It was all eerily immaculate, as if someone had redecorated in a forty-year-old style only a week ago. From the kitchen I could see the garden. In the back was a patch of regimentally straight rows of pink tulips.

Tony followed me in. His heavy boots clumped through the hallway.

'Have a seat,' Job said. 'Where's Mum?' he asked Tony.

'She's gone to bed. She was upset when Kars brought her back.'

Job frowned. 'Where is he?' When there was no reply, he put the kettle on the gas.

I sat down at the kitchen table. The skirting boards were a light brown that hadn't been fashionable since the seventies. A black clock with red hands ticked away the seconds. There wasn't a single scuff mark on the walls. The window ledges had been newly painted as well.

'Have you lived here a long time?' The straw seat of the chair dug into the back of my legs. At one point my mother had had a fridge just like the one that hummed in the corner. She'd replaced hers.

'My wife has lived here since she was a little girl,' Job said. 'We can't really leave. She gets confused.' The kettle came to the boil with a loud whistle that sounded like a high-pitched scream.

'It's because you've never moved.' Tony stirred sugar into his tea with a spoon with a little Delft-blue clog attached to the end. The spoon looked dainty in his enormous hand. His neck was triangular above the collar of his polo shirt. 'Maybe you should think about it.'

Job raised his eyebrows. 'That's a change of heart. You said we should stay. I wanted to put it on the market before I went to the hospital. The stairs are murder on my hips.'

'Love your garden,' I said. 'It's huge.' A property developer could have built three houses on that piece of land. I turned on my seat to face it. 'You must have spent a lot of time getting it like that.' The pink tulips dominated one corner. The flowers that had spilled their pollen on both sets of bones.

'Something's happened to it.' Job stood up. 'What have you done to my tulips?' He stared at Tony.

'I haven't done anything,' Tony said. He looked down at the spoon. His face was that of an obstinate teenager. His biceps bulged from the short sleeves, more tensed than holding the spoon demanded.

'They weren't like that. They weren't in rows.'

'Dad, shut up.' Tony looked at me.

'Does she know what's out there?' I made the words deliberately confrontational. 'Your mother? Is that why she's crazy? Because she's got a dead body buried in her garden?'

The impact of Tony's fist against my mouth knocked me off my chair. My head smacked on the linoleum floor and the thump reverberated inside my skull. The sound came before the pain. As the metallic taste of blood hit my tongue, I thought that at least Mark was innocent.

Chapter Thirty-seven

'Hi, Francine.' Her father looked at the wall calendar that kept track of which visitor was coming in. It helped him remember who had been to see him. 'I didn't know you were coming.'

On the table, she saw Thursday's paper open to the interview with her. She pointed at it. 'What did you think? Just tell me the truth, Daddy. Please just tell me the truth.' She had to fight to keep her voice under control.

Her father, a shrunken figure in his chair, nodded. 'Yes, maybe it's time.' He got up and took his bible from the bookshelf. He removed the cover and got a photo out. He pushed it across the table. She recognized the uniform. Of course she recognized it. Even though the photo was black and white, there was no mistaking it. The black uniform, the flame on the sleeve, wasn't this the uniform that the evil people wore? The traitors? Even worse than the Germans, this was the uniform of those who betrayed their own country. Those who were on the enemy's side. Those who took advantage of the situation and sided with the rulers:

Dutch Nazis. She gripped the top edge of the photo, ready to tear it in half.

She stopped. The man in the photo was the spitting image of her father. The eyes were the same, the nose was the same. It could have been a younger version of her father wearing that uniform. 'Is this . . .' She couldn't get the words out.

'Your grandfather, yes.' Her father looked away.

'All those years you told me he'd been a hero.' She found it hard to talk through the tears that tightened her throat. 'You told me and Sam. How he'd been a hero and we should be like him. Well I guess Sam is.' The press were going to have fun with this one. They were already calling the hooligans 'neo-Nazis' in the papers.

Her father stared at the photo. He didn't touch it. 'I have dreams,' he said. 'About my father. There's a group of people, my neighbours, my colleagues. I have a shovel in my hand. There's a hole. I've probably just dug it, and at the bottom is my father, dead, in his uniform. The other people look at me. They finally understand what I am. They don't say a word, they just push me in beside my father, look at me with hate in their eyes and spit on me, big gobs of phlegm, as they fill in the hole.' He smiled, an insincere smile, the corners of his mouth lifting but his eyes staying sad. 'So ever since you told me they'd found his body, I've been waiting for this moment. Waiting for someone to say that they now know what I am. And to fill in the hole.'

'What about Grandmother, was any of that true?'

'Any of what? That she died in a concentration camp? Yes, that's true.'

'What happened? Why did the Germans—'

'The Germans? The Germans didn't do anything to her. Were you hoping that at least my mother stood up against them?'

'No, I meant—'

'She was a member of the Nazi party until her death. But they lost, of course. That's when the neighbours came.'

'The neighbours?'

'Yes, they came, dragged my mother away and killed my father. The evening before Liberation Day, when it was obvious how the war was going to end. I thought they would kill me too, so I ran.' He frowned. 'Later I found out that after my mother was driven away in a truck, they moved into our house.'

'Daddy, I'm—'

'They put her in Westerbork. When all the Germans had gone and the Jews had been freed, they reused the concentration camp. Did you know that? They put all the NSB-ers and their wives and their children, if they were old enough, into those same camps. Scores died. My mother was one of them.'

'And you?'

'I was lucky, I guess. I told you the truth from there on in. I walked north to my aunt and uncle. I was lucky that I was so young. They took me in and nobody ever knew.'

'You didn't tell?'

Her father laughed. 'If you'd seen how the children were treated. The teachers were beating them up, the other NSB children. They would line them up outside the school and give them each a kicking. The teachers! Until the children were bruised all over. There were two children in my class, their parents weren't even full NSB members, but everybody knew they had been "wrong". They were beaten up every day, by staff and other children alike. What did you think I was going to do? Give them another punchbag? Or invent a war hero? I was seven years old. What would you have done?'

'But later—'

'I should have told you? Even your mother didn't know.' He hung his head. 'I'd told the same story so often, it didn't even feel like a lie any more. It felt as if my father really had been a hero. Only at night, only in the dreams, do I remember what he really was.'

'I'm sorry.'

'I should have stopped you. When you did the interviews. But I almost didn't remember and I didn't think anybody else would. It's so long ago.'

'You didn't do anything wrong. It was your father—'

'He was so proud of his uniform. I still remember that he came into my bedroom in his black uniform and his cap. He was never allowed to be a member of anything else before.'

'Proud. That's so hard to believe,' Francine said.

Her father ignored her. 'What are you going to do?' he asked instead.

'We should bury it. Christiaan can help, that's his job.'

'Bury. That's an interesting word.' He lifted his teacup to his mouth. His hands were shaking. The brown liquid slopped against the sides. It almost spilled over the edge, but was just about contained.

'What should we do?'

'I had hoped I would . . . that I would be . . .' He put the cup down. He took his glasses off and wiped a hand over his eyes. 'At least your mother's dead. It's the first time I've been happy about that. Happy that she's no longer with me.' He got up, using both hands to lift his body out of his comfortable chair. He looked out of the window. 'I know what will happen here. When they find out.' His voice was faint, and Francine had to strain to hear him.

'Nobody needs to know.' If only she could see his face, but she was talking to his back. He seemed to slump forward at her words, his back bent. He moved further forward until he was resting his forehead on the window. She got up. Put her hand on his back. Slid it further forward, around his waist, and gave him a hug.

'But *I* know,' her father said.

'Dad, we can keep this quiet.'

'I know where they buried him.'

'You do?' Francine pulled back and turned her father round. 'Oh Dad.' However much she wanted to protect her good name, she couldn't keep that quiet. Even though her grandfather hadn't been in the resistance, she still felt this overriding need to do what was right. She hated that about herself at that moment. Knowing full well that this was the last time anybody would think of her grandfather as a hero, she called Thomas.

'Hey, Francine, I'm in the middle of something.'

'This won't take long. Listen, my father just told me that he knows where my grandfather was buried. Where Dollander probably still is.'

'Give it to me.'

'Bloemenstraat 82. I'll meet you there. I'll get you the search warrant too. We're going to have to dig.'

Chapter Thirty-eight

A kick connected with my stomach and pushed its contents into my mouth. I doubled over. I was on my wrong side. I needed to turn. The old man screamed at his son. Tony kicked my shin.

The doorbell rang.

Tony's assault paused and it gave me the chance to roll on to my left-hand side. I undid the holster on my right hip and got my gun out. I pointed it at Tony's face. 'Have another go at kicking me now,' I said softly. 'Go ahead.' I swallowed thick goo.

He breathed hard and carefully kept both his steel-capped boots on the floor.

I rolled on to my knees. Something trickled from the side of my mouth. I wiped it with my shoulder without taking my eyes from his, the barrel of the gun firmly aimed at a spot just north of his nose. I touched the side of my face gingerly. Everything to the left of my mouth was tender and swollen. I had trouble focusing and it felt as if someone were pushing a skewer through my eye. My gun never wavered from Tony's face.

The doorbell rang again. 'Police, open the door!'

With relief I recognized Thomas's voice. My gun still pointed at Tony's head, I told him to open.

Thomas had his gun drawn so I could lower mine. Behind him I could see he'd come with the backup that I should have brought.

'Fuck, Lotte, why were you here? What the hell happened?' he said.

It had been worth it. 'Just cuff him. Get him out of here.' I dangled the gun by my side. I hugged my stomach with my other arm and moved carefully. I shook out my leg, but it was fine. There would be some bruises, but that was all.

Ingrid secured Tony's hands behind his back and led him to the car. She read him his rights.

I joined Thomas outside the house, to get some air. He held my chin and tipped my face into the thin sunlight. He took out a tissue and wiped the blood from my mouth. It made me want to cry.

'Assaulting a police officer, along with moving human remains.' I licked my lips and tasted the metallic tang of blood. I brought the back of my hand carefully to my mouth and it came away stained red.

'I had nothing to do with that Nazi,' Tony said just as Ingrid put a hand on the back of his head to guide him into the car.

I signalled to Ingrid to hold on. 'What Nazi?'

'We found a box. It's on the table in the kitchen.' He looked at me. 'I'm sorry.'

'For what?'

'You said something about my mother. I—' He stopped himself. 'No,' he said, 'there was no excuse for doing what I did.' The words sounded like a mantra, as if he'd been going to an anger-management course. Maybe there were other victims of those red knuckles.

'You're in a whole world of trouble.'

'All because of my brother moving a dead Nazi.' He sounded bitter.

'What about Tessa?'

He frowned. 'Who's that?'

'Frank Stapel's widow.'

Tony shook his head. 'Never met her.'

'Young, long hair, gap between her front teeth? She's missing.'

'No, sorry, no idea.'

'Okay, put him in the car.'

Ingrid nodded, locked Tony in the back of the car and started making calls.

As I went back into the house, I heard a sound. It came from upstairs and went from a moan to something louder, a scream, a grown-up version of a toddler having a tantrum: attention-seeking, but the fear behind it sounded real. The screaming stopped. It became a whisper. A woman came down the stairs, swaying side to side like a flower buffeted by the wind. It was the woman from the nursing home. Now she wasn't wearing a miniskirt and high heels but thick trousers and slippers. She shuffled towards me until she stood next to me in the hallway by the open door.

'Have you come for Barbara?' she said. Her voice was clear, like a young woman's.

'Good afternoon, Mrs van Wiel, my name is Lotte Meerman.' I started a reassuring smile, but stopped when the movement caused a shooting pain through my lower lip. 'I'm a police detective.'

'What are you doing with my husband?' she said. 'Where are you taking Job?'

'That's Tony.'

She shook her head, pursed her lips. Her long straight hair flew around her face. 'Barbara's come back, you know.'

'She has? Can I talk to her?'

'She can't come to your daughter's party.'

'Mrs van Wiel,' I said.

'She's got to study. She can't come outside.' Her voice grew louder. 'She can't leave her room.' She shouted the words. Her husband moved to her side and held her, her eyes tearing over.

'Conny's confused,' he said. 'It was difficult when I was in the nursing home.'

'Who are you?' the woman said, removing his hand from around her shoulder.

'Conny, I'm your husband.'

'You're not my husband. My husband is right there. Why is he handcuffed? You're not my husband. You're an old man.'

'That's your son. That's Tony.'

'My son's at kindergarten. Who are you?' Her voice was shrill and made my head thump. She brought her hands to her mouth, her eyes wide as she stared at her husband. 'Who are you?' She looked at me. 'Who are *you*?'

She blinked a few times, rapidly, and it seemed to clear the clouds from her eyes. 'She's come back. Barbara. I never thought she would.'

'Conny, darling,' Job said with his eyes closed, 'Barbara isn't back. I spoke to her last week. She's in the States.'

'She's back. I saw her.'

'I'm sorry, Conny, she isn't.'

My heartbeat sped up. If she thought Tony was her husband, then maybe the girl wasn't Barbara but another woman. 'Mrs van Wiel, where did you see Barbara?'

'In my room. She was staying with me.'

I rushed up the stairs and pulled open the door to a bedroom. A green bedspread on a double bed, copper lights with white lightshades on either side. A large wardrobe filled with suits and dresses emitted the smell of mothballs. The bedroom was empty. So was the second. So was the bathroom. A wooden staircase led to the attic. I held my gun out in one hand. I was very aware that I hadn't seen Kars in the house.

'Lotte, are you okay up there?' Thomas shouted.

I kept quiet, counted to three in my head and pushed the hatch open.

Chapter Thirty-nine

My gun entered the attic before I did. It was empty. An even layer of dust showed that nobody had been up here in months. I closed the hatch behind me and went down the stairs. I checked every room. Tessa wasn't in the house.

Conny van Wiel's words, that her daughter had returned, hooked themselves into my brain. Yes, she was crazy, so maybe she'd just been rambling, but why could I not shake the thought that she'd been talking about Tessa? At the moment, what else did I have to go on?

After the fruitless search, I joined Thomas in the sitting room. The clock on the wall ticked slowly. The sofa was covered in brown corduroy. It was easy to tell which seats had been used most. Two shiny circles were worn out of the fabric on the two closest to the arm rests. Only the middle cushion was still ribbed. If this had been my mother's sofa, she would have rotated the cushions so that they wore out evenly.

'Mrs van Wiel,' I forced myself to stay calm and my voice to be even, 'where were you last week? Did you go on a little holiday? Stay with one of your sons?'

She frowned. 'I didn't go anywhere.'

I rested against the windowsill, where there was space between two azaleas and a peace lily.

'How long has your wife been like this?' Thomas asked.

'A long time. It's slowly getting worse. She gets upset when I correct her. I normally just go along with her, but when she gets me and Kars, or me and Tony, muddled up, I don't know, too Oedipal to let pass, I guess.'

'Frank Stapel,' I said. 'He gave everything a new coat of paint here, didn't he?'

'He hated the colours.' The old man bent over to pet a sleek Siamese cat who'd come into the room. 'He did a nice job but wanted to paint it yellow or white or magnolia. Anything but this. Light brown wasn't to his taste.' He picked the animal up and put it on his lap. 'Or so Kars told me anyway. He did it while I was in the nursing home.' He scratched the cat behind its ears. It started to purr loudly, stretched out its claws and hooked them through his trousers, into the knees. Job van Wiel grimaced, undid the claws from his legs. He stroked the cat. It started milking the flesh on his legs again.

I looked at my watch. How long would it take for Forensics to turn up? I hated the waiting but I also knew I shouldn't start digging in the garden until they were here. 'It must have been tough for Kars, looking after his mother.'

'I don't know how he did it, I really don't.' The cat turned on its side, stretched out along the length of the old man's thighs. 'He did an amazing job. His wife probably helped, but still.'

'Your wife always lived at home?'

'No, she was in an institution for a while. Early on. We missed her, the boys and me.'

'Was Kars here, in your house, when you were in the nursing home?'

Job didn't answer, because a fleet of cars had turned up outside and screeched to a halt. The digging could begin.

'Job,' I said more urgently. 'Your wife, where was she?'

Edgar Ling came in with a team carrying equipment, shovels. The old woman keened in a high-pitched tone at the army marching through her house. Job didn't answer my question.

I followed Edgar to the garden and Job stood beside me. He had a piece of paper and a pen. He was drawing something. I asked him what he was doing and he said that he wanted to be able to put the garden back exactly the way it was. For his wife.

Edgar Ling's first step was to cut some of the tulips' stamens, taking samples of the pollen as evidence to match with the bones. I shouted at him that he was being unnecessarily careful, that all he had to do was dig. The sooner we had this second skeleton out of the ground, the sooner I could start looking for Tessa again. And the sooner it would be obvious that Mark was innocent. Edgar straightened his back and walked over to Thomas with some of the tulip pollen in a plastic bag.

'You might want to get the old man out of here,' he said. 'For when we start to dig.'

The clouds were gathering in the sky; the dry weather

wouldn't last. The sun's rays peeked around the edge of the clouds and hit the ground exactly on the tulip patch, a spotlight to show where they should be digging.

'I want to stay,' Job said.

Thomas shook his head.

'Mr van Wiel, where was your wife while you had your hip operation?' I said.

Job didn't respond, but stood there with his eyes glued to the patch of tulips.

'Come inside,' I said. 'Could you give me Tony's address? Or Kars's? Or was your wife somewhere else?'

'I'm staying here,' Job said.

I wanted to grab him by the shoulders and give him a shake. Edgar looked at me with his bulging eyes. 'If we find nothing, we're destroying his garden. If we find something . . .'

Frustrated, I threw up my hands. I'd tried. Job was not going to leave until the garden had given up his secrets. All I could do now was wait and observe his reaction. I'd seen Tony's flash of anger; I'd more than seen it, I'd actually felt it. Job had a dangerous criminal buried in his garden. Had he known about that?

Edgar took out a device shaped like a flat, square metal detector. He floated it over the ground. The garden looked freshly weeded. The plants were neat: tulips grew in unnaturally shaped squares, busy Lizzies and sweet Williams edged a smartly mowed lawn.

I walked over to the tulip patch. The squares were regimental, with equal distance between plants in each direction.

Edgar signalled that there was something there, in the back corner behind the tidy row of bedding plants, underneath the tulips. He took a shovel. I couldn't take my eyes from the blades as they carefully dug their way to the skeleton. The old man started to sway but continued drawing the location of each tulip. The result was strangely like my drawing of the raindrops on the CI's window. Thomas grabbed the sleeve of Job's coat. I wanted to look away, to avoid seeing another set of bones being dug out of the earth, but somehow the shovels were like magnets to my eyes. I followed the plants as they were removed and the tulips taken away and put on a pile. Kars must have done the same thing; he'd dug up a natural-looking patch of tulips. When he put them back, he had used a tape measure in each direction and planted them equidistant. And Frank Stapel watched Kars dig up the skeleton as he decorated this house.

'Stop!' Edgar shouted. 'Careful.'

I moved forward. Pushed someone out of the way. The sooner I did this, the sooner I would prove Mark's innocence.

'Lotte, get away from here.'

I ignored him and moved closer. Behind me I heard a soft keening that turned into a loud moan. A clatter as the notepad hit the ground. I looked round. Thomas's hand on the old man's arm had been enough to break his fall. He hadn't fainted, but his hip seemed to have given way, tipping him sideways and on to his knees.

Someone passed me a pair of nitrile gloves and I slid them on. I took a large stone out of the soil with my fingers and put it behind me. I found more stones. There was a layer of them. I wiggled my fingers underneath the biggest one. A sudden sharp pain hit as my nail gave way under the pressure, but I dug my fingers in deeper until I felt the stone loosen. I lifted it and saw a flash of ivory underneath. I paused. Edgar crouched beside me. He lifted a skull with a clear bullet hole right between the eyes. I straightened and looked at Job's face. It was so pale it was almost blue. He grabbed his chest. I got my mobile out and called an ambulance.

Chapter Forty

I supported Job van Wiel and helped him back inside the house. He sat heavily on the corduroy sofa.

'Lotte, now that it's confirmed that the rest of the skeleton is still here, we're going back to the police station. Coming?' Thomas called out to me from the open front door. 'We'll interview Tony. He'll talk now.'

'I'm going to wait here with Job. Make sure he gets in the ambulance safely. Our priority now is finding Tessa,' I said. 'If Tony says anything about her, call me straight away.'

He nodded. 'We'll find her.'

After they'd left, I sat down on the sofa next to Job. His face was as pale as Tessa's had been when we first told her that her husband had died. Outside, the Forensics team were digging up the rest of his garden. Conny stood by the window overlooking the activity, humming contentedly to herself, as if they were a group of landscape gardeners that she had employed to create this destruction.

'Where did your wife stay?' I asked for what felt like the tenth time. 'She wasn't here, was she? Your son Kars, why couldn't he pick you up earlier on? Where is he?'

Job's eyes opened. 'I didn't know,' he said.

'I understand, Mr van Wiel. You were in the nursing home. There's no way you could have known what Kars—'

'The Nazi I knew about. Not that second body.'

'The Nazi? What Nazi?'

He closed his eyes.

'What Nazi?' I repeated. I'd forgotten about the box that Tony had mentioned. I went to the kitchen. It was there as he had said. I put on a pair of gloves and opened it with trepidation. The lid was rusted and the hinge at the top bent where someone had forced it open. Soil was stuck in the hinges, as if it had been buried with the body. Edgar Ling would be able to confirm that later. There were a number of photos in the box. Photos of a couple, the man in an NSB uniform with a woman on his arm. Photos of multiple NSB-ers together. Who were these people? Were they people that Francine's grandfather had killed? Was that why he had been shot? Then I looked more closely at the face of the woman in the photo. She had wild dark hair. I saw the family resemblance.

'That's how you knew,' I said to Job. 'That's why you asked me when I was going to check that story.'

Francine drove with her father to the small house where her grandfather's body had been buried. She parked behind the police cars. Her father got out and stood outside the house: an old man with tears streaming down his face. 'I remember it so well.' His voice was steady through the tears, as if his vocal cords and his eyes weren't driven by the same brain and emotions. 'I was there,' he said. He rested his hands on the gate next to the climbing roses. 'I was here when my father died. I dug the grave.'

'Oh Daddy.' She put a hand on his shoulder. 'I'm so sorry.' She worried about her father most on these clear days. She'd read somewhere that most people with dementia got stuck mentally in their twenties and thirties, in the days when they had been most active. She'd hoped her father would just think he was going to work, with her mother still alive and she and her brother young. Happy days before Sam went off the rails but long after the war had finished. She remembered her own childhood as a happy time. She couldn't imagine what it must be like for her father, to have memories of his father being shot, of digging his grave, of his mother being dragged off and put into a concentration camp, of the long walk north to escape, of changing his name and identity to hide from the political choices that his parents had made. Of knowing that his parents had been on the wrong side. The evil side. All at seven years old. How could he have left his father buried here all these years? But then she remembered his reaction when she'd told him there'd been no clothes. He'd thought his father had still been wearing his uniform. He could never have unearthed his father, because that would have shown the world the lie he'd told to his wife and children and all his friends.

'You dug the grave but never saw what happened after?'

'There was someone else too,' he said. 'Conny, she was called, I remember. We used to play together. Just a little girl, my age, six, seven years old. Her father was the one who shoved the gun under my father's chin. I didn't think he was going to do it, but he pulled the trigger. He made her watch. He said that she should learn what they did to traitors. Then he looked at me and I was sure I was going to be next. But I got away. Only later did I find out that he was the one who took our house.'

I showed Job the photo. 'You knew this man was buried in your back garden?'

'Conny told me. When we got married.'

'You didn't want to tell anybody about that?'

He shrugged. 'Her father killed a Nazi. So what.'

'To give him a proper burial?'

'Why? How many people had this man killed during the war?'

'At least to get the skeleton out of your garden?'

'My wife was worried that . . .' He shook his head. 'It was stupid. But that we would have to give the house back. To the family.'

'The family of the Nazi?'

'We thought it was better to keep quiet. That's why we thought we'd always have to stay here.' He rubbed a hand over his bald head. 'But the stairs, I couldn't go up them any more.'

'So you asked your son.'

'He works on a building site. An old skeleton. What difference does it make? Conny told stories . . . more stories recently. About how her father shot a man and then had her help him strip the body. He burnt the clothes but buried some photos.'

'How did she know? Did she see it?'

'Yes, he made the children watch . . . That wasn't right.'

'Children? Does Conny have brothers or sisters?'

'No, she's an only child. It was the man's child. A boy, she said. What she says about the past is clearer somehow. More true than the present.' Some colour had returned to Job's face. The ambulance seemed less necessary, but I wasn't going to cancel it.

'Unlike what she said about Barbara being back.'

'Yes, she's not.'

'There's a young woman missing. I think that's who she might have seen.'

Job frowned. 'What young woman?'

'Tessa Stapel. Frank's widow. Is there anywhere that your wife could have met her in the last couple of days?'

'She stayed at Kars's house.' Now that all other questions had been answered, he finally responded to this one.

'Give me the address.'

He wrote it down on a piece of paper. I didn't wait for the ambulance to turn up but left immediately. Outside, I saw Francine and her father, but I didn't stop to talk to them. I called Dispatch, gave Kars's address and asked for urgent backup there.

Chapter Forty-one

I had both my hands folded, almost like in prayer, and the index finger of my right caressed the trigger of my gun. I only took my left hand away to ring the doorbell, then it went back to supporting the wrist of the right. The ring was a five-note chime that intercut the fast beat of my heart pounding in my chest. I stepped sideways so that I was protected by the pristine door frame. There was no answer. The house was as big and broad as Kars himself, with that same facade of respectability: two storeys high, a slanted roof, freshly painted window frames surrounding spotless glass. A property developer's business card. There was no way of telling what was inside.

A woman on a bicycle saw the gun in my hand. I waved my badge at her and put my finger to my lips. The last thing I needed was for her to call the police and a fleet of my colleagues to turn up with sirens blaring. When my backup got here, they would at least not try to shoot me.

I peered through the window. Through a gap in the net curtain I could see a tall standard clock ticking away Tessa's time, and a plasma screen on the wall where sixty years ago there would have been an oil painting. I didn't see Kars. I scanned the house from top to bottom for an open window, but found none. I skirted around to the back. Behind me, the ducks in the narrow canal that edged the garden quacked their concern.

The back door was closed too. The house kept its secrets closely hidden. All the windows were shut. I looked around in the garden. The circular lawn had a bird bath in the middle. A small blue shed with white trim that reminded me of a beach hut seemed the right candidate to yield up what I was looking for. I opened the door and found pots of old paint, a Black & Decker Workmate, a full set of tools hanging neatly on the wall, some lengths of wood and, finally, a small pile of bricks. I picked one up.

Most of the windows were double-glazed. The kitchen door had a single pane of glass. I wanted to smash my brick through it and destroy the glass with a loud shattering. As a last precaution before doing that, I tried the door handle. It opened. I felt stupid about the brick now and dropped it on the ground. I went into the kitchen. The marble countertop and fitted cabinets seemed to have stepped right out of the pages of an interior design magazine. Apart from a mug and a teapot on the work surface, there were no signs that anybody ever cooked in here. I waited with my gun drawn to see if anybody would come running. Nobody. I touched the teapot. It was cold. Had Kars popped out? Left the back door open by mistake? The house was filled with silence. Still, I wasn't taking any chances: gun in both hands, I swung into the lounge. It was empty. The open-plan layout of the house allowed me to check most of the downstairs area in two swings. The large clock didn't make a sound and showed a time that was two hours and twenty minutes wrong. There was a cupboard under the stairs, but when I pulled it open, it didn't reveal a person. The downstairs bathroom was all mirrors and stainless steel, but no sign of Tessa.

The barrel of my gun was cold against my cheek. I took the stairs without making a sound. The doorbell would have drawn everybody's attention to my presence already, but I didn't need to make it any easier for them. At the top, I had to take a couple of breaths to steady my nerves. I swung into the hallway, gun drawn. It was empty. I sneaked over the rug that covered the wooden floor, to dampen the sound of my footsteps. I stayed behind the frame as I opened the first door on the left, then swung in. Empty as well. Two teddy bears on the windowsill, a pink bedspread and a poster of One Direction on the wall. First door on the right. Also empty. Four glass tanks with lizards. The scaly creatures blinked slowly at me. The next door on the right was locked. A flimsy padlock kept it closed. I was about to move on when I heard a sound from behind the door. Not a voice as such, but a groan. I rammed the door with my shoulder but it refused to budge. Then I took a step back and kicked right next to the handle with all my force, frustration and weight backing my foot from my hip. The wood cracked and tore with the sound of a branch breaking off a tree in an October storm. The door swung open, the padlock dangling and the hook it had been tied to torn out of the frame.

Tessa was barely conscious. I was at her side immediately,

crouched between two single beds. She was still breathing. Under my hand I felt a faint heartbeat in her chest. I tapped her face but there was no response. I could see an empty pot with a white prescription label on the front. I put my gun on the floor and tried to get her upright.

'Tessa? Tessa!' Was I too late again, as I'd been for Mark's sister? I could have guessed sooner that she was here. Why had I stayed at Kars's parents' house? Fuck, fuck. I grabbed my mobile from my pocket and dialled Dispatch again. Kneeling next to Tessa, I moved her hair out of her face. Her eyelashes flickered but she didn't have enough strength to open her eyes. She whispered something. I brought my face close to hers and felt her faint breath touch my chin.

The same operator answered and I told him I needed an ambulance too. 'It's an emergency.'

'Most units are attending a large accident on the ring road but I'll get you one,' he said. 'And I've got someone on their way to you.'

I disconnected the call and stuck my phone in my pocket. For a second, I closed my eyes. This time I hadn't been too late and Tessa would be fine as long as we got her to a hospital in time.

Then I felt a solid weight pressing against the back of my head.

'Don't do anything stupid,' Kars said.

I couldn't get to my gun. I'd put it down when I tried to get Tessa upright and it was now a metre or so away. It seemed like a ravine separated me from it. Whatever Kars was holding against my skull, it felt as if it was metal. Knowing his background, I was pretty sure it was for real.

'Did you do this?' I gestured at Tessa.

'What does it matter?' Kars's hands were steady. The pressure against my head didn't waver.

'It matters to me.'

'She did it. I only gave her the necessary means and opportunity, if you know what I mean.'

The sensible thing was to do nothing, I knew that. I was out of options. I had to wait until my backup turned up. Or the ambulance. That would be my window to act. 'We got the skeleton. Dollander. We found it.'

'I knew that would happen, ever since your colleague came to ask questions about him. I always knew this day would come. I'm prepared.'

'You won't get far.'

'No? Easy with all these open borders.'

I'd called it in as an emergency, so the ambulance would arrive with sirens blaring. It would give Kars time. Time to pull the trigger and make his escape. I was aware of everything around me as if my brain wanted me to savour this room. Tessa was pale and her breathing seemed even shallower. The duvet covers on the two single beds on either side of her matched the curtains. Tea-rose pink. The kind of decor you would choose for an old woman. The padlock on the door. He didn't have this installed for Tessa. It dawned on me who had stayed here before her. 'You had your mother in here?' I said. 'Locked up like this?'

'She was safe here.'

'Did your father know?' It was impossible to keep the anger out of my voice, even though I didn't want to antagonize him. I remembered his father saying that he didn't know how Kars had done it, looking after his mother so well. Here was the answer.

He laughed. 'It was fine for him, being pampered by everybody in that nursing home. All the old women doting on him. I had to deal with my mother. She's not easy.'

'He's dealt with her all his life.'

'He should have put her in a home years ago.' His voice sounded rough. I remembered how she held his hand when I saw them together in the nursing home. She'd adored him. 'He should have put her away when we were still kids. You think it's the dementia, but she's always been crazy. It's what made my sister leave. Turn round. Slowly.'

I felt the barrel of the gun scrape my scalp as I did as he said.

'Just making sure you know what's against your head.'

His face was pale. His eyes were on mine. I had my hands out by my sides. He should have kept me facing the other way if he was planning to shoot me. 'You locked Tessa in here too. That's why your mother thought her daughter had come back.'

Kars smiled. 'Mum liked her. Called her Barbara. The girl was scared enough to play along with it.'

The casual tone made me even more angry, but the minute I moved, he'd put a bullet in my brain. If I didn't move, he'd kill me anyway. My heart refused to accept what my brain was telling me: that I was out of options.

Then I heard something downstairs. Was it my backup? I forced myself to keep looking at Kars and not turn my head towards the sound. Every muscle in my body tensed.

'I've got it all figured out,' Kars said. 'I've got a house.'

He was stalling. It was difficult to kill someone in cold blood. Pulling the trigger wasn't that easy. Had he not heard the sound? Was his hearing damaged from all those years in the noisy building trade? Or was I imagining it? The door behind Kars opened slowly.

I'd never been happier to see Ingrid's spiked-up hair.

'Police, put the gun down,' she said.

Relief coursed through my veins with the thought that we were done. My shoulders dropped. Kars lowered his gun and moved round to face Ingrid. Even though it was probably unnecessary, as soon as the gun moved away from my head, I dropped down. Crouched low.

'Drop it. Drop the gun,' Ingrid shouted.

I fitted my fingers around my own weapon. The heft of it had never been more delicious.

Kars had his gun pointed at Ingrid's feet. 'It's funny,' his voice was soft, 'this is what I had been trying to avoid. I turned my back on this, but it came looking for me again.'

'Kars, this is over,' I said.

'All because I wanted to keep my life the way it was. Away from the violence.'

'Put the gun down, Kars.'

'My wife, my kids, they never knew. Never knew about my past. And then Dollander came back with his demands. I paid him for a while. But he didn't stop. They never stop.'

'So you killed him.'

'For two years after he'd been released from prison, he came to my door every month like a rent collector. Demanding money. Then I shut him up permanently. That was six years ago. Six years.'

'Is that why you didn't meet with Frank and Eelke?'

Kars laughed. 'I thought they had the bones of a Nazi. Why would I want those back?'

I looked along the barrel at the head on the thick neck, which was bent forward. 'You knew about that?'

'Yes, though I never knew for sure that it wasn't just one of those stories. My parents never dug that patch over, not even when they were really into gardening. They had those tulips growing there but didn't even lift the bulbs. I found the other skeleton. Buried Dollander beside it.' He grinned, but he was still looking down at the floor. 'It was fine for years. Then my father had to have his hip replaced. If only he could have stayed in that house. I thought they would live there for ever, but no, he was talking about moving into a bungalow. So I had to remove the bodies. I started with the Nazi. The one that didn't matter.' The gun was still pointing at Ingrid's feet. 'Only that little red-headed bastard saw me. Still, I thought it was under control, as it was only the Nazi's skeleton, but then you,' he nodded towards Ingrid, 'turned up to ask about Dollander.' He grinned ruefully. 'That's when I realized I had messed up. Even more so when Tessa turned up on my doorstep, screaming that I had killed Frank. I hadn't.'

I moved to the side of Kars. 'Put the gun down. There's

an ambulance coming for her.' The sound of the siren was audible in the distance.

He seemed to nod. 'I had to keep her here to make sure Eelke wouldn't tell on me. It was a stupid idea.' He grinned. 'But it worked for a bit, didn't it? You arrested Mark Visser.'

I thought that was it. But then his gun arm moved up. 'Sorry,' he said to Ingrid. He took the safety off. She had to take the shot. He raised the gun until it was pointed at her head. She stood there, frozen. For a millisecond I wasn't sure what he was trying to achieve, then I saw his finger twitch on the trigger and I reacted before my brain was even in gear. The bang reverberated through the silent house.

Kars fell to the floor.

Some of his blood had splattered on Ingrid. She lowered the gun, still clutching it in both hands. 'I couldn't do it,' she whispered. 'I knew I had to and I just couldn't.'

The previous times I'd pulled the trigger, a certain adrenaline rush had coursed through my veins. Now I was just filled with an enormous sadness.

'I'm so sorry,' Ingrid said. 'I heard the call from Dispatch, that you needed backup. I wanted to be the one to help you.'

'If you hadn't come, he would have killed me,' I said.

The ambulance pulled up outside. I put my gun on the dressing table. I had never taken a life before.

'Lotte, wait,' Ingrid said, 'you could never have saved Agnes Visser. I checked in the file: he killed her the day he abducted her.'

She offered it to me as a consolation prize. There was too much going on in my head to take it in properly.

Chapter Forty-two

I would have liked to go with Tessa in the ambulance, but I knew I should stay at Kars's house until the rest of the police turned up. I was taken to the police station and answered seemingly endless questions as through a cloud of fog. What had happened still didn't feel real.

It was two hours later that I finally made it to the hospital. It was the same one from where I'd picked up my mother only a few days ago. I normally hated the smell of disinfectant, but right now it seemed in tune with the way I was feeling. I tried to tell myself that this was the outcome I'd wanted. That this hospital visit was proof that I hadn't been too late this time. It was just that the price I'd paid for it was too high. The price that Kars van Wiel had paid.

Tessa seemed small in the hospital bed. She was pale and curled the edge of the blanket with nervous fingers. 'This was all my fault, wasn't it?'

'No.' I sat down by her side and took her hand. 'Not at all.' If anything, it was mine. 'How are you?'

'They pumped my stomach.' She grimaced. 'Everything hurts. And it's a surprise to still be here, you know? How's the old lady? Where did that man take her? Your colleague was here earlier but he didn't tell me much.'

'She's fine. You know she was Kars van Wiel's mother, don't you?'

'She was so confused all the time. I didn't know who she was. She called me Barbara.'

It was because Conny had continued to think that Tessa was Barbara that I had found her in time. It was odd to feel grateful for an old woman's mental problems.

'How can he have locked his mother up like that?' Tessa continued. 'She was crazily grateful whenever he came round. Told me not to shout at him.'

'Why did you go there anyway?'

'You told me about the leather jacket, and there was only one person who had a key. I knew Eelke had put the jacket in the flat. He was the only one who could have. So I went to see him, to ask him what had happened.' She coughed with a dry hacking sound. I poured her a glass of water and she drank greedily. She gave the glass back to me and wiped her mouth with the back of her hand. 'I didn't want to believe it, that Eelke could have killed Frank. I thought there was an explanation and I was relieved when Eelke said that it was Kars's fault. That Kars had killed him. But that wasn't true, was it?'

'In a way it was.' It wasn't even a complete lie. It would make things easier for Tessa to think that. It was so hard accepting that you had been totally deceived by someone. Plus if there hadn't been problems on that building site, if they had installed the glass panels correctly on the roof terrace, Frank wouldn't have died.

'I wanted to believe Eelke so much,' Tessa said, almost more to herself than to me. 'I wanted that to be the truth, so I went to Kars's house. Just to have a chat.'

'A chat?'

A nurse looked around the corner of the open door to check on Tessa. She seemed content to let us talk because she walked away.

'Maybe not a chat,' Tessa said. 'I was very angry. I shouted at Kars, said I would call the police, call you, and tell you what he'd done. Then I heard this noise from upstairs. Screaming.' She closed her eyes.

I thought she'd fallen asleep, but she continued talking.

'I got my phone out and I called you.' She didn't open her eyes. 'Kars grabbed my phone and locked me up with his mother. He was giving her Valium, to make her sleep most of the time. The pot of pills was there and I didn't know what was going to happen, I just knew it wasn't going to end well. I thought he would keep me locked up there for the rest of my life. When he took his mother away, I got really worried and I decided that it was much better to end it there rather than go through years of abuse.'

'Did he touch you?'

'No. No, he never did. But I thought I only had one opportunity to do it. I took the pills. It felt like the best thing I'd ever done. The best thing I'd done since Frank had died.'

I smoothed some hair away from her face. 'It's all fine now.'

'No.' Tessa looked at me. 'No it isn't, is it?'

'You're right.' Didn't I understand only too well how she felt? 'It will get better. I promise you that. It will take time, but it will get better. Kars is dead.'

'Good. That's good.'

Mental exhaustion made my body feel as if it weighed ten kilos more than usual. Tiredness intermingled with emptiness as I opened the front door to my apartment. I hadn't heard from Mark, even though I'd sent him three text messages after I'd been debriefed.

I'd discharged my weapon.

That official police euphemism used to annoy me, but now I understood. I found it hard to admit to myself that I'd killed someone. I dragged my tired body up the first flight of stairs. Was I any better than Eelke? He had punched his brother with no intention of killing him. Had it been justified to shoot Kars to save Ingrid? To save Tessa? Even if, in the back of my mind, I thought it was what he'd wanted to happen. That was why he'd apologized to Ingrid. Why he'd raised his gun.

I heard a commotion from the top of the stairs. The sound of a cat's screams and something heavy falling on the floor pulled the skin on my arms into goose bumps.

I suddenly found the energy to take the stairs two at a time. What was happening to Pippi? The door to my flat was open, which was probably why the noise had managed to travel down. It sounded as if someone was strangling her.

Even when she'd been thrown in the canal a week ago, she hadn't sounded this desperate. Her cries resembled those of a hungry baby.

'I've nearly got it,' a man's voice said. 'Can you just hold this?'

'Not really,' my mother said. 'I've only got one hand. Well, I've got two, but you know what I mean.'

The words were interspersed by loud meows.

'What's going on?' I pushed the door open wide. A man in a courier's uniform, wearing a pair of pink Marigolds, was holding Pippi by the scruff of her neck. Her eyes were bulging out of her head as the skin was pulled back tight. 'Put her down.'

'Lotte, the cat needs to go back to her owners,' my mother said. 'I called the removal company.'

'I'm in so much trouble for losing the bloody thing.' The man's face was deeply wrinkled underneath short grey hair. 'I need this job.' The Marigolds gave his sincere statement a ridiculous edge.

'I'm sorry about that,' I said, 'but I can't let you have her.'

'Lotte, be sensible. This man's job is on the line, and it isn't your cat.'

Pippi looked at me from the man's grip and meowed as if she knew that I would rescue her. 'I'll call the Americans. The owners. I'll tell them I've got her.'

The man shook his head and pulled the pet carrier closer to him with a booted foot. Pippi sprawled out as much as she could, as if she were dropping from a high building and needed to break her fall.

'Can you at least put her down?'

He laughed with a grimace. 'You wouldn't say that if you knew how long it had taken us to catch it. If you open the carrier, we can put it in and it will stop this almighty racket.'

Her claws were out. I reached for her. Her nails hooked in the sleeve of my coat as if it were a life jacket. I put my arms around her shivering body. The man still held her neck with his Marigolds. We locked eyes.

'It's just a cat,' my mother said. 'You can get another one. Her owners will be missing her.'

'Don't do this,' the man said.

'Did they call you? Her owners?'

'Of course they did. Wondered what had happened to kitty.'

'Look, whatever I need to sign, just give me the forms. I'll call your boss. This is my responsibility, not your mistake.'

He sighed and let go.

I put Pippi on the floor and she rushed into my study. She would be hiding under the desk. 'Your mistake was a week ago. What happened?'

'There was a whole bunch of stuff that they wanted to throw away. Furniture that they didn't want to ship back to the States. There were some chairs, a sofa, and I put the cat down on those chairs. We had so much stuff to carry. I just forgot to pick it up later. The cat.'

It seemed such a long time ago: that night that I jumped into the canal to rescue her. 'Without me she would have drowned.'

'Could you just sign this form?'

'Give me the number of the Americans.'

'I can't do that.'

I had lost so much today, I wasn't going to lose the cat. 'Give me the number and I won't report you to Animal Protection. You left a cat in a carrier. You nearly got her killed. Losing your job will be the least of your problems.'

The man paled. Maybe my argument had scared him, or maybe what had happened today showed in my eyes.

'Or you can give me the number,' I said, 'and your problems will go away.'

He gave me a piece of paper with an international number on it. I checked what the time was in the States. It was afternoon. I dialled. The phone rang with that foreign tone.

A woman picked up.

'Hi, Nancy, this is Lotte from upstairs. From Amsterdam. I have Pippi. Your cat.' My cat.

'Oh, I'm so glad. I've been worried about her. Is she all right?'

'She's okay.'

'Excellent. Can you talk to the couriers to get her here?'

'I don't . . . I don't think that's a good idea.' There was no way I was going to put her in a carrier again and give her to that man. 'She's been quite traumatized. I don't want to put her through that.'

The woman laughed. 'She'll be fine as soon as she gets here.'

I could hear the kids in the background. 'Can we get a dog?' the boy shouted.

'Jonathan, be quiet. Anyway, Lotte, thanks for looking after her. Let me know when she's on her way.'

I shook my head, even though I knew she couldn't see it. 'I'm not going to do that. It wouldn't be good for her at all. She's . . . she's just settling in here. I'd . . .' I swallowed. 'I'd really like to keep her.'

'A dog, Mummy, can we get a dog?'

'Please, Nancy,' I said, 'please can she stay here?'

There was a moment of silence as she weighed up what to do. It seemed to last a long time.

'I know what you mean, but I want her back.'

'She's an old cat. The stress of the travel. Do you really want to put her on a plane?' I paused. 'I'm not sure I can do without her now.'

'And my husband was already complaining about the cost of flying her over. Okay,' Nancy said finally. 'I'll miss her, but it sounds as if she's got a good home.'

'She does,' I said. 'I'll look after her.' I put the phone down and turned to the delivery guy. 'We're done here. I won't report you.'

After he'd left, I smiled at my mother to show that I wasn't angry with her. Her ideas of right and wrong had always been too black and white. She would hand in a ten-euro note that she found on the pavement to the police, even if she needed the money.

'I'm sorry,' she said.

'It's all right.'

She went into her room and I picked up my book. Turning the pages seemed to be a signal for Pippi to come back in and jump on my lap. Nowhere in *Surviving Your Elderly Parents* did it talk about arguments over pets, but there was a chapter on the difficulties that could come up when grown-up children had more knowledge than their parents. That was to do with modern technology, but I thought some of the advice would work in our situation too. The doorbell rang and I lifted Pippi off my lap and rushed to the intercom. 'Hello?' I said, almost breathlessly.

'Did I catch you in the middle of something?' Not Mark.

'Hi, Thomas, what's up?'

He laughed. 'I can hear you're disappointed it's me. Can I come up?'

I pressed the buzzer and let him in. I stood with my hand on the door handle and watched him come up the stairs. He wasn't out of breath. In better health than Ingrid had been. 'This is late for a visit,' I said.

'Yeah, well. We found something at Kars's place. I didn't want to call you. I didn't want it anywhere on record that I'd talked to you.'

'Not during the investigation. Sure.'

'This is going to be a short one. I watched everything.'

'Watched?'

'He had a camera rigged up in that room.' Thomas sat down on the sofa. 'Not a nice man, that Kars.' He picked up *Surviving Your Elderly Parents* and turned it over.

I reached out to take it from him. 'I've only got that because my mother is staying here.' I put it back on the bookshelf. 'Can I get you a drink?'

He looked at his watch. 'Sure, why not. I'll have a beer if you've got it.'

'Yup. Just wait here.' I went to the kitchen and opened two bottles of Grolsch. I handed one to Thomas and we tapped the necks together in a collegiate salute.

'Kars's version of this would describe how to lock your mother in a room and leave her alone for whole days at a time.' He rubbed the top of the bottle and took a gulp. 'It was actually better for her when Tessa was there. She looked after her. The two of them talked. Even if it was only for a day, the mother was calmer then. But she became hysterical when Kars took her out of the room.'

'This morning, you mean? When he took her home?'

'He came back an hour or so later. I think you missed him at Job's house by ten minutes at most. Anyway, what he did to his mother and to Tessa, that's on there as well as your stand-off with him. And him threatening Ingrid.' He shook his head. 'Should never have put your gun on the floor.'

'I know, I know. It was stupid.'

'Ingrid is very upset. She's blaming herself. She said she should have shot. She also said something about Agnes Visser, that it had been in all the papers that she had been dead for over ten months when Mark found her body. You never saw these?' He took a handful of printouts from his bag. They were copies of newspaper front pages of the time. The headlines were only too clear: *Ten-year-old brother more competent than police*, *Schoolgirl strangled by neighbour* and *Police fail to find hidden body for ten months*.

'My mother hid those from me. For my own good,' I said with a wry smile. That had worked out well. I drank from my beer.

'Anyway,' Thomas said, 'Kars must have seen you on the screen.'

'I didn't think he was in the house.'

'He was in the basement. That's where he had the monitors rigged up. Tony became a lot more talkative after his brother's death. Told us how they got involved with Dollander in the first place. They ran some of his property projects in the early days. You can watch it when you get back.'

'Thanks.'

'That other stuff is recorded too. Exactly how you acted and what happened in that room.' He paused. 'Are you all right?'

'I think so. I didn't have a choice.'

He looked at me, his pretty-boy face serious for a change. 'I know. You'll be back at work soon. There's just one problem.'

'What's that?'

'I had some other tapes of yours. A couple of recordings of you interviewing that murderer. The ones that were . . . let's say the ones that made me question you in the first place. I seem to have accidentally destroyed them. We all make mistakes.'

'Thanks, Thomas.'

'Sure.' He put the empty beer bottle on the table.

'Want another one?'

'No thanks.' He looked at his watch. 'Time for me to go home.'

I closed the door behind him and sat down, and Pippi jumped back on to my lap. She turned in circles to find the most comfortable position against my stomach. I scratched the top of her head, between her ears, and she purred. My book, back on the shelf, was out of reach, but maybe I didn't need it. Maybe my mother and I were doing just fine. I stared out of the window to the darkness outside. Compared to the van Wiel family, we definitely were.

Then my phone rang. It was Mark. I closed my eyes for a second before I answered it. Happiness stabbed my heart. Hope is hard to kill.

Acknowledgements

My mother was eight years old when she saw the Nazis arrest my grandfather. When he returned from the concentration camps, he was so emaciated that my grandmother failed to recognise him. But when I was checking some details at the Netherlands Institute for War Documentation (NIOD) I read about what happened in the Netherlands to the families who'd been on the opposing side. After the war, many children of Nazi sympathisers were beaten and bullied on a daily basis by teachers and classmates alike. This inspired me to create the character of Francine's father.

Many people helped me with this novel and I'm grateful to you all. I'm fortunate that in Allan Guthrie I have a fantastic writer as my agent. Thanks to my editor Krystyna Green and all at Constable and Little, Brown for helping me make this novel the best it could possibly be.

Finally, I'd like to thank my parents for sharing their stories.